A SMALL-TOWN WESTERN SINGLE-DAD ROMANCE

Greta Rose West

COPYRIGHT

PRESS

ALSO BY GRETA ROSE WEST

Wild Heart: Welcome to Wisper

Subscribe to the newsletter for this short introduction into the Cade Ranch world and for extra goodies and scenes. Sign up at gretarosewest.com.

THE CADE RANCH SERIES IN ORDER

BURNED

BROKEN

BUSTED

BRAVED

BLINDED

THE WISPER DREAMS SERIES IN ORDER

RIVERS BETWEEN US

STORMS INSIDE US

MOUNTAINS DIVIDE US

LIGHT BETRAYS US

MIDNIGHT SURROUNDS US

ROADS BEHIND US

FOREVER FINDS US

WYOMING LOVE EBOOK BOXSETS

LOVE AT CADE RANCH (Cade Ranch Books 1 - 3)

CADE RANCH IN LOVE (Cade Ranch Books 4 & 5)

LOVE IN WISPER, WYOMING (Wisper Dreams Books 1 - 3)

ACKNOWLEDGMENTS

The person I most want to thank isn't around anymore for me to say it in person, but my own belief in woo-woo tells me he knows. Still, I want to type it: Dad. Walter J. Finklefarkle. I love you and I miss you. Thank you for inspiring me. Thanks for all you lost and all you gained, for all the pain and the joy. And the upside down glasses and terrifying Cessna Gs.Mom, this book wouldn't exist if you hadn't gone through what you did. I'm sorry for what you lost. Things haven't been perfect between us, but I love you, and I carry Tawny around with me in my heart. Sometimes I wonder if she were here and she was the oldest, would I be so bossy? But then I laugh, cuz, yeah, I totally would.

Thank you to Peter Senftleben for editing this book. Number 11, baby! Number 12 will be headed your way before Roads is even published.

Sarah Kil, you killed it with this one. 😜 Sometimes I just gaze at the cover and wish I was the heroine of this story. Lol.

To Sarah W, thank you for my pretty pink bison! I love your rendition of Wooly Wally. And thanks for reminding me that Aspens are called quakies. I totally put that in the book!

To my beta readers, Geri, MJ, and Barb, thanks! Your insight and feedback helped this story bloom. And MJ, you know I love you, but I wanted to say it again and tell you that I admire your strength. This book was hard for you to read, but you did it for me. You couldn't be a better friend. 🥹

ARC readers, thank youuuu! Thanks for hyping me up, for all the shares and DMs. I love you!

To the following musicians and dreamers, plus so many others who inspire me hourly—GAI, Penny & Sparrow, Ella Langley, Zach Bryan, Bon Iver, Shane Smith & The Saints, The Lumineers, Chris Stapleton, Stephen Wilson, Jr., and The Pixies (I never imagined I'd be addressing you in a book, but WHOA!):

THANK YOU.

Tawny:
You are a hole I feel in my soul. I can't see you, but I know you're there. Say hi to Daddy, Grandma, and Graddy for me.

PROLOGUE
SWEETIE

Two Years Ago

As the only woman on a thirty-man construction crew, I pulled my misogyny repellent around me like a superhero's cape. I needed a thick skin and a foul mouth to fit in with the guys at my new job with Lee Construction.

Sure, the company employed other women, but they worked in the office. I was the only female with blisters on her hands and a hammer engraved with her name, a gift from my daddy from the day after I graduated high school and he offered me my first real job on his crew.

But that was seventeen years and one failed marriage ago. Taking a last, deep breath, I wrapped strength around me like a second skin before I knocked on my new boss's front door, opened it, and strode in like I owned the place, ready to beat some men's asses in a game of Texas Hold 'Em.

"You made it," Brand Lee said with a kind smile. The man who'd hired me on the spot three weeks ago, nodded and addressed the four other men in his modern, well-lit kitchen.

"This is the new hire I was tellin' you about. Y'all haven't been formally introduced, so Sweetie, meet the guys."

"Hey," was all I said, but steel pulsed through my posture. I stood straighter and reached forward to shake their hands.

"Sweetie, these are my three project leads. Meet Milo Chalk, Tam Corbin, and Tweety."

Three of the men I'd seen Brand working with over the last few weeks shook the hand I offered. Two of them looked to be in their late thirties or early forties, and both said, "Nice to meet you." They said it, but I saw the looks, the sweeping gazes of my short stature and long hair. They were thinking, "What's this little woman doing in our world? What's wrong with the boss? Why'd he invite her?"

The third man, Tweety, was a heavy-set guy with a scraggly beard that looked like he'd dipped it orange Kool-Aid. He'd made the choice when he got dressed this morning to wear a Hooters T-shirt. I hoped it was a decision made out of irony, but I had my doubts. He couldn't have been more than twenty-five. He said, "What's up."

But all of my senses had focused on the fourth man, an extremely handsome guy I'd never seen before wearing a straw cowboy hat down low over his sky-blue eyes. From the kitchen chair he seemed to have poured himself into, he flashed me a smile, and I swore I felt my knickers literally twist. His jeans fit him like they'd been made to hang from his clutchable hips in just the right way. Every woman in a five-mile radius was no doubt hyperventilating, and I hadn't even seen his backside. I had a feeling his Wranglers did a fine job of wrangling *everything* he had to offer.

Don't be daft, Bea. This dude's trouble on a sexy stick. You can see it in his eyes, just like every other guy you've ever known.

With his arm slung over the back of his chair and a short tumbler of clear liquor sloshing around in his hand, he was the picture of a bad boy, and somehow, I knew he could bring me to my knees with just one soft whisper in my ear.

He said, "Sweetie? My brother call you that 'cause you got a sweet little ass?"

My coworkers all groaned or winced, and my boss laughed under his breath as I took three steps closer to his brother. He'd only known me a few weeks, but Brand could probably guess that my bitch mode had just been activated. I wasn't worried about offending my boss by addressing his brother, and honestly, brother or not, if he didn't have my back in this kind of situation, I would be moving on.

I planted my hands on my hips and bent at the waist, surprising the cowboy with my sudden closeness. He was already one sheet to the wind and well on his way to two or three, but I noticed the symmetrical features of his face and the sharp cut of his jaw, which had only been enhanced by the soft cerulean blue of his irises and the fine laugh lines at the edges of his eyes.

Letting my approval and attraction show on my face, I hinted at what he already seemed sure of—if he wanted me, he could have me. I rolled my lips together, then pinched the bottom one between my teeth.

I smiled, but with my thumb and middle finger, I flicked the hat up an inch. "My name is Bea," I said, and I nodded over my shoulder, "but my ass is pretty sweet, ain't it?"

Mutely, he stared into my eyes and nodded.

"Wanna see what happens to your face if you put your hands on it?" I lifted a brow and waited for his answer.

When none came, I straightened, and my boss introduced us. "Sweetie, this is my big brother, Bax. He came up to visit from Wisper, our hometown down south of Yellowstone." Annoyance rang loud and clear in Brand's voice. *Good.* "Please excuse his idiocy. He's drunk."

"No worries," I said. "If he makes a habit out of belittlin' me, I'll deliver his balls to the pearly gates of Heaven myself *and* take all his money tonight."

Pain flashed across Bax's face, and Brand pulled at my elbow. When I tore my sharp gaze away from his brother's and looked back at him, Brand shook his head discreetly, his eyebrows dipping, and said, "Don't," under his breath.

Shit. It was then I remembered Brand mentioning that his sister-in-law had passed away the year before and his brother hadn't been handling it very well.

My daddy's face flashed in my head. Looking down at the broken man in front of me now, I had a hard time not seeing my dad breaking down at my mama's funeral and sobbing over her open casket.

"I'm sorry," I said. I didn't make a habit out of apologizing to rude men often. Not anymore, but God. There was so much sorrow in Bax's eyes.

Although, he hadn't apologized to me for his sexist and extremely inappropriate comment about my ass.

"Fuck your sorry," he said, his voice low, thick like molasses, and slightly slurred. He stood, and I rose slowly, noticing his tall height as he straightened. He towered over me, but not in a menacing way. It was a challenge, and then he tossed back the drink still in his hand and handed me an unopened box of playing cards from his back pocket. "Deal me in."

So, no apology then? Okay. I see how this is gonna go.
Fine.

Swirling my misogyny cape around me once again, I imagined it whipping Bax in his smug face as I turned.

"Okay, cowboy, but I hope you came prepared to have *your* sweet little ass handed to you by a girl."

We hadn't even started playing yet, but I figured the score had already been skewed in my favor: one point for me, negative 367 for Bax Lee.

CHAPTER ONE

BAX

Present Time

FORGET THE REST.

Remember the good times and forget the rest?

I'd been trying, but losing my wife, best friend, and the mother of my daughter had been… soul bending. And so fucking hard. Sometimes, it felt like it had only been three days and not three years. I knew it wasn't her fault, but every morning when I opened my eyes, I looked at the ceiling in my bedroom and asked, "Why'd you leave us?"

If I could avoid it, I never thought about the baby boy she'd been carrying when Candy died seven months into her pregnancy. His memory triggered a shield and a hardening to descend down around my heart the instant I tried to imagine what his laughter would sound like.

Who was I if I wasn't Candy's husband? She'd been my world for twenty years, and she gave me the best gift I'd ever been given when she gave birth to Athena. If I hadn't had our daughter to look after when Candy and the baby died suddenly, I probably would've dissipated into the ether, would've ceased to exist anymore.

Fortunately, having a kid on the precipice of her prime teenage years meant I had to get up every morning, had to shower and cook and interact with the world because if I didn't, there'd be hell to pay. How in the world was my daughter about to turn fourteen? In my head, she was still a little girl with sticky fingers, dragging her dirty tiger stuffie around the farm.

The grown-up sound of her voice now shook me right out of the memory. "Daddy, I need new shoes. I told you last week."

"Oh, right. Sorry, Road Trip. I forgot. Here." Teetering precariously on one foot and trying not to let my crutches fall, I pulled my wallet from my back pocket and snagged three twenties.

One damn day I'd been in this stupid, full-leg cast, and it had already become the bane of my existence. Until my incisions had healed enough to be covered with a cast, the brace the doctor had me wearing right after surgery let me maneuver through my house easy enough. I still hadn't tried to venture upstairs to my bedroom. I'd been sleeping on my living room couch, but now that the rigid, plaster monstrosity was in place, it was bulky and unforgiving. And it weighed a ton. I was exhausted just thinking about trying to lug it up there.

I handed the money to Athena, but she held the bills up next to her sweet face. She'd braided her hair this morning, and she looked like she used to when she was little and Candy would French braid a twist down either side of her head. Candy had tried to teach me how to braid our daughter's hair more than once, but I'd proved useless with that kind of stuff. Besides, I was busy with our farm, and I never thought I'd need the skill.

The regret I still felt every morning for that stupid thought ate at me. What I wouldn't have given for a second chance to learn. YouTube could only show me so much. What I wanted — What I *missed* was watching the gentle glide of Candy's fingers through Athena's silky hair as she sat, patient and relaxed in front of her mama at the kitchen table, and the quiet way Candy would ask Athena what she'd dreamed about the night before or how excited she was for the day. They'd plan dinner together in soft voices, sleep still evident in Athena's eyes and voice.

Holding the cash in front of my face, Athena asked, "What am I s'posed to do with this?"

"Buy shoes?"

Athena laughed. "Okay, Daddy. Should I walk to the store? In *Idaho Falls*? These are special shoes. They cost twice that much, and we'd have to go to, like, a whole other state to get them. You know that, right?" When I shrugged, she stuffed the money in my back pocket. "Check your texts, old man. I sent you a link. Just order them—women's size seven—but if they offer rush shippin', do that."

"Okay. Thanks. What kinda shoes are these?"

"Trainers. Remember, I told you I joined cross country this year? We've already started, but the shoes I have aren't cuttin' it. The soles are practically nonexistent."

"Right, yeah. No, I remember." Athena turned to head out the kitchen door. Hopefully she hadn't figured out that I'd completely forgotten. What kind of shitty parenting was that? "Wait. Didn't you tell me you needed somethin' else too?"

She stopped with her hand ready to push open the door. "Yeah, but don't worry about it. I'll have Aunt Abey take me to get new riding boots. At least those we can get in town, and she said she'd get them for me for my birthday."

"Okay, cool. You know you're expensive?" I smiled, but she already knew I was kidding. It didn't matter what she wanted; Athena had me wrapped around her little finger since the moment she was born.

She scoffed. "It's not my fault I keep growin'. It's kinda yours and… Mama's."

It broke my heart that she felt she had to be careful with me when she brought up her mom. It was getting easier to hear, but I still avoided the subject. I knew I needed to let go of some of the pain, but the loss had changed me, and I clung to it like a best friend.

I'd have to remember to thank my sister again for basically being a fill-in mom these last few years. I really needed to stop depending on her. I thought I'd lose my mind after the funeral when Athena announced to a room full of family and neighbors that she'd started her period. For a split second, I thought God was coming straight for me. Sometimes I still thought that. Like a week ago, when a bull tried to kill me but broke my femur instead.

Thankfully, Abey knew all about PMS, sanitary pads, and tampons, and she'd tried to educate me. Unfortunately, at the time, my mind held onto only every fifth or sixth word she'd said. She had to explain it all again the next month.

But my baby sister had her own life. She was engaged to be married to her girlfriend, Devo, they were building a new house half a mile away from mine, and she'd recently become the deputy sheriff of our small town. She had enough to deal with.

Getting bodychecked by a bull hadn't made things any easier. That day, my mind had been fixed on the complicated logistics and details of starting a sustainable cattle farm and luxury rental-cabin business, but as soon as the bull charged and my ass hit dirt, my mortality smacked me in the face. The realization that if the bull had been any meaner, Athena might be without a mother, a brother, *and* a dad, had struck me like lightning.

My head had been in the clouds ever since, my thoughts on a constant loop, worrying about Athena's future, the stability of my brand-new businesses, and oddly, the fact that I hadn't painted my house in years and now it looked like one of those shacks you see in documentaries about the fall of a former metropolis.

I'd be forever grateful for my family's help, but being the oldest of four siblings meant I needed to get on with life, get my shit back together, and get to work. No rest for the wicked.

"You okay, Daddy? Does your leg hurt?" Athena asked, worried because she realized she'd reminded me of all we'd lost.

She dropped her backpack on the kitchen table and came to slip her arm beneath mine, and she hugged me gently. She knew not to pull on me 'cause, since I had to rely on the crutches, my balance had pretty much gone out the window.

"It's not too bad this mornin'," I said. "I'm good. Promise." I wanted to caress her hair, but I didn't want to mess up her braids, and if I let go of the crutches, I'd fall on my ass.

"Okay." She turned her head, tucked it against my chest for a second, and took a deep breath. I breathed her in too. Nothing could comfort me like the smell of my daughter's shampoo. "Oh, don't forget, Shaylene's mama's pickin' us up after school today. We're goin' to the U-pick place to do the hayride thing and get apples."

Squeezing my baby the best I could while still holding onto the crutches, I nodded over my shoulder, at the sixty bucks sticking out of my pocket. "Take the money. Get me some apple donuts and half a bushel of Granny Smiths, and we'll beg Auntie Aubrey to bake us a pie." I winked down at her, and Athena wiggled her eyebrows conspiratorially and nodded.

She reached up on her toes to kiss my unshaven cheek and snagged the twenties. "Deal. Have a good day, Daddy, but you might wanna do somethin' about this scruff." She patted my cheek, stepped back and dipped her head, then speared me with a judgmental look. "Love you," she said, and she smiled and dashed from the kitchen, off on another road trip, this time to school.

Man, how had I lucked out with this kid? She was smart, resourceful, and funny. She struggled with losing her mama just like I did, but she was tougher than me by a mile.

"Love you, Athena! See you tonight," I called after her as the kitchen door slammed closed behind her. I heard the truck door slam shut, too, when she jumped in my sister's county cruiser outside, and they honked when they took off.

As they drove away down the dirt lane leading from my house and past Spitfire Ranch and the future Lee Valley cabins, I listened as a dead quiet settled in around me.

I was still so pissed at myself for letting that damn animal get the better of me. Now, not only could I not help my best friend, Rye, work our ranch and tend to our new stock, I also couldn't help my brother finish the cabins he'd agreed to build for our new business. I couldn't do shit. Couldn't drive. Couldn't work. Couldn't take a goddamn shower. I would have to sit and stew in three inches of bath water with my leg sticking up over the edge of the tub so I didn't get the cast wet. It would be better than the sponge baths I'd had to give myself the first week, but I already knew it was going to be the biggest pain in my ass.

Before that overly aggressive animal had pinned me between the barn and the fence gate and then kicked at it with his hind legs like he had been trying to launch himself to the moon, I could stay busy. I'd gotten really good at distracting myself with work or Athena or anything in between to occupy my mind so I didn't think about shit I didn't want to think about.

But now, thinking was all I did. I'd even started dreaming again about Candy and the baby I never got to meet.

In my dreams, they were both alive and vibrant and whole. There was no deadly blood clot lurking beneath the shadows, catching me unawares to knock me numb when it lodged in her brain and killed the only woman I'd ever loved and my son, who, if he'd been born, would've been named Baxton Brennen Lee II. Duo for short.

In my head, I could see him so clearly. He had brown hair like mine, kind of wavy but not curly. He'd love four wheeling with his old man and his big sister, and his eyes would be the same light blue as mine. He'd call me Pops or something similar that would make me feel twenty years older than the thirty-eight I'd lived so far.

But I'd love hearing it every time.

The pain in my chest every time the realization washed over me that I'd never know the sound of my son's voice *leveled* me. The wall around my heart cracked enough to let the pain slither in, and I staggered back, forgetting the cast on my leg, and fell into a chair at my kitchen table.

Losing him was different than the loss I felt for Candy because she had been a real-life person. Her kind smile and the tender lilt to her voice when she read bedtime stories to Athena had been branded onto my memories. And the belief and faith she'd had in me after my dad died and left me in charge of our family's sheep farm was probably the reason it had taken me so long to let it go and focus on a new dream, one that could actually make a profit.

The baby was different because he'd gotten stuck in my head as an abstract idea. I'd never held him. Never heard the sound of his coos or hiccups. Never got to feel his heart beating inside his little body as I rocked him to sleep.

I'd long ago stopped crying. What good did that do besides make Athena worry about me? But it hurt, and I always had to take a few minutes to breathe and find gratitude for all the good things I still had in my life.

Athena. My family. My friends. Sunrises. Sunsets. Laughter. Athena's laugh. Her smile. Her spirit. It's crazy how different she is than her mama. Candy would've loved who our little girl's turning out to—

My phone rang on the table in front of me—*thank God*—and I breathed a sigh of relief when I grabbed it and saw my brother's name on the screen.

"What's up, little bro?" I said, trying not to let him hear the croak in my voice or the sound of me trying to clear it from my throat. "You make it out of Jackson yet?"

"Yeah, just turned onto Highway 26. Only six more hours to go till I get back to Sheridan. I talked to Sweetie. She'll be on her way to you in a few hours. She got off to a late start today, but she'll be there tonight. I'm not sure exactly what time. She's already complainin' about the drive, so just beware."

"Beware?" I laughed, remembering vaguely the night I'd met Sweetie up at my brother's place in Sheridan, and how feisty she could be. I also remembered her green eyes. And I remembered getting rip-roaring drunk when those eyes and the way they'd stared into mine made me realize I was attracted to a woman who wasn't my wife. "You're warnin' me about the person you've sent to live here with me and your innocent, defenseless niece? What exactly should I be wary of?"

"Please," Brand said. "Athena's anything but defenseless, and Sweetie's harmless. She's just a little stressed about the job. I've put a lot of pressure on her, and she can be a bit… intense."

"Okay."

Whatever. With this godforsaken broken leg, it wasn't like *I* could finish all the work Brand had started but couldn't finish because he'd been called back to Sheridan for some kind of legal hogwash. But I guess that was what happened when you became a big, successful contractor like my little brother had.

Brand's forewoman, Sweetie, would be staying in the first finished cabin. She was our best hope of getting three half-finished houses and nine more cabins completed before the end of autumn.

If winter hit before then, we'd all be screwed. I'd have to spend the next half year holed up with my teenager, my mama, who'd just put her trailer up for sale, and my derelict brother, Dixon, if he ever showed his face at home again. If their studio rental fell through, my sister and her fiancée might be forced to live here, too, and probably my best friend Rye and his girlfriend Aubrey. Until his house was ready, Rye had been sleeping on my couch some nights, on the barn floor in a sleeping bag on top of a blow-up mattress other nights, and at his girlfriend's house in town, which she'd just sold.

Added onto that would be five to ten various animals, going in and out my kitchen door at their leisure. In an old, three-bedroom farmhouse with only one standing shower and a fifty-year-old tub?

If I had to endure Sweetie and her "intenseness" to avoid all that, I wouldn't complain. Not one bit.

CHAPTER TWO

SWEETIE

"CHICKEN-FRIED STEAK."

Chicken-fried steak and grits. Ham hocks, salty greens, grape jelly. Ooo, pepperoni rolls, buckwheat pancakes, pawpaws, and fried mushrooms. Oh, how I miss Mama's fried morels.

Driving alone down a lonely mountain highway, listing foods I'd eaten growing up, wasn't making my seven-hour drive down to Wisper, Wyoming go any faster. This foggy bullshit was a bitch, and my truck radio was dead. My phone's battery had just about kicked the bucket, and for extra funsies, my charging cord decided to quit today too. I had a spare in my suitcase, but I didn't feel like stopping to get it out of the bed of my truck.

Maybe if I counted off all the places I'd lived since I left North Carolina?

"Iowa… what was that place called? Fredman? Yeah, Fredman, Iowa. Middle of nowhere, Nebraska. North Dakota." Ugh, I was getting frostbite just remembering that winter hell. Whoever made the movie *Fargo* hadn't been far off the mark.

To the silence inside the cab of my truck, I said, "Lust, Wyoming. Now there's a place I'll never go back to. Five cowboys to every woman per square mile, more cows than I ever want to see again in my life, and dirt. Dusty, dirty foothills and vistas." Lust was pretty in a barren-landscape kind of way, but I liked trees. Coming from a dead-end Appalachian holler, trees were a necessity. I felt exposed without them.

Since I left home, I hadn't lived in any one place longer than six months, but then two years ago, I found Sheridan, Wyoming, met my boss, Brand Lee, and he gave me a job.

He probably shouldn't have. Until the day Brand offered his handshake and changed my life, I had no steady work experience. Flitting between waitress gigs wasn't what I considered a career. I worked as a bank teller for a short minute, and I'd cleaned enough office buildings to be awarded a gold medal for being "that bitch who empties your trash cans and accidentally bumps your computer with her Swiffer but is never surprised to find a porn site loaded up. You know, the one you jacked off to during a muted conference call?"

But I knew how to build houses, knew how to fix and rig shit when it broke. And I had an innate ability to boss men around.

"Now *that* you came by honestly," I told myself.

Before he broke his back and got hooked on pills, then ran his business to the ground, my daddy had steered a tight ship at our family's construction company. Even before he started showing me how to work the job, doing my homework in whatever build had been going up that month taught me to be a builder simply by osmosis. And I watched and listened to my dad's guys arguing about how to do something, which team played the best football, or who'd slept with whose girlfriend.

The answers to those questions were always: The way I told you to do it, Chicago (bear down!), and lastly, you're all a bunch of morally defunct horndogs, and you're probably all passing syphilis back and forth between each other with your girlfriends acting as the superspreader highway.

A bunch of grown men bickering and barking like a pack of prairie dogs got old fast. Figuring out how to put them in their place so they'd go back to work came naturally 'cause I'd grown up watching my dad do it.

Too bad it hadn't worked on my ex-husband. I could only hope that by now he'd fallen off the edge of a cliff or had contracted some rare, extra painful disease. No, I didn't wish him too much ill will. I was relieved just to have gotten out when I did, and I thanked the Lord I'd had the sound foresight to not have children with Lincoln Louis Jr. If I had kids, my cross-country search for a new place to belong would've been a hell of a lot more complicated.

It made me sad sometimes, not being a mom. I'd always pictured myself as someone's mama, but pushing thirty-five as a single, emotionally unavailable woman kind of made the whole motherhood thing difficult.

I didn't aim to be emotionally unavailable, but running from your past and men who were weak or mean or just plain stupid always seemed harder when you wore your heart on your sleeve.

Changing my name back to Beatrice Baker before the ink had even dried on my divorce decree had been my saving grace. I was able to see myself again. Really see and feel the old me. I could look in a mirror and steel myself again to pain and loss and disappointment.

Was love really more important than strength of self? I

used to think so, but in my recent experience, the answer to that question was no.

Never.

For too long, I'd been someone's wife, which then made me a secondary character in the story of my own life. Nothing I did mattered as much as how everything I did or didn't do or say affected my husband.

Utter fucking bullshit. But wasn't I the dipshit who'd let it happen? Hadn't it been me stuffing down my opinions and emotions to please a man who hadn't considered once what might please me?

Unfortunately, it was how I'd been raised, and the loss of my only remaining parent after losing Mama at such a young age made me so fucking desperate to feel special to someone that I'd given up what made me special in the first damn place.

It hadn't helped that all my daddy had left me was debt and pissed-off customers. I'd needed my ex-husband's family's legal counsel. His father owned a chain of dry cleaners. Lincoln would inherit the entire empire when his parents passed. Maybe they already had by now. I wouldn't know because I left North Carolina almost five years ago and hadn't looked back once.

Catching a glimpse of myself in my rearview, I asked my reflection, "Does that make you shallow? Are you a gold-digging asshole?" But my eyes were clear. My conscience clean.

I thought I loved Lincoln once upon a time. That had to count for something. And after we'd dug Daddy's company out of its hole and sold all the equipment to pay off debts, I'd tried to make it work. I tried my hardest to be the wife my husband had thought he wanted.

It took way too long for me to realize I'd never be that

woman, and finally, after ten years, I walked away. Lincoln and his family had been paid back in full, plus I'd left him some cash to ease his ego.

My ex was another reason I had been so surprised when Brand offered me a job. Lincoln hadn't wanted me to do anything besides waitress or stay home and clean, so technically, when I met Brand, I hadn't been on a build site since I was nineteen and didn't exactly have the credentials he'd been looking for.

I guess Brand had seen something in me. He must have since he paid for me to get recertified in a handful of skills I needed to freshen up, and then he set me loose. He watched me work, watched how I interacted with the rest of the crew, and six months later, he'd titled me his number one, his foreman. Two of the leads I'd met when I first started had threatened to quit because of my promotion, but Brand showed them the door. He didn't care that I was a woman. He wouldn't have cared if I was from Venus. He only cared that I did the job right.

"Forewoman?" I nodded to myself in the rearview. "Yeah, I like that better."

How was it possible that Brand was so kind and accepting, but his older brother Bax, who incidentally, I'd be living with for who knew how long, was a snarky pain in the ass?

Technically, I wouldn't be living *with* him because Brand had hurried to finish and set up the smallest of the new cabins for me on his family's property. I'd never been there before, but I'd seen the blueprints when Brand had his architect draft them, so I knew the cabins were less than a mile from the main house where Bax and his daughter lived.

I wasn't all that excited to see Bax every day until Brand finished dealing with the bullshit court case he'd been plagued with back in Sheridan, but I was a little excited to get to know Brand's niece. When I met her on a Zoom call last week, Athena reminded me of myself when I was her age.

Too bad her dad was an annoying, poker-losing fuck twaddle. A sexy fuck twaddle, but still. I'd only met him the one time, when I demolished his ass in a game of Texas Hold 'Em, but he was pretty drunk and, to be fair, no one beat me at Texas Hold 'Em. I'd become too good at reading men's faces. They all thought they hid their tells so well, but excitement about winning anything, including poker *and* women, was so goddamn evident. It was like a bright, flashing red light every single time.

Bax had a somewhat interesting tell; he licked and then bit his bottom lip when he had a good hand, and when he didn't, he pursed those lips and swallowed. I'd had a hard time looking at anything besides his neck muscles flexing, Adam's apple bobbing.

Still to this day, my reaction to the tall, annoyingly handsome single dad pissed me off.

But none of that mattered. He'd never apologized to me for the "sweet little ass" comment, and two years later, it still pinched under my skin, like a splinter you could see but couldn't remove.

Back then, I knew Bax had been struggling with the loss of his wife, and it was the only reason the words "I'm sorry" had passed my lips.

Despite the playboy air he'd tried to give off the night we met, I understood where he'd been emotionally. I saw a lot of my own dad in him, the aura of his loss of love and direction. When Mama died, Daddy had tried to figure out how to raise a thirteen-year-old on his own at first, but he'd been just as adrift. He'd lost the love of his life. Nowhere to go from there.

But Bax still tanked every hand we'd played at his brother's house that night. It wasn't in me to give up the goods. And then Brand had taken a very drunk Bax to pass out in his guest room, and I hadn't seen Bax Lee again till a week ago on my computer screen, when Brand begged me to make the trek to Wisper to finish all the projects he'd committed Lee Construction to.

Bax had looked different somehow on that laptop screen. Granted, I didn't know him well, apart from what his brother had told me, but he seemed… tamer—quieter—than he had the night I'd beat him at poker. The same night I'd had a hard time keeping my cards straight because the color of Bax's eyes had mesmerized me and the shine on his lip left there by his tongue had me sawing my legs together beneath Brand's kitchen table.

Whatever had changed for Bax Lee or the wetness level of his full lip, it didn't really matter. For the next couple weeks, he was nothing more to me than a landlord and my boss's older brother. Brand had appointed me project lead for all the builds on his family's property; he expected excellence and efficiency, and I intended to do the job justice. Bax couldn't help because the idiot had gotten his leg broken by a cow. Or a bull? Whatever. If it went "moo" and shit where it ate, it was a cow.

My phone rang. *Speak of the devil.*

"What's up, boss? You make it home yet?"

"Yeah, been home for an hour or so," Brand said. He sounded exhausted.

Tapping the speaker button, I set the phone on my dash.

"Are you close to Wisper yet?"

"An hour out, I think," I said. "I'm glad you called. I just wanna reiterate that I'm *not* goin' to your brother's place to be his nursemaid. You know that, right? It's not my job."

"And I wouldn't ask it of you," Brand assured me. "All I

need you to do is supervise the crew finishin' the houses. They shouldn't need too much of your energy. All three houses are almost done. What I really need you to do is use your motivational services to whip the cabin crew into shape. If those don't get finished before the snow hits, Bax and Rye's whole business plan might go up in smoke."

I snorted. Right. Me, motivational?

"You know what I mean."

"I do," I said, "and it'll be done."

"Thanks. I better go. I need to unpack and grab a shower. The lawyers estimate that the case will take two or three weeks. We're meetin' tomorrow to go over everything. They want me to settle with this guy, but I'm not sure I can do that. To me, a settlement means admittin' fault, but it wasn't our damn fault."

"Okay," I said, "but Brand, listen to the lawyers. At least hear them out, and then you do what's best for you and your company. To hell with everyone else."

"I will. Thanks, Sweetie, and listen, go easy on Bax. I know the two of you didn't exactly hit it off when you met, but he's been through a lot. You're gonna be seein' a lot of him. Might as well make the best of it. And Athena will be there. She's a great kid. She'll have you bustin' a gut in no time, but be careful where you step. She has a habit of adoptin' abandoned animals and they crap everywhere."

"Sounds like… fun?"

Brand laughed. "Thanks again. You're savin' my ass."

"Yeah, yeah. You're welcome."

"Text when you get to my brother's."

"Will do. Bye."

Brand had downplayed the job he'd asked me to do, just a smidge. There was still a ton of work left. The three houses Brand had agreed to build for his mom, his sister, Abey, whom I met last year and loved, and her fiancée, and a third house for his friend and business partner, Ryder, and Ryder's girlfriend were almost done. All they needed were roofs, drywall, and exterior siding. Plus, then there was all the interior stuff and electrical. But a lot could still go wrong. And if the houses weren't enough, the nine rental cabins left to finish were all in varying stages of completion. The two biggest structures had only recently had their foundations poured.

Cabins were a hell of a lot less involved than houses, but they still needed sturdy floors, working toilets, and kitchens. And these were fancy cabins, so each build was like a mini house. The two crews on payroll, not including the specialty guys who'd pop on and off the property until the jobs were done, had been split between the houses and the cabins all summer. But in my opinion, separating them further would be more efficient. The crews would be smaller, yes, but more specific to the tasks still needing to be finished.

Brand had given me the go-ahead to make changes because the work had to be paused for him to prepare for court, and any time I could buy back for us would help. I'd spent the last several days working out the new crew configurations and schedule. The delay was a problem, but time would tell if I had put my money where my mouth was. If I could get all the projects on track to be finished before the end of October, I'd consider that a win and a job well done.

Brand had personally overseen all the preliminary work on the cabins while I stayed in Sheridan to run the projects we had going up there. He'd done a good deal of the groundwork himself, but the enormity of the overall project was a little intimidating. And then there was the fact that I was a woman. A five-foot-two woman who had been nicknamed Sweetie. At least in Sheridan, I'd worked with the crew for a long time. They knew me, knew I had the skills to lead them and that I didn't take any shit.

The mostly male crew in Wisper didn't know me from Eve, and I couldn't even put into words how excited I was to deal with their whistles and catcalls and all the blowback they'd give me once they got a good look at me.

Right.

Brand had handpicked the cabin crew, and those were the guys I worried most about. If they fancied themselves special or irreplaceable, that usually came with attitude. Not always, but enough to make me bite my nails and stress about hitting our deadlines. As a woman, trying to lead those guys could sometimes be a little like wrangling self-important cats. A lot of the guys had grown up with Brand, though, so I hoped they were down to earth like he was.

He would've managed the whole thing himself, but he'd tagged me in when he knew he'd need to be away for the stupid legal crap he was dealing with. Who the fuck injured themselves—on purpose—on a construction site hoping to get a payout?

Brand was a good boss. Everybody in and around Sheridan knew it to be true. If they worked for him and they needed something, all they had to do was ask. So why this douchebag, Jim Culver, felt the need to "fall" from the second floor of an unfinished house onto a pile of lumber and risk breaking his neck was a mystery to me. If the idiot needed money, Brand would've gladly helped out. The dude would have quite literally given Jim the shirt off his back and all the cash in his wallet, so the fact that the whole thing had ended up in a formal court hearing was just plain—

"Shit!"

Slamming on my brakes, my tires screeched to a stop when a gargantuan bison stepped out from the row of trees lining the highway and stood in the middle of the road thirty feet in front of my truck. It was definitely a male, with huge, thick horns, a long beard, and a boulder-like shoulder hump on his back.

As my heart rate increased to dangerous levels, I whispered to myself, "Like you'd know a male from a female bison. Have you ever even seen one in real life?"

But I felt sure the animal was male. There was just something about his kingly stature and the way his deep brown eyes saw into my soul. He had to be old. Maybe wise too.

Glancing in my side and rearview mirrors, I checked for cars behind me on westbound Highway 26. The road was empty as far as I could tell, and there were no cars coming from the opposite direction either, but I flicked on my hazards to be safe.

It was just me and my new best friend, a bison. Was he part of someone's herd, or was he one of the free-range ones that wandered out of Yellowstone?

Damn. "If he attacks, you're screwed."

How much did a full-grown male bison weigh? Two-thousand pounds? I imagined his horns tackling my truck's front end and winced. His head was huge! I doubted I had a cell signal out here. I'd just passed over the Continental Divide and hadn't yet made it to Moran, and from what my maps app told me, that was where civilization would start to make a comeback in this part of the state, but I was too afraid to move to grab my phone and check the distance.

My new friend's legs seemed breakably skinny, but the rest of him was truck-sized, and all I could do was watch him turn and square off with my rusted-out Chevy. I could've tried to back up, but I had a feeling his reflexes would be quicker than mine right now. My hands on my steering wheel shook.

The bison stared past the windshield, right at me. I didn't get the feeling he was mad or he wanted to ram my ride, but he just kept staring.

Like he was… trying to tell me something?

"Are you mental, Bea?" I whispered into the deafening silence. "What's wrong with you? This is a very wild animal. He could crush you quite literally. He didn't stop to shoot the shit."

In my defense, a bison stopping traffic wasn't a super common occurrence up in Sheridan. I'd never been down to the Jackson Hole area before, and I hadn't yet taken the time to wander Yellowstone, but humungous mammals didn't usually hang out on the side of the highways up in the northeast part of the state. Actually, we did get moose and elk occasionally, and sometimes wild turkeys, but definitely not bison.

"What do you want?" I asked the wooly brute, but my voice sounded insignificant in the magnitude of the moment, and he couldn't hear me anyway.

He turned his head, like he wanted to direct my attention to the mountains behind him I could barely see peeking through the fog to the northwest. Was there something I needed to know about my destination? Something a humungous bison felt the need to stop traffic to tell me… or, like, impart through nonverbal communication?

Wooly Wally swung his head back in my direction. He kept his eyes locked on mine and moved slowly—and pretty gracefully for an animal his size—and stepped to the graveled side of the road, and then he lowered his shoulders and dipped his horns, as if in the last minute he had judged my character and was saying, "Go ahead. I give you my blessing to continue forth on my land."

Quickly grabbing my phone from the dash, hoping he

didn't get spooked by the movement, I snapped a picture of the mountain protector, this once nearly extinct behemoth and guardian of the West.

He grunted a breath, and it turned to steam in the cool, fall air, and then he lumbered back into the trees and was gone. With him went the fog I'd been battling through the last two hours. It rolled in waves off the hilly, winding highway, leaving Togwotee Pass and lifting back into the sky like steam rising from hot coffee in the cold.

As the sawtooths of the Teton Mountain Range revealed themselves to me, I sat in awe, holding my breath, still barely daring to move as the deep blue-green roadside fence of evergreens with their wood-post trunks led my eyes to the orange sunset deepening in the distance. The impending twilight lit up those impressively tall peaks and darkened their sharp valleys, washing them in a powerful peach and dusky lavender glow.

And now I got it. I finally understood why Brand had been so homesick, and how, when he talked about the mountains surrounding his home, he got this cheesy, faraway look in his eyes.

It was silly, but I felt Wooly Wally's approval of my reaction to his land, and somehow, it felt like I'd been called home too.

CHAPTER THREE

SWEETIE

THE BISON really shook me up, and I gripped my steering wheel like it was the only buoy in a sea of mountains and sharp, switchbacking roads.

He'd been there to welcome me. I was sure of it, and how ridiculous was that?

If you asked anyone who knew me, they'd laugh in your face if you told them Beatrice Baker had been seen communing with a very large land mammal. In fact, I'd earned the nickname "Sweetie" initially because everyone at Lee Construction thought I was so nice, but I had just been settling in and learning my way around my new job. Once my coworkers realized I really wasn't that sweet and that I tended to be a bit of a Brunhilda on the job, the irony made the nickname stick, not that any one of those knuckleheads knew the actual definition of the word irony.

The guys probably thought I didn't have a nurturing or animal-loving bone in my body. I'd never had a dog or a cat. Not even a goldfish. Why on earth I thought I'd felt a connection with a bison was beyond me.

Driving slowly through the Jackson Hole valley, I found

my way in the intensifying night. The road to Bax's place rose in elevation quickly, and the fields and open areas I'd driven through earlier disappeared and gave way to climbing pine forests with dark mountains bookending them in every direction.

For a good twenty minutes, I'd been convinced I was lost and that any moment I'd hit a deer or an elk or something. There were wildlife signs everywhere, not that I could actually read them because apparently the entirety of Teton County had taken an anti-streetlight stance.

When I took my second-to-last turn onto Old Fish Creek Road, I breathed a sigh of relief. Brand's directions told me I was only five minutes away from the house he'd grown up in, and finally, I saw the new sign he'd just installed at the start of the Lee's property that had thankfully been backlit and read "Spitfire Ranch at Lee Valley."

Like it was on tiptoes instead of tires, my truck crept up the graded and graveled drive slowly, and I scanned the still darkness for animals, but when I saw Bax's big, two-story farmhouse and parked in front of it, stress left my shoulders and I took a deep, steadying breath.

You made it.

Standing on the small porch, Bax Lee was also backlit by a warm glow coming from inside the house Brand told me his brother had inherited when he took over running the Lee's family farm.

Bax held himself upright with a crutch beneath each arm. A thigh-to-toes plaster cast encased his right leg. He'd covered it with a pair of loose jeans, but I knew it was there, and it made his leg look twice as thick as the non-broken one.

In the dark, I couldn't see the house well, but it felt a little run-down to me, which surprised me since Brand's house in Sheridan was new and modern.

Bax squinted, trying to get a better look at me. "Thought you got lost," he said as I stepped out of my truck. "I expected you a little earlier."

The night we'd met flashed through my head, when he'd said in front of my coworkers, *"My brother call you Sweetie 'cause you got a sweet little ass?"*

Still waitin' for an apology, asshole.

"No," I said. "I wasn't lost, but there's no streetlights around here. I had to drive five miles an hour 'cause I'm terrified of hittin' somethin'. I mean, the least y'all could do is put some road reflectors along your driveway."

"Oh."

I laughed into the quiet between us. "You never thought about it?" The stillness in the dark was a little unnerving. Sheridan wasn't some big, busy, bustling city, but it wasn't *this* quiet.

"Honestly? No, which is dumb, but it's just that I grew up out here, you know? I don't need lights."

Wanting to see him better, too, I climbed the porch stairs and stood in front of him. His eyes traveled the shape of my face, and mine did the same to his.

Yup, the fucker's still gorgeous.

I'd forgotten how sexy Bax was. His hair looked the same as it had last week on my computer screen, thick and light brown and kind of messy, and he had the same strong, athletic build I'd noticed back in Sheridan two years ago.

And those baby-blue eyes? *Damn.* Women had been brought to their knees with far less.

But I was right that something was different about him. It wasn't only his reliance on crutches curving his shoulders inward a little.

"But your future customers didn't grow up here, and you want them to be able to see so they don't trip over a rock or crash their cars into a tree and break their necks. I'm surprised Brand hasn't suggested a lighting plan."

"Maybe he did. He could have." Bax looked down at the cast on his leg. "I've been a little distracted, I guess."

"Yeah, I heard. Got yourself beat up by a bull?"

He nodded. "Sorry I can't help with the cabins."

"It's cool. I don't really need your help."

He didn't like that. His eyebrow jumped the tiniest bit, which made me realize that maybe I'd been a little harsh. It was habit. When I met a man in a work situation, my instinct was to prove my dominance and worth. *And that goes double for Mr. Smart Mouth Lee.*

"Right. Well, I guess you'll probably wanna get settled in. Brand set up a cabin for you, and my sister stopped by with some grocery staples earlier. If you need anything else, please feel free to come up to the house anytime. There's people comin' and goin' at all hours."

"Where is it?"

Both eyebrows rose this time. "The house?"

I rolled my eyes. "The cabin?"

"Oh, right." He chuckled. "Uh, it's… Well, if you turn around and drive half a mile back down the lane, it's the second right you come to… Ah shit, but it's not lit, like you said. You might not see it. I'll drive you."

He looked at his cast again.

"I mean, you can drive. I'll ride with you. Show you where to go, but you'll have to drive me back." He sighed. "Fuck. That's sounds like too much work. I'm sorry. I'm sure you're tired from your drive."

"It's fine," I said, watching exhaustion take over his features, like candlelight being snuffed out in a pitch-black room. "C'mon, let's go and then I'll get you back here. Tomorrow, we're gettin' some damn road reflectors."

Bax was not graceful with the crutches. He almost fell off his porch when he lost his balance. I imagined him landing on his ass and snickered to myself, but then I felt bad about laughing. Memories of my dad after his back surgeries came back to me. He couldn't do anything for himself for a long time. I'd had to help him with everything. And the pain? God, I couldn't even imagine. I was sure Bax was in pain now, but he tried not to show it.

He had to sit turned toward me a little in my truck because the cast was completely unbendable. For him to fit, I had to adjust the bench seat as far back as it would go. Even sitting forward at the edge of the seat, I could barely reach the pedals, but Bax's leg still looked like a long, denim log stuck through my floorboard. And he wouldn't let me help him, not even to shut his door, but soon enough, we were bumping along back down the gravel lane.

"Where's your daughter?" I asked.

"Athena's asleep. She's got school tomorrow. I don't usually stay up this late either, but lately…" He looked at me, stopping himself from saying whatever he'd been about to admit. "Anyway, I watch a lot of late-night TV these days. Turn here."

He motioned out his window to a barely recognizable dirt road to the right. He hadn't been lying when he said I would've missed it without his help. The road looked more like a hiking path, until I realized that the trees and brush hanging over the dirt just needed to be weed whacked a bit. I added it to my mental to-do list.

We drove almost another half mile, and when he pointed to a cabin coming into view off to the right side of my truck, with cozy golden light spilling out its windows, I pulled in twenty feet from the front door and parked.

I couldn't see any other structures nearby because the

night was lightless besides the twinkling of a few stars, but I knew from the blueprints I'd studied that the frames of the other cabins were near. Not too close so guests would have privacy, but not too far so they wouldn't be completely secluded in the forest, although, each cabin's location had been chosen for its proximity to a lake on the property and to offer the illusion of seclusion and stunning views of the mountains.

Breathing deeply as I got out of the truck, I let the perfume of the pine trees ground me. I heard a stream or river running close by. It reminded me of when I was a little girl and my dad would go hunting and come home with a deer, and then my mama cooked the steaks over a fire behind our house while I played in the creek back there, trying to catch minnows with my bare hands and waiting for supper.

Bax watched me over the roof of my truck. It was as if I could feel the direct stare of his eyes on the back of my head. For some reason I couldn't name, I felt self-conscious around him. It wasn't a feeling I was accustomed to. I didn't usually give a shit what people thought of me, as long as they knew I was confident and competent, so why would I care now? Besides, Bax had to know that about me already or else he wouldn't have agreed to let me stay on his property and finish the builds. Or maybe he hadn't agreed. Maybe my boss put his foot down and insisted, and Bax hadn't really had a say in the matter.

"It's nice out here," I said. "Quiet."

"Yeah."

He dragged my backpack from the front seat, slung it over his shoulder, and then took off with his crutches toward the cabin. I grabbed my suitcase from the bed of my truck, and when we were standing on the little ground-level log porch, he turned back to me.

"There's a fire pit out back. You can see it from the slider in the kitchen. Brand left a load of firewood out there for you. It's relaxin' at night, sittin' out here with a drink."

"I don't drink."

"Oh, well, then… tea?"

I grimaced and Bax laughed. The weightless sound changed his face, and for the first time since I'd arrived, I noticed a light in his eyes. He looked the way he had in the pictures I'd seen in his brother's office, before life rained hell down on him, with his beautiful, tall, blond wife by his side and little Athena flashing a goofy smile with dirt stains on the knees of her leggings.

Maybe it was Bax's height making me suddenly worried about how I appeared to him. He towered over me with his solid six-one or six-two frame. Compared to my measly five feet and two teeny, tiny inches, he was a giant, and my southern upbringing had tried to ingrain in me that a big man was the guy in charge in most situations. What a load of horse shit, but still, the urge to defer to him for safety or knowledge was there.

And it pissed me the fuck off.

"What do you drink then?"

"Water or coffee."

"I don't know if my sister brought coffee, but if not, come up to the house when you wake up. I've always got some brewin'."

"Thanks," I said as he unlocked the cabin's door with a key.

He handed it to me, swung the door wide with the bottom of one crutch, and then hobbled back two steps to let me go ahead of him. "There's another key up at the house, in case you lose this one. I hung it next to the kitchen door on a hook. The keychain is leather with the number one on it."

The comforting smell of Western red cedar filled my nose as I stepped over the threshold. "Okay. Thanks."

"Athena picked out the sheets and pillows and stuff for you." He moved behind me and stood to the side of the little loveseat in front of the cabin's front window next to the door. "And she said we *had* to get you this blanket. It can get pretty cold out here early in the mornin'."

I turned and saw a thick, fuzzy, sage-green throw draped over the back of the loveseat. Sitting carefully on a cushion, I touched it with the tips of my fingers, then let them flatten over the softest thing I'd ever felt. My best friend Bree from grade school let me hold her pet chinchilla once, and I remembered marveling at how soft his fur had been.

Athena's blanket was softer.

Closing my eyes, I smoothed my hand back and forth over the fabric, brushing uneven lines in the fleecy softness.

What a nice thing for a kid to do. In fact, it was the nicest thing anyone had done for me in a very long time, to think of such a sweet comfort for me, a complete stranger. It never would've occurred to me to leave something like a soft blanket for a guest I'd never met. I couldn't wait to snuggle up beneath it in my PJs.

Bax cleared his throat. "So, the bedroom's over there." He pointed to his right with his crutch.

The cabin Brand had set up for me was the only habitable structure so far of the ten Lee Valley cabins, and the smallest of the lot. The layout reminded me of a corporate apartment, but the place was all mountain-cabin vibes, with lots of wood and simple, timeless features. The open living room and kitchen set-up, with only a five-foot-wide wall to hold the fireplace and separate the spaces, took up the majority of the floor plan.

To my right was the bedroom with just enough space for a

queen bed, a long dresser, and a rocking chair in the corner. A shallow closet lined one bedroom wall, and a soft light shone out from the attached bathroom featuring a bath and shower, a toilet, and a single-fixture sink, with storage for towels and toiletries underneath.

The cabin really was perfect for a single renter.

Athena had decorated the bed simply with another green blanket and matching pillowcases, but the comforter looked poofy and lush, with red and rust-orange fall leaves printed on top. A Mason jar sat atop a basic, solid-wood bedside table with real wildflowers dropped into three inches of water, and a traveler's guide to the Grand Teton National Park lay next to it.

When I turned back to him, I caught Bax watching me move around the bedroom. He shifted his weight onto his good leg and gripped his crutches' handles tightly.

I get it, buddy. This ain't the most ideal situation for me either. At least I'm gettin' paid to be here. What's your excuse?

Clearing his throat, he said, "There's a temporary power pole outside, about a hundred yards down the lane. Everything runs off that till the power company connects the cabins to the grid. It's in the works. Hopefully they'll get it done in the next few weeks, but if the lights go out—"

"I know what to do. Brand said he'd leave a portable gas-powered generator for me in the closet." I walked past Bax and slid open the closet door. "It's right here."

"Oh, okay. Good," Bax said when I backed out of the way so he could see the little square generator on the closet floor. "Brand thought of everything."

"It's kinda his job."

"Right. You know, now you're here, I'm not sure it's a good idea for you to stay—"

"This is perfect," I said, cutting him off before he could get all chivalrous. Looking around the cabin again, I nodded. "I'll be fine."

Besides, Brand knew me well. I lived alone and preferred small spaces. Empty rooms, in my opinion, were a waste, and they kind of freaked me out in the dark. My apartment back in Sheridan was a studio, and it suited me perfectly.

"Okay, but seriously, if you change your mind, you're welcome to stay up at the house if you'd be more comfortable."

"Thanks, but I prefer the solitude, and I think it'll be better if I'm closer to the work. I'm not too worried about the houses gettin' done, but the cabins are another story."

He shrugged, and his crutches lifted off the floor for a second. "Okay then. Just a little warnin', though, in case you don't know: don't leave food outside. Don't leave it in your truck either. Not even a package of trail mix. When you have trash you need to get rid of, bring it up to the house. We don't have bear-proof cans out here yet. They can smell that shit from miles away, and right now, they're looking for anything they can find to eat before it's time for 'em to bed down for winter. We've got electric fences in some places, but they don't reach the more remote corners of the property."

Oh shit. What the fuck? Now I'm totally gonna sleep soundly, alone, out here in the middle of the forest with bears circling my cabin like hungry sharks in the sea.

Fear must've shown on my face because the side of Bax's mouth tipped up a little. "Scared? Still think you wanna stay out here alone?"

"Absolutely I do," I said, trying to assure him and to reassure myself I could handle a harmless grizzly. I knew there had to be construction equipment close by, and I'd packed a bunch of my own tools behind my seat in my truck. If I had to, I could nail-gun the fucker in the ass to scare him off.

Good plan.

Bax cleared his throat again. "What'd you say?"

"What?"

"You said somethin'."

I shook my head, and Bax watched as my hair fell over my shoulder. "No I didn't."

He laughed under his breath. "Okay, you didn't."

"I just said that. Anyway, guess I better get your gimpy ass back up to your TV. Reruns are callin'."

"Yup. Guess so."

CHAPTER FOUR

BAX

SWEETIE DROVE me back to the house and dropped me off, and as I watched her drive away, my attraction to her slapped me across the face. It surprised me that I didn't have a black eye after all the reality knockouts I'd had lately.

I'd thought admitting to myself that I was attracted to anyone would feel weird. I hadn't really felt it since Candy, or I thought I hadn't, but now, fuzzy memories of the night I'd met Sweetie flashed in my head, her piercing green eyes, sexy smile, and big attitude like a wake-up call I didn't ask for.

There was no denying I'd felt a pull to her when she parked in front of my house tonight and stepped out of her Chevy in tight jeans and an oversized sweatshirt.

I wanted her.

That in itself was some kind of revelation. That I could want something again, other than time to move backward. Athena got older and more independent every second of every day, and Candy and the baby became hazier and further away with every breath I took. I was afraid that soon I wouldn't be able to remember them at all.

But Sweetie was sexy in a different way than Candy had been. Candy was my first and only love. I knew her body because we'd grown up learning each other together. And she was the mother of my kid. To me, Candy's body had been a holy shrine. Even fourteen years later, I was still in awe of what it had been capable of.

Until it betrayed us all.

Sweetie tempted me in a completely different way, a more seductive way. Vaguely, I remembered feeling something similar when I first met her up in Sheridan, but grief had me trapped in its heavy haze back then. The gin had a pretty good hold on me that night too.

Seeing Sweetie again wasn't the first sign that the haze had passed, but until tonight, I hadn't wanted to admit it was true. What an odd thing, to know I'd been holding onto pain just because it was familiar. It kept me company. How messed up was that?

And what did it mean that I'd finally let some of it go?

Sweetie's much smaller size made me feel protective of her. Maybe it was just the possibility of grizzly bears "circling her cabin like hungry sharks in the sea." She seemed not to realize she'd said it out loud. It was cute, and hilarious, to hear the thoughts she meant to keep to herself, and it fought against the hard-ass persona she tried so hard to project.

But it was clear she didn't want or need my protection. Or my company, which made it really inconvenient that, in some fucked-up way, her movements and the way her body seemed to ground her with every step she took only made me want her more.

Her confidence was sexy.

Her deep, dark brown hair and the way it fell down her back had my hands itching to touch, to caress and wrap around my fist. Her pink lips and the habit she had of rolling them together when she was thinking about what she wanted to say had me imagining how good it'd feel to slip my cock between them, for her to suck and roll those soft lips over my hardness.

I'd never had that particular urge with someone I didn't even know. It felt a little dark, but exciting. And different.

As I hobbled through my kitchen to the living room, not even bothering to turn off lights as I went, I thought, *different's good.*

Not like it mattered though. Sweetie had been clear that she was here to work. She wanted to be left alone.

And, like, what was I planning to do anyway? If I had any notions of getting her in my bed, those flew out the window real quick when I realized Athena would be around, and I couldn't even bend my knee. How exactly did I think I'd take Sweetie if I had to rely on crutches to keep me standing upright?

I mean, if you really want her, you could get creative.

Whoa. My mind had gone straight to sex. That hadn't happened in years.

It was good, though, that Sweetie seemed focused on her job and couldn't have cared less about me, because being in a relationship with anyone, or even just having sex with someone, would feel like a betrayal.

I couldn't do that to Candy. I wasn't ready. Maybe I never would be.

Turning on the TV with the volume set low so I wouldn't wake Athena, I fell onto my couch and flipped channels till I found a familiar motorcycle show with a bunch of gruff-looking guys in leather cuts fighting each other in a parking lot in California, and my mind began to drift.

My eyelids grew heavier as I imagined Sweetie bent over my kitchen table, her long hair tumbling over her naked back, ass at just the right height for me to pound into her from behind.

The eerie, thin consciousness of a dream settled around me. I wasn't sure when I'd fallen asleep, but static showed on my TV, which was how I knew with certainty I was dreaming because TVs didn't show static anymore. It wasn't 1994. If the show had ended, the next episode would've played, or the TVs screensaver would've popped up from inactivity.

The static was loud, though, and I startled. My eyes popped open, and immediately I felt a presence. When I looked to my left, my dead wife was sitting next to me on the couch. I covered my mouth with my hand so Athena wouldn't hear me scream.

"I'm not really here," Candy said.

But the heartache and surprise seizing my breath rendered me speechless. And the guilt I felt for wanting someone other than my wife threatened to swallow me whole.

"It's okay, Bax," Candy said. "You're just dreamin'. You know that."

Trying to slow my racing pulse through force of will alone, I sat up. "Yeah, I know. Dead people don't come back to life just to watch TV."

"That's not why I'm here," Candy said, "but I mean, that Jax guy is hot."

"Hey now." I scoffed. She'd been gone three years but decided to haunt my dreams from the beyond just to lust after some other man?

Her tinkling laugh soothed the pit in my stomach I'd been feeling since she left me. I knew she was only a manifestation of my imagination or subconscious, but I was so relieved I hadn't forgotten the sound.

"But there is a reason I'm here, Bax."

"What is it?" I asked. "Is it Athena?"

Candy shook her head. She wasn't pregnant anymore in my dreams. She looked like she had when we were eighteen and full of hope for our future, and I wanted to reach over to touch her, run my fingers through her hair like I used to, but I was too scared to feel the emptiness when she disappeared if I tried.

"Athena's good," she said. "She doesn't dream about me anymore. Not like she used to." Sadness crossed Candy's face quickly, but then it disappeared. "She's movin' on as much as a young woman can from losin' her mama."

"Is the baby with you?" I whispered.

She didn't answer, but she smiled softly, and I hoped the answer was yes. Every time she came to me in my dreams, I asked her, and she always smiled. Sometimes she'd nod. But she never actually said it. Not with words, but something told me he was safe wherever he was.

"I miss you both."

God, she looked so real as tears filled her eyes, but abruptly she said, "Stop that."

"Stop what?"

She shook her head quickly. "Stop it."

"Candy? Stop what?"

"Just stop," she said, but this was the worst part of my dreams. She had already begun to fade away.

"Please stay," I begged, but she had already gone.

All that remained was her quiet voice in my head. "Stop changin' the channel. There's a good show on."

I felt hollow when she left, and just like every time she'd appeared to me, I wondered why she didn't bring our son with her. Why wouldn't she let me see him?

Athena's shrieking voice ripped me right out of the fog. "Daddy! Stop that. You're layin' on the remote. It's so loud!"

When I opened my eyes, squinting against the lights I

hadn't turned off last night, Athena stood in front of the couch in her koala pajamas with her hands pressed tightly over her ears. I'd passed out with the TV remote in my lap, which was now under my butt, and it seemed my ass cheeks couldn't hear the bikers on TV so they turned the volume up as loud as it would go, except now the SAMCRO guys were in a shootout with the Mayans, and it sounded like it was taking place in my living room.

"Shit, sorry."

I pulled the remote out from my under my ass and turned off the TV just as there was a knock on the kitchen door.

Athena rolled her eyes at me. "I'll get it."

"Thanks, Road Trip. Sorry about the noise. What time is it?"

Over her shoulder, she called, "It's not even five yet."

Groaning, I fell back into the permanent indentation my lazy bones had recently made on my couch, but when I heard Athena opening the door, I remembered that the person knocking would probably be Sweetie looking for coffee. I'd forgotten to set the machine on a timer. Not thinking, I tried to jump up, but I touched my foot to the floor, and pain shot up through my right leg like a flash of furious lightning. I yelped and fell back on my ass.

"Shit!"

The patter of Athena's slippers and a set of boots filled my ears.

"Daddy," Athena said, "what in the world—"

Sweetie's low chuckle made me open my eyes. "Put too much pressure on that leg?"

I nodded. *Damn.* I'd fallen asleep before I brushed my teeth last night, and it had been two days since my last self-inflicted sponge bath.

"Don't get up," Sweetie said to me. To Athena, she asked, "What time do you need to leave for school?"

"Seven."

"Do you need a ride?"

"No, Aunt Abey's pickin' me up."

"Cool. We've got time then. Go upstairs," she told Athena. "Do whatcha gotta do, shower, finish homework or whatever. I'll start some coffee and see what y'all have for breakfast."

Surprise washed across Athena's face. Probably mine too.

"I usually make breakfast," Athena said.

"Well"—Sweetie shrugged—"today you get the day off."

"No, no," I interrupted, "you don't have to do that. I can—"

Both women turned my way and broke out in giggles.

"Yeah, right, Daddy." Athena turned to Sweetie and held out her hand. "I'm Athena, by the way. We met on Uncle Brand's computer last week."

Sweetie shook my little girl's hand. "I remember. I'm Bea. Nice to meet you IRL. And thanks for that fluffy blanket in my cabin. I love it. Now, go do what teenagers do. Text your friends, change your outfit fifteen times and throw all your clothes on the floor, and I'll start breakfast for you."

Athena smiled and reached out to surprise Sweetie with a hug. "Thank you."

Sweetie stiffened. She didn't say anything at first, but slowly, she brought her arms up and hugged Athena back. They were nearly the same height, so it was a perfect fit. "Welcome. Now git."

Athena turned to do as she'd been told, but she stopped her forward motion and looked down at me still trying not to let out a string of really foul cuss words from the pain. "Need me to get your toothbrush or help you to the bathroom?"

"Of course not," I snapped. How embarrassing! Was this what my life had been reduced to, being cared for by my little girl like I was ninety-five? "Sorry, baby. I meant no thank you. I've got it. Go ahead, get ready for school. Sweetie and I've got things covered down here."

"Her name is Bea, Daddy. She doesn't like her nickname."

"You don't?" I asked, looking up at Sweetie, surprised Athena had picked up on it.

Sweetie pursed her lips and shook her head. "Funny your kid figured that out in one conversation over a laptop, but you've known me two years and it never occurred to you a woman wouldn't like to be called Cupcake or Sweetie Pie?"

I winced. "Shit. I hear it now. Sorry."

Athena turned again, looking back and forth between Sweet—between Bea and me.

"What's so bad about that?" she asked. "My mama's name was Candy."

Regret washed over Bea's features in an instant. "There's nothin' wrong with your mama's name, Athena. I didn't mean to imply that there was. I'm sorry. A person's name is their name, and they can and should be proud of it, whatever it is.

"But mine is a nickname, and my problem with it is that men have often nicknamed women after foods or animals because they think it makes them sound like the dominant person in the room. But I am almost always the most dominant person in the room or the person in charge, so it's just a stupid joke that they nicknamed me Sweetie."

"Oh." Athena twisted her lips, thinking it over, but then she smiled. She was a good judge of character. She always had been. She knew Bea wasn't making fun of her mama's name.

"Okay." Athena skipped over to the staircase and then

charged up. We heard her turn on the shower and stomp around her room, deciding what to wear as the water heated up.

I wondered how long I had left until the sweet softness of childhood disappeared from my daughter's expressions and the hardness of teenaged angst took over.

"Sorry," Bea said again.

"Really, it's okay. You didn't know. And I'm sorry. My brother always calls you Sweetie. I guess I assumed you were cool with the nickname."

"Now you know."

"Got it," I said, tapping the side of my head with my index finger, like it was a locked vault.

She held out her hand, nodding to the rat's nest on top of my head. "C'mon, you look like you just woke up. I'm sure you need to pee."

With an awkward laugh, I accepted the assistance and took her hand. The pain could be unbearable in the mornings before I'd had a chance to load up on ibuprofen, and that was when I hadn't tried to walk on my leg.

Maybe having help wasn't the weakness I'd always thought it was. I'd accepted my brother's and Rye's help with the ranch and the cabin business, and that had been going really well. But I hadn't had help around the house—*female help*—since Candy passed. Other than my mother, I hadn't let anyone get close enough to me or Athena for that.

Besides my sister, thinking about someone else trying to mother my daughter made me angry. No one could replace Candy. Not even a sexy, green-eyed contractor my brother trusted fully.

But Bea hadn't come all the way to Wisper to try to move in on my family, I reminded myself. In fact, in my head, I could hear the things she'd probably shouted at Brand when he asked her to come here. She was probably the last person I'd think to ask for help, but here she was, helping me anyway.

Bea pulled me up onto my good foot, and I bent to grab my crutches leaning against the side of the couch. She walked ahead of me, motioning to the bathroom door with a swing of her arm. "Bathroom?"

"Yep," I said as I followed slowly, trying not to fall over. "Thanks, but I can take a leak on my own."

"Mm-hm."

She flipped on the light and then dug through the medicine cabinet for my toothbrush and paste. I'd been keeping them in the downstairs bathroom just for the ease, plus, the tub was in there. Dragging myself upstairs wasn't my favorite thing to do at the moment. It took too long, and the standing shower was of no use to me anyway. The doctor had said I could shower, as long as I used a cast cover, but the standing part was the issue. On one leg in a slippery shower stall? Uh, no thanks. If I broke my other leg 'cause I lost my balance and slipped, I'd be in a wheelchair for the foreseeable future, and then I'd really be screwed.

Twisting the hot-water knob on the sink, Bea let the water flow over her hand as it warmed up, and the need to relieve myself made its presence known. If I could've hopped up and down, I would've.

She looked at the chips in the enamel on the side of the old sink, the yellowing grout between the tiles surrounding the tub, and the ancient toilet I'd been meaning to replace for years. "This bathroom needs a facelift."

"Yeah," I agreed. The whole house needed one. It hadn't been updated since my parents had lived here years ago. "Brand keeps sayin' he's gonna do it, but he's got so much on his plate."

"Can't you do it? I mean, once your leg heals?" When the water was hot, she turned on the cold water and swiped her hand beneath till she was satisfied with the temperature, still scrutinizing my dingy downstairs bathroom.

"You know," I said, "people have been brushin' their teeth with cold water since the dawn of time."

She rolled her eyes, wet my toothbrush under the now lukewarm stream, squeezed a bubble of toothpaste on the bristles, and held it up to my mouth. "Open."

My mouth popped open before my brain had given its permission, and Bea shoved the toothbrush in. I bit down on the bristles to hold it in place as she gripped my waistband and began to unbutton my jeans.

"What're you doin!" I garbled. Heat churned in the space between us, and it rose from where her hand hovered over my body. It crawled quickly up to my neck, and I felt my cheeks flush.

"Helpin'."

"I can do it."

She speared me with a look, then unzipped my zipper. "That's all I meant to do. You can whip it out yourself. I'm gonna go find the coffee."

"O-okay. Thanks. Um, coffee's in the cupboard closest to the fridge, filters are on top of the machine, and there's milk in the fridge. Sugar's in a jar next to—"

"Don't need it," she said before she closed the door behind her. "I don't do sweet."

I chuckled, my rapid heart rate decreasing, and my toothbrush almost fell out of my mouth. "'Course you don't."

CHAPTER FIVE

BEA

SUBTLETY HAD NEVER BEEN my strong suit.

Laughing at the incredulous look on Bax's face, I rooted around inside his kitchen cupboards, looking for the coffee he'd said was in one place, but I found the package of light-roast grounds sitting on the top shelf in the fridge. The guy really was out of his head.

As I had so vehemently stated to my boss yesterday, helping his brother was at the bottom of my list of priorities, but when Bax cried out in pain this morning after trying to put weight on his broken leg and I caught him defenseless on his couch, I kept seeing similarities to my dad after he'd broken his back. I didn't think Bax's titanium-fortified femur was quite as complicated a medical issue as five broken vertebrae, a compressed spinal cord, and fuck-tons of pinched nerves, but he was in pain. That was easy to see.

And the disrepair Bax's house had fallen into was familiar too.

For a guy who built houses for a living, my dad had certainly let the ball drop on his own home. It was the reason I'd started teaching myself to fix broken things. Daddy lay on the couch watching TV most days after his accident, long after the doctor had said he could resume light activity. He never noticed the world passing him by.

If I wanted something fixed, I had to figure out how to do it myself. That included infuriating dripping-sink faucets, patching holes in roofs, and replacing old floorboards so they wouldn't trip him when he shuffled to the fridge for another beer to go with the buzz from his pain pills. I could've called one of twenty guys to fix those things, but Daddy wouldn't let me. He was embarrassed he couldn't do any of it himself and didn't want any of the men from his crew to know.

Bax didn't seem quite as pigheaded as my dad had been, but he was definitely stubborn.

And I hadn't missed how Bax's cheeks had pinked when I went for his zipper, a dark look flashing in his baby blues.

Unfortunately, sex with my boss's brother wasn't the reason I'd come to the middle of bear country. And besides that, Candy was everywhere in this house. There were framed pictures of Bax's dead wife on the fireplace mantel, hanging on the walls, and the way Athena had jumped down my throat when she thought I was dissing her mom's name told me she wasn't ready for her dad to be with anybody anyway.

Still though, the desire was there. At least on my part, but I'd gotten pretty good at denying myself things I wanted. I could do it again. I had to. The alternative would be messy, and anyway, I had no plans to be one of those women who bulldozed their way into a single dad's life and stomped all over his kid to get what she wanted.

I set the coffee to brew, searched around for clean mugs and a spoon, and when I found them, sat at Bax's kitchen table and checked emails on my phone while I waited, but it wasn't long until I heard the bathroom door click open and the rubber feet on the bottom of his crutches squeak on the floor as he made his way to the kitchen.

When he got there, he stopped and looked down at me. "Can I ask you to do me a favor?" The pinched look on his face said he didn't like asking for help, and the resigned sound of his voice convinced me I was right about it, but whatever the favor was, he needed it.

"Sure."

"There's a laundry basket on top of the washer." He nodded behind us to a closed door, where I assumed his washer and dryer set would be. "Can you throw the clothes from the dryer in there and bring it out here, please? I forgot to ask Athena to do it, but all my clean clothes are in there."

"Sure."

I brought the basket into the kitchen and set it on the table, then went to pour two cups of coffee. I heard Bax digging through the basket, and I heard the *thunk* when he dropped a pair of jeans on the floor.

"Need some more help?" I asked as I poured a little milk into my Spitfire Ranch mug, stirred it slowly, and then turned and leaned against the counter, blowing on and sipping the hot coffee, watching him drop a T-shirt and a sock.

He really needed to keep both hands on his crutch handles. I assumed his left leg hadn't been injured, but constantly putting all his weight on it had to start to hurt at some point, and I had a sneaking suspicion he'd been trying to hide the amount of pain he was really in from Athena.

"Naw, I'm good. Thanks."

He dropped a pair of black boxer-briefs, and I rolled my eyes.

"You've already asked for my help once. What's the harm in askin' again?"

"Uh." He turned a little, his cheeks reddening in chagrin.

"You know, male pride and all that. I've been on my own a long time now. It frustrates me to no end not to be able to do the simplest shit for myself. Plus, I didn't think you'd wanna touch my underwear."

"Please. They're clean, right?"

"Yeah."

"Sit down."

He did it. Didn't argue this time as he pivoted on his foot and lowered himself into a dining chair. He looked the picture of male pride, but it didn't make sense to me, because if his wife were still alive, surely he would've let her fetch clean laundry.

Looking at his shirt, I noticed wrinkles, and was that dog hair clinging to it? Cow hair? I knew the cattle were close. I smelled the dirty buggers, but I hadn't seen a dog anywhere.

But male pride aside, I remembered how it felt to be thirteen and depended on like I had been thirty. It wasn't fun, and that made the decision for me. I called into the living room and up the stairs. "Athena, are you in the shower?"

"About to be," she yelled back. "Why?"

"Don't come downstairs for a few minutes. I'm gonna help your dad change his clothes, okay?"

"Umm… Yeah, okay, I think?"

"Good. Thank you!" Bending in front of him, I grabbed the jeans Bax had been failing to pick up off the floor, but there was no way the thick cast on his right leg would allow itself to be covered by denim, not even boot-cut denim. "How did you plan to get these over your cast, and how the hell did you manage the ones you're wearin'?"

"Aw, shit. I forgot. My sister's future mother-in-law fixed the jeans I have on. She sewed these wide panels in the leg so they'd fit over the cast." He touched the side of his leg, and I finally noticed what he was talking about. "But I've only got the one pair, and they're dirty as fuck. I've been wearin' 'em for two days."

"Yeah, your T-shirt ain't much better. Got sweats?"

"Uh, yeah. There should be some in the basket." He watched as I dug through the pile of clothes until I found a pair of heather-gray sweatpants. They looked roomy enough to fit over his cast, and I lifted the boxers he'd dropped in my other hand.

"Strip."

"Okay." He puffed out his cheeks and released the breath slowly. "Guess we're really doin' this."

"Please. You think I've never seen a pee-pee before?" I rolled my eyes. "But I won't look. I know you can do this on your own, but how long would it take you, and can you promise me you won't fall over in the process? Your daughter might kill me if you break your arm too."

More color rushed into his cheeks. He smirked, and in a low, rasping voice that reminded me of the night we'd met, he said, "Probably not."

I set the boxers and sweats on the kitchen table as he unzipped his zipper and popped open his fly, then shoved the denim as far down his thighs as the chair would allow, and I whipped my head away. Just that one little motion, the sound of the fabric snapping open, and the way he looked right in my eyes when he'd pushed it down his legs— *Oh, Bea. You're in trouble.* The small glimpse I'd gotten of his strong, uncasted and hair-dusted thigh was enough to make me salivate.

I hadn't seen a man's thighs in two years, since my last deeply disappointing one-night stand before I landed in Sheridan. The sex had been adequate, but the happy ending I'd had to give myself when I got home let the sting of disappointment linger. Girls got blue balls too.

Blue ovaries?

Bax cleared his throat. "What'd you say?"

"Nothin'. You ready?"

His chair creaked, and out of the corner of my eye, I watched as he slid his boxers down with his jeans. He made no move to cover himself with the many articles of clothing at his disposal.

He coughed awkwardly. "Yeah. Help?" he said, but there was teasing in his voice.

I took a deep breath, turned back to him, and crouched in front of him, refusing to allow my eyes to focus on bare skin. I tugged at the leg of his jeans, working it over his cast. It took a minute, but I finally managed to get it almost down to his ankle, and then I slipped the other leg down, catching his boxers with the jeans.

He grabbed a clean tee from the laundry basket, set it in his lap, and lifted the dirty one he'd been wearing and pulled it over his head. It messed up his hair, and I wanted to run my hand over it to calm it down, and maybe feel it slide between my fingers. It looked downy and soft.

He tossed the dirty shirt next to the basket and lifted the clean one, working his arms through the arm holes so that the rest of the fabric stretched tightly across his chest.

And then this man was essentially naked in front of me for a hot second.

You are denying yourself right now, Beatrice. Do not look. Don't look. This is your boss's brother. Do not look at his abs, and don't you dare look at his wooly wally!

Shit. I totally looked. How could I not? And of course he was big. And hard. My head cocked to the side just a little as I considered his sizeable girth. *Would it fit?*

Oh God, but wouldn't it be fun to try?

He said nothing, but the smirk at the edges of his lips let

me know he wasn't too embarrassed about popping a boner in the middle of his kitchen at five in the morning while his kid was upstairs.

It told me two things: 1.) he was turned on by me, or nervous around me—or he still had morning wood, and 2.) Bax was comfortable with his body and his virility.

And I liked that just fine. He had a *great* body.

Visions of riding him, of being taken by that big, strong body clouded my mind. A thick vein ran the length of his arm, from the inside of his bicep down to his forearm, like one of those dudes on an airport runway, waving their orange wands to direct large aircraft, or in this case, my eyes, to where they wanted to go. Bax's large hand flexed into a fist on his knee, and I imagined it wrapped tightly around my hair while he pounded into me from behind.

I'd never understood when women spoke of a "swimmer's physique." Sitting around watching guys swim laps on TV every four years wasn't my thing, but now I totally got why those women loved the Olympics. I didn't know if Bax swam, but his shoulders were broad and defined, but not with bulk. They'd been sculpted in sleek muscle, and they led down to clavicles made for licking and a chest so goddamn sexy, I was having a hard time not leaning my cheek against it just to feel the dark hair there scruff my skin.

I bit my lip, rolled it under my teeth as I daydreamed about taking his nipple into my mouth and biting it too.

The memory of his "sweet little ass" comment and the sound of Bax's deep voice cleared the sexy fuzz from my head. "Thought you weren't gonna look?"

"I didn't!"

He laughed when my eyes snapped up to his, and he handed me the sweats and clean boxers from the table.

As I unfolded them, I looked only in his eyes. I would not

look at his dick again. I couldn't 'cause if I did, I'd be tempted to lick it like a lollipop. A salty, man-flavored, delicious…

But a moment passed, and I was still looking in his eyes, still holding the clean clothes between my hands. Again, just like on the highway with the bison, I felt like my character was being contemplated.

Bax blinked.

I moaned.

The sound was so soft and quiet that I hoped he hadn't heard, but he smiled earnestly, and I felt something inside my chest crack and burn a little.

"I'm ready," he whispered, and finally, he pulled the clean tee over his head.

"Right." *But I'm not.*

"THANK YOU FOR MAKIN' breakfast," Athena said, sitting across her kitchen table from me, right before she shoved a forkful of veggie scrambled eggs into her mouth, "but this is weird."

Between us, Bax arched an eyebrow. Just like in poker, he couldn't hide the irritation he felt, relying on my help.

I ignored him. "What's weird? I mean, I know you guys are probably used to eatin' breakfast with just the two of you, but I'm sure Brand or that other guy who lives around here eat here sometimes, right? It's no different than that."

What a cute kid. Her light brown hair was a carbon copy of her dad's, down to the thick waving texture, but her mama's contributions to her DNA showed in the wheat-blond highlights streaking through the hair around her temples and through the knots of her braids. Her smile was genuine, warm and teasing.

"Uncle Rye? Yeah, he eats with us sometimes. Actually, your eggs taste like his. He's a pretty good cook."

"Thanks," I said. "I usually only cook for myself, so I'll take that compliment."

Athena took another big bite and washed it down with orange juice.

Suddenly, the kitchen filled with new morning sunlight and unfamiliar voices as the door banged open behind us and two women walked in. Then a big dude, bigger and a little taller than Bax, followed after them.

"What's this?" the guy said. "I thought it was my turn to cook."

"You're late, so Bea made breakfast this mornin'," Athena told him. "Rye, this is Uncle Brand's forewoman, Bea." She nodded over her shoulder and to me, said, "That's Uncle Rye. He's not really my uncle, but we adopted him, and the lady in the funny hat is my actual Aunt Abey."

"Hey," Abey said, smiling. She tipped her brown sheriff's hat. "Good to see you again."

"Hi."

I'd met Abey once before when she'd come up to Sheridan with her mom to visit Brand, but she hadn't been wearing a uniform then. She looked good in it, and the woman standing next to Abey agreed with me. She checked out Abey's ass, then smacked it playfully.

"Glad to have you here," Rye said. He was a character, I could tell. Every word out of his mouth came coated with a smirk. "Alright, since I'm off the clock, I'm takin' my food to go. I've got so much shi—stuff to do today. And Aubrey's on her way over. She said she wants to talk to me about somethin', but I think she just wants a hot little… Uh, hug. I think she wants a hug."

"And I'm Devo," the dark-haired woman said as she leaned down to kiss Athena's cheek, rolled her eyes at Rye's self-interrupted sexual innuendo, and snagged a piece of bacon off Athena's plate. "You must be the woman who's come to finish our house."

"I am," I said. "Nice to meet you."

"Have you seen it yet? The house?" she asked, and her deep brown eyes twinkled as she tucked a lock of her hair behind her ear and delivered the bacon straight into her mouth.

"No. I got in late last night, but I'm plannin' to head over there after breakfast."

"Mind if I come with?" Devo asked as she chewed. "I can be a little late to work. It makes me so happy to see it. I can't wait to get in there and start decoratin'."

"Sure. I don't mind the company, but from what Brand has told me, there's still a lot of work to be done before you can live there."

"Oh, I know," Devo said. "I'm just excited."

"Hey." Rye's head popped up behind Devo's. She was about my same height, so he probably could've stepped on her and wouldn't have noticed, and in his hand, he held a plate that he'd scooped enough of my eggs and bacon onto to feed a small town. "Bax, you think you're up to a little work today? I've got some phone calls I've been meanin' to make. You could do it since you're stuck in the house. I mean, if you feel up to it."

"*Please*," Bax said. "I'm so fuck— I'm so sick of lookin' at the TV."

Athena snorted. "Guys, it's really comical the way you all try to hide the cuss words, but I know exactly what you mean to say. You're not protectin' my innocence. I hear y'all swearin' up a storm when you think I can't." She shook her head, and I laughed. This kid was sharp. She looked around the room. "Can I go with Devo and Bea? I wanna see the house too."

Devo looked at me, and I looked at Bax. He was staring at my mouth, though, and he didn't answer. Did I have green peppers stuck in my teeth?

Looking back at Athena, I sipped my second cup of coffee and tried to free the green peppers with the tip of my tongue. "Don't you have to get to school?"

"I mean, technically," she said with a grin.

"No way," Abey chimed in. "You're goin' to school. Devo can pick you up later and show you."

"I can't," Devo said. "I have a meetin' this afternoon about that big fundraiser for the community center. Sorry, Road Trip. Maybe this weekend then?"

Athena sighed in defeat. "Okay, I guess."

I blurted, "Why on earth do y'all call this child Road Trip?" What a weird nickname. I'd heard Bax use it twice this morning, and now again. "Is it like my nickname," I asked Athena. "Do you hate it?"

She smiled and shook her head.

Finally, Bax woke up. "She can't sit still. She's always off on a road trip, a new adventure."

Athena beamed at her dad. "That reminds me. I need fifty bucks for drama-club dues."

"Drama-club dues?" he repeated woodenly, like the words Athena had said made no sense strung together. "They charge for that shi—stuff now?"

"Yeah, it's just for snacks and field trips. Stuff like that. We're goin' over to Jackson in early December to watch an adaptation of *"A Christmas Carol."*

Rye turned and set his plate on the counter behind him. He pulled his wallet from his back pocket and handed Athena a fifty.

She tugged it from his fingers. "Thanks."

I'd been feeling sad for Athena that she'd lost her mom, and since I knew what that kind of devastation felt like, there was still a lump in the back of my throat, but as I watched her with her dad and extended and found family, the sadness began to disappear.

When I agreed to fill in for Brand, I hadn't expected to be included in his big family. I'd never had a family like the Lees. I'd had my mom and dad before Mama passed. And when my dad died, I had my ex-husband, kind of, but I'd never been part of a family this loving and involved supportively in each other's lives.

I kind of... liked it?

CHAPTER SIX

BAX

"THE CURSED WHEELBARROW that started it all," Rye said with a grin.

The metal pushcart I'd turned to grab when Red Pepper the bull tried to maim me waited by the base of the porch stairs, and Rye helped me down them.

"Hold on," he said, and he left me teetering on my crutches. He jumped the stairs and grabbed a pillow from the wooden chair I used to rock Athena in, then jumped back down and tossed the hot-pink puff into the wheelbarrow. "A cushion for the king's tender ass."

"Ha. Funny," I said, but it wasn't the worst idea in the world. I sat on it and let my good leg hang over the side. My cast kept my right leg straight out in front of me, and I rested the crutches over my thighs.

I heard Rye grunting behind me as he began to push. "Damn, man. Lay off the pound cake, will ya?"

"Ha! You know we've got tractors, right? You could've picked me up in the skiddie, and by the way, you weigh more than I do."

"There's no way you're ridin' in my brand-new skid steer.

You're bad luck. And now you got them rods and pins in your leg. They probably add twenty pounds. Anyway, I'm just glad you decided to get out of the house. A little sun on your face ain't a bad thing."

"Please," I said. "You're taller, and you got at least ten percent more muscle mass than me, at the very least."

"Whatever. You're just jealous 'cause I'm more handsome than you."

"You're delusional," I said, laughing with my best friend who was as much a brother to me as Brand.

He pushed me through a dip in the dirt on the path to the barn that he easily could've avoided. "Now, I know that's not true. Aubrey tells me I'm the hottest guy on the planet, and she's very knowledgeable. She reads lots of books."

I snorted. "Sure she says that, when she wants somethin' from you."

"Fine by me," Rye said, "'cause what she wants is my hard c—"

Throwing my hand up in the air, I yelped, "Stop! I got no need to hear about your red rooster."

"Your loss. My red rooster can cock her doodle doo somethin' fierce. Hey, so how you feelin'?"

"Yeah, I'm… okay."

"How's the pain?"

I sighed. "Sucks. But it's better than it was right after surgery. Now it's more about aches and pains. It's so damn frustratin'. I'm sittin' around, watchin' the world go by without me. You know me. I like to stay busy."

"Have you finished that picture I saw you workin' on the other day?"

Every pebble he rolled the cart over made me clench my jaw in pain. "Naw, man, that's just sketches and scratches."

"Well, you oughta make it more than that. Spend some time on it. Let your creativity out. What else you got to do?"

He had a point.

"Well apparently, today I need to make some phone calls. Who am I callin'?"

"I need you to put in an order with Bob at the feed store, and it'd be great if you could call the vet and hash out the herd health-check appointments and the immunization schedule for the next year, and if we wanna go organic, we gotta start talkin' about probiotics. Yola's expectin' our call. We've already talked about it, but I've been waitin' to get anything down in their books till the new stock got here, so we'd have a better idea about numbers."

"Done. That's it?"

"I mean, I've got a whole list of shit that needs doin', but just tackle what you feel up to. Don't push it."

I rolled my eyes. "It's not like I broke every bone in my body. I can make calls or do whatever else as long as I can sit while I do it."

"This is a cattle ranch. If we're sittin', we're not makin' money."

I laughed. "We ain't made a penny yet, but it's good you still got two workin' legs."

"Touché. By the way, why'd Athena name the bull Red Pepper?"

As he wheeled me under the shade of the big balsam tree halfway between my house and the new barn, the wheelbarrow's tire hit a good-sized rock, and the creaky contraption tried to tip me into the dirt. I held onto the sides with a death grip and sucked in a breath. I released it slowly through my nose so my mouth would stay shut and the sharp stab of pain in my leg wouldn't make me scream.

"Sorry," Rye said, grunting and trying to tip me upright.

"We really need to clear and level out this path. My fancy new Bobcat will do the trick. I'll get started on it later today."

Making a conscious effort to slow my heart, I answered, "'Cause Athena's still angry with that damn bull for breakin' my leg, and she hates red peppers. Give her green peppers or yellow, and she'll eat the crap out of 'em, even raw, but red? No go."

"Your daughter is weird," he said.

I settled back into my rickety bucket and adjusted the crutches over my legs. "We refer to it around here lovingly as 'unique.'"

He chuckled. "Seriously, she's a really cool kid, Bax." He parked me next to the open barn door and held out his hand to help me up as Figaro, Rye's cattle-herding German Shepherd, came out of the barn to tug and bite at my good foot. "You're doin' a great job with her."

"Thanks," I said, ignoring the hand he offered. I gripped his forearm instead and used my own weight and momentum to launch my ass out of the wheelbarrow. Rye snapped his fingers at Figaro and pointed to the dirt, and Fig sat with his tongue lolling out the side of his mouth. He was still a puppy, a big fucking puppy, but definitely a puppy.

But had I really been doing a good job with Athena?

Every other word out of my mouth was a curse. Even before I broke my leg, I rarely remembered to take the laundry out of the dryer. There were always dirty dishes in the sink, and our house was falling apart. My friends and family had been better parents than me since the Red Pepper incident, and I forgot about cross country and drama club. What else had I forgotten?

"So what's up with Bea?"

"Oh, um, who?"

"You know who."

"Nothin's up," I said. "She's here to do a job. End of story."

Rye laughed again. "Mm-hm. Sure that's the end of it."

Fig and I watched as Rye led his horse Blue from a stall into the barn aisle, then set about saddling him. Fig had already proven to be hell on four paws around the cattle, but around the horses, he was a perfect gentleman, maybe because Blue was side eyeing the dog, like he was thinking, *"Get in my way, you squishy little fruit, and see what happens."*

I'd already caught Fig napping a few times, curled up with a couple of our calves in the sun. He fit in on the ranch like he'd always been here.

"Whatcha mean?" I asked.

"Bea's a beautiful woman," Rye said as he hefted his saddle onto Blue's back.

"Mm."

When he had it strapped down and tightened, he turned. His dirt-stained, tan hat shaded his eyes, but the pity was evident in them all the same. "You know it's not wrong if you wanted to… date again."

I shook my head as I reached for my own hat I'd left hanging from a hook by the door the day I broke my leg. I fixed it on my head and tugged on the brim to shade my eyes too. "Not ready."

"Okay, if you say so. But still, it wouldn't be wrong. Candy wouldn't want you to be alone."

"I'm not alone. I've got Athena."

A rare flash of irritation crossed Rye's face. "That ain't what I meant, and you know it. And are you really gonna put that on a kid? All that weight?"

"What weight?"

"The weight of your happiness," he said as he turned

again and stepped his boot into his stirrup. But before he pushed up, he asked, "Need help before I go? I won't be gone too long. I just wanna do a quick paddock check. One of the new heifers is due any day. Just wanna make sure everything's goin' okay."

"I'm good."

"Alright, well, it's just you and me today, so text me if you need me. My to-do list is on the table in the tack room next to my laptop, and I wrote down all the stuff we need from the feed store on there too."

I nodded and shuffled back to lean against a stall door as he turned Blue in the aisle and headed out.

The weight of my happiness?

How much did happiness weigh exactly?

CHAPTER SEVEN

BEA

"IT'S TAKIN' forever," Devo said as we stood half an acre away and looked at her framed and soon-to-be-drywalled house. The roof was next to go up, and the windows and doors would be delivered later in the week.

"I know it may seem like a long, chaotic process," I said, "but this is what Brand's really good at. He can manage the shit out of simultaneous builds. Actually, I think he thrives on the chaos."

"Oh, I know he's bustin' his butt for us. I didn't mean it that way. It's just that this will be my home with my *wife*, after we tie the knot anyway, and I'm so ready to live out here with her."

"Home is where the heart is," I said.

"Yeah."

Devo gazed out at the view as we took in the land and the blue morning sky high above us. An eagle soared in the distance. It screeched, and then we watched it dip and descend into the trees, probably to eat a mouse or something.

"So," she said, "if Brand's the chaos coordinator, what's your job?"

"I'm the dipshit director."

She laughed. "Huh?"

"I boss the crews around, make sure they're doin' what they're supposed to. I take all the supplies Brand brings us and direct my guys so all those supplies turn into houses."

"That sounds kinda fun."

"I love it."

She turned to face me, shading her eyes with her hand and squinting against the sun's glare. "You single?"

"Yeah, why?"

"Just curious. You seem like a pretty rad person. I was just wonderin' if anybody's figured that out yet."

"Ha!"

"What?" she asked when I barked my laugh in her face.

"No, I don't think so. I used to have a husband, but he never got wise."

"That why he's not your husband anymore?"

"No, it's 'cause I murdered him in his sleep."

I fixed my hands on my hips and cocked my head to the side. Devo squeaked and covered her mouth with her hand.

"Kiddin'! Jeez. Do I look like a murderer?"

She scanned me up and down. "I'm not sure. I think you're too short to do any real damage, but I like you." She laughed. "Where you from? Your twang is a little twangier than we usually hear around here."

"Appalachia. The mountains and valleys of the majestic state of North Carolina."

"Ah, that explains it."

"The town I'm from, Mays Hollow, isn't much bigger than Wisper."

"I bet it's pretty this time of year."

"Oh yeah," I said, picturing my childhood home and the surrounding fall foliage that would be peaking right now. I could hear the babbling brooks and see the stones beneath the slow water, glittering in the sun as orange and yellow leaves danced and floated down the streams.

Memories of those rivers and trees were really all I had left of my home.

I took a deep breath, forcing myself to see the beauty in front of me in the moment. Western Wyoming was no wilting daisy. There was a lot here I could see myself getting used to.

"It's gorgeous here, though."

"Yeah," Devo said, bending to pick a purple wildflower from the meadow we stood at the edge of.

The fields seemed to go on forever in the distance. They swayed lazily in the autumn breeze, all the blades of grass and flowers flowing in one direction, but then the wind would shift, and they'd sway back the other way.

Aspen trees glittered like gold at the edges of the meadows. The white and black trunks reminded me of wood elves, standing guard beneath the gilded canopies so winter wouldn't come to steal the gold too soon. The evergreens sprinkled throughout the aspen groves stood like blue-green soldiers sent to protect and defend the elves and their forests' bounties.

And the mountains? The Tetons had to be female, if mountains could claim a gender, because I'd never seen anything more terrifyingly beautiful and commanding.

"Well," Devo said, "guess I'd better get to work. Can I drop you somewhere on the way?"

"Yeah, thanks. I'll just have you drop me back at Bax's house, if you don't mind. My truck's there. The crews won't be here till tomorrow. Brand gave 'em a few days off so I could get my bearings, so today, my to-do list consists of findin' a hardware store."

She nodded. "You'll wanna head to Jackson for that. Bob

over at the feed shop sells some of that stuff, but I'm guessin' you'll have more specific hardware needs than he can provide."

"Actually, today I just need road reflectors and some solar garden lights."

"Oh, perfect. Bob will have those for sure. You can follow me. I drive right by there on my way to the community center."

"Cool," I said as she turned, and I followed her back to her truck. "So what do you do at the community center?"

"Lots of things. I'm the assistant director, which basically means I do everything. There's a lot of management to my job, but I also work with the community on different projects. We offer education and employment services, and we do a lot of outreach and fundraisers and things like that, but the best part of my job is bein' there for people when they need a helpin' hand or guidance or they just need someone to talk to."

"That sounds awesome, and like you work your tail to the bone."

She laughed. "Yup. Every day, all day, but it's worth it."

"You and Abey both work in town. Why didn't you build your house there?"

"Oh, 'cause this is our dream. Abey grew up on this land. She loves it and her family, and we're startin' a community garden out here. See there?" She stopped and turned to point to a plot of land beside her future house, where I now noticed rows of small plants growing. "That's where we started. It's our first growin' season. Right now, we only have carrots, onions, radish, and some squash, but we've got big plans for next year." She smiled with so much pride, I felt it inside my own chest. "Abey left some of the spoils in your fridge in the cabin before you arrived. Hope you like veggies."

"Thanks," I said, feeling like the kindness I'd experienced in the last twenty-four hours since I'd hit the Wisper town limits would soften me to the point of crying, or at the very least, make me reluctant to yell at people as much as I normally did. "Where's the grocery store? I'll get some noodles and chicken stock and make soup."

BOB'S FEED AND TACK, a dusty little store on the outskirts of Wisper, owned by Bob himself, whom I met along with his wife, Linda, sold everything but the kitchen sink, including but not limited to hay, horse/sheep/cow tack and feed, cowboy hats, plastic wading pools filled with baby chicks, jerky of all varieties, and WD-40. If you needed to stop somewhere to pick something up real quick on your way home, no matter what it was, chances were Bob had it. Or he could get it, and he'd send Linda to deliver it to your house for a small fee.

Bax had asked to tag along. He said he needed to pick up a few things from the grocery store and put in an order at the feed store, but when Bob and Linda fawned over him as we entered, I would've bet my favorite tape measure he regretted the decision.

"Bax," Linda said in a pitifully sweet voice. "How are you, honey? How are you and Athena holdin' up?" She patted his shoulder over the checkout counter when we stopped to ask if they had road reflectors, her big, teased gray hair bouncing with the movement.

"We're good, Linda. Thanks for askin'. This is Bea. She's workin' for Brand on the new cabins out at my place."

"Nice to meet ya," Bob said, offering his hand. I shook it while Linda offered a "Welcome, hon."

"You too. Thanks."

"Bob," Bax said, pulling a crumpled ball of paper from his pocket. "I've got an order for you."

Bob took the paper and smoothed it out over the counter. He read it and said, "Some of this stuff won't be here till tomorrow. We'll get it all ready for you when it comes in, and Linda can deliver it."

"Thanks," Bax said. "Sounds good. You should have a card on file for us."

Linda focused her eyes on Bax's cast. "You poor thing. I've been meanin' to get out to your place to bring y'all some food."

"Thank you, Linda. That's very kind of you, but I promise, we're okay."

"Nonsense," Linda went on. "Big man like you, raisin' a daughter on his own no less? I'll make up some casseroles and bring 'em out tomorrow when I deliver your order. You can freeze them…"

She droned on and on, and the more she babied him, the tighter Bax's hands gripped his crutches' handles, so I hurried to the aisle Bob had said I'd find the reflectors in, grabbed every last one they had, and rushed them up to the counter.

"Girl, you sure you need all these?" Bob asked when I plopped the open box and the second unopened box in front of him.

"Yes, sir," I said. "Ring 'em up."

It seemed glaringly obvious to me that Bob's and Linda's concern made Bax uncomfortable, but they hadn't caught on. He was polite and kind to them, and he answered their questions the best he could, but he kept tossing glances my way, hoping I could help him somehow get out of the awkward conversation.

I pointed behind Bob to a poster hung on the wall of a

landscaped backyard that had been lit up with solar pathway lights. "You got those?"

"Yes, ma'am," he said "Just came in."

"They come eight in a box?"

"Yup, as is standard."

"I'll take six boxes, please."

"Six?"

"Yes, sir," I told Bob. To Bax, I said, "*Sweetie*, why don't you go ahead and wait in the truck while I check out." I tried really hard not to laugh because the look of surprise on Bax's face was priceless, and I had a feeling he was having a hard time not laughing, too, when I called *him* Sweetie. "I'll only be a minute, babe, and then we can swing by the grocery on our way home and pick somethin' up for dinner."

But it shut Bob and Linda up.

Like a good boy, Bax crutched himself out to my truck after he thanked them, told them how nice it was to see them again, and promised to say hi to his mama for them. I watched him go, fixing my eyes on his ass in an appreciative manner and then turned back to Bob, who was now blushing, and miss Linda seemed to have lost her voice.

I used my company card and bought the lot and then skedaddled right on out of Bob's Feed and Tack. I dumped my bags in my truck bed, and then Bob and Linda crowded together in the doorway to watch us go as I reversed out of their parking lot. Bax waved and smiled at them through his open window, but as soon as we hit the highway, he let out a wild, "Yeehaw!" and slapped his good thigh with the flat of his hand.

He whooped it up for a minute, laughing and stomping his foot on my floorboard.

"Watch it! Your big boot's gonna poke a hole in my truck."

"That was so much fun!" He chuckled and relaxed back in his seat, tossing out directions as I drove.

When I parked and shut off my truck in front of the Food Mart in town, I asked, "Is it like that all the time?"

He sighed. "Pretty much."

"That sucks."

"Yeah, I mean, it's nice people care, but it's been three years since my wife died. And what the hell did Linda mean? 'Big man like you all alone?'"

"I know, right? Men can't boil a pot of water for macaroni?"

"Hey now, I make a mean steak, and I can cook you up the best spaghetti and meatballs you ever ate. The secret is pork ribs. You gotta let them flavor the sauce while it cooks down, and I serve it with a boiled egg. Well, I *could* make it for you if I could stand on my own two feet." He eyed me cautiously. "You know the whole town's gonna think we're together now."

"Yeah, I'm from a small town too. I know how it works, but gossip's better than people feelin' sorry for you."

"You ain't lyin'. C'mon, let's get the shoppin' done. The grocery store is worse. I guarantee you we'll see at least five people I know in there. Best just to get it out of the way."

CHAPTER EIGHT

BEA

"SO," I said as we walked the grocery store's aisles, tossing ingredients into our cart for soup and odds and ends Bax said he needed. "You used to raise sheep."

I hadn't framed it as a question, so he asked, "What about it?"

"Why'd you quit doin' that?"

He laughed. "Have you ever had the pleasure of shearin' a sheep?"

"No."

"Consider yourself lucky then. It fuckin' sucks. I hated it my whole life, but that was the family business so…"

"If you hated it, why'd you decide to go into business with Rye? Athena mentioned you're waitin' on a new flock to be delivered."

"Yeah, a *small* flock. It's just for the soil. When you have large numbers of cattle, they pretty much destroy the land. That's why we'll be movin' 'em from pasture to pasture throughout the year, and then we'll replant the fields they've just eaten and trampled. The sheep will help. Their manure helps fertilize, and we'll plant cover crops to protect the soil after that. Then, the cows will get rotated back to that pasture once it's ready again.

"There's a whole science behind it."

"Huh. Cool."

"Yeah," he said. "It is. I thought my eyes would gloss over when Rye first started talkin' about it, but it really is interestin', and the work is good. I like bein' outside, workin' with my hands, you know? And it's not so bad this time around 'cause I've got help. After my dad died, it was all on me. My brothers and sister had already moved on. They weren't interested in raisin' sheep, and I didn't blame 'em. We all had to suffer through it growin' up. At least now I've got people to commiserate with when we have a bad day, people to bounce ideas off of. It's nice, havin' a community."

Bax lifted his crutch and pointed to a box of Cookie Crunch cereal.

"This is garbage. You eat this?" I said.

He grinned. "Yes, ma'am, but don't tell anybody. I'll get yelled at by at least four people. Rye's not a health nut per se, but he's got somethin' against sugar, and if Athena sees it, I'll have to sit through another PowerPoint presentation on heart disease."

"Then we should get two boxes," I said, and I tossed two in our cart.

"Bax Lee?" a woman said in a honeyed voice as she passed us in the cereal aisle. "Is that you?"

"Hey, Felicity," Bax said to the very well endowed, tall, bottle blonde.

She pushed her purse strap up her forearm and anchored her hand on her cocked hip. "Honey, what'd you go and do to yourself?" She pointed to Bax's broken leg, her eyes flicking back and forth between Bax and me, and she angled her body so she faced him straight on, and poor little ol' me got pushed to the side.

"Yeah, I broke my leg."

"Well, now I can see that. How're you gettin' on then? You know, I'd be happy to stop by your place if you need anything." Finally, her stare landed on me and stayed there. "I could help around the house, wash the sheets, cook you up a little dinner some night."

"Thanks, Felicity," Bax said, and he leaned closer to me, balancing on one crutch. He held the other beneath his arm and rested his hand over the waistband of my jeans above my hip, letting his fingers caress beneath my sweatshirt. He slipped them into my belt loop and tugged me closer, using *me* as his crutch, and a thrill rushed through my body. I didn't mind so much being bossed and tossed around by Bax. If any other man had done it, I would've nailed their balls to a wall. "But I've got all the help I need. Ain't that right, Sweetie?"

Actually, Bax might've still been a target for my nail gun. I hadn't decided yet, but it seemed we weren't done playing house.

"Sure is," I said, jumping back into my role, "but thanks so much for the offer, Felicity. You're too kind."

A sour look flashed across Felicity's face, her eyes narrowing the slightest bit. "Alright then," she said. "Guess I'll see you around, Bax." She tossed me one last look, her shrewd gaze landing on Bax's hand still on my hip, and then she sighed and walked away.

When she was gone, I asked, "Who was *that*?"

"Felicity Flanigan." He leaned closer and whispered into my ear. "She's the president of the widower-slash-divorced-dad club. Doesn't matter who the guy is, if his wife leaves him or dies, she's on him like white on rice. I went to school with her, but she was three or four years behind me. She actually showed up at my house a month after Candy passed. Athena and I hid behind the couch till she was convinced I wasn't home and left."

I snorted. "Oh my God."

Bax laughed and his breath rushed past my ear. "Trust me. It was the right move. Even Athena said so."

I tried to disguise the shiver that skittered down my spine, but then he pulled his hand away and his fingers trailed across my back beneath my shirt, and that just made it worse.

Three minutes hadn't even passed and another woman called Bax's name. He winced, and I pulled my truck key from my pocket and slipped it into his.

"Go. If you could run, I'd tell you to do that, but just crutch yourself out of here as fast as you can. I'll check out and catch up."

He grinned. "Thank you, ma'am," he said, smirking. He tipped his hat and dashed off, and I laughed when the woman poked in and out of the aisles, calling his name and trying to find him.

When I walked out of the Food Mart with two full paper bags balanced in my hands, Bax couldn't stay hidden beneath his cowboy hat in my truck. His manners got the better of him, even though with his broken leg he was no help to me at all, but he climbed out and tried anyway.

"That was a close one," he said as we pulled away.

"Don't you worry, *sweetie*," I said. "I got your back."

He grinned at me. "You're like my very own four-leaf clover."

"Oh yeah?" I lifted an eyebrow and looked down at his cast. "Well you ain't no lucky penny."

AFTER DROPPING Bax off and lugging the bags into his kitchen, I spent the rest of the morning walking from Bax's house down to Old Fish Creek Road and back again, along the winding gravel drive with my measuring wheel, zigzagging back and forth across the lane, staggering reflectors and sticking them into the dirt every three-tenths of a mile.

Normally, I would've spread them a little further apart, but Brand had said they got a lot of snow in this part of the state. I wasn't sure if Bax and Rye planned on welcoming guests in the winter, but at the very least, they'd have service people and delivery drivers coming and going down this lane, plus all the cowboys who'd work with the cows, and those guys would appreciate my overzealousness until Brand could install permanent lighting.

The Lee property had been bisected by the main road. Technically, it was more like a driveway, just a really long one, but on the north side to my right, the property stretched out in fields and meadows, and Rye and Bax's cows dotted the hillsides. The southern side was like a whole different world, packed densely with trees and forests that slowly climbed into the mountains, and Bax and Athena's house was at the end, where the two worlds met.

As I meandered, I saw squirrels with fluffy tufts of fur on the tips of their ears, or maybe it was just the one squirrel, but if so, the little shit had been following me, chittering at me the whole way. I saw some kind of rodent or weasel that looked a lot like a ferret, but smaller and his coat was pure white, his face brown, with brown speckles down his white back.

After pausing to place a reflector, I stopped and tipped my face up to the sun in the center of the sky, peeking through the high tops of the trees. God, was it possible to fall in love with air? The faint breeze caressing my skin and warming me in the middle of the day smelled so damn good. Some of the coniferous trees around Bax's place gave off a citrus scent. When I happened upon a spotty cell signal, I looked it up and was surprised to learn that the sweet smell came from white fir trees.

I also looked up the whole bison thing, and it turned out there was a wild herd that roamed northwest Wyoming, so my Wooly Wally really was a wandering free spirit.

The white firs were so pretty with their waxy, silver needles, and I wondered if I could have one for a Christmas tree. I hadn't had a tree in many years. What was the point? I lived alone and worked long hours. Things slowed down at Lee Construction in winter, but there was always work to be done. But now I could picture my apartment back in Sheridan, flooded with the orangey scent and glowing lights on a tree. But then I'd have to actually buy the lights and decorations, and it all seemed like an unnecessary expense just to entertain me for a month.

The lane wound its way back to Bax's house, and when I got there after placing the last reflector, my rust-and-silver Chevy reflected midday sunlight. It was old and barely hanging onto its dignity, but it ran like a beast.

When we returned from the store, I'd parked next to Bax's currently unused big ol' blue Ford. The two trucks next to each other reminded me of the differences between Bax and me. I was short and little compared to him, and kind of beat up and used. Bax was handsome and tall and proud, but he'd been covered in dirt lately, just like his truck was covered in a healthy coat of dried mud. The windshield looked like someone had smeared muddy water over it with their hands, but I figured Bax hadn't had time to wash it before he got clocked by the bull who'd snapped his femur in half like a pencil.

I wondered if anyone would mind if I popped inside the house to fill my water bottle. The day was cool, but the sun was scorching when I didn't have trees as cover, and I'd gulped down the last of my supply half a mile ago. Bax had said I was free to stop by anytime for coffee, so I hoped the invitation would extend to water too. Hopping up the porch stairs, I intended to knock, but I heard grunting coming from behind the house. For three seconds, I thought it was a bear, but then Bax's voice became discernable when he yelled, "Aw, fuck!"

I jumped down the stairs and jogged in that direction, and I found him sprawled on the ground, covered head to toe in yellow paint with a long, extendable roller still gripped in one hand.

"What the hell did you do?"

"Can you please go away and pretend you never saw this?" he asked dejectedly, releasing the roller from his hand and flinging his arms out to his sides. Paint plopped into the grass beside him, and he wiggled his left boot out of the five-gallon bucket he'd stepped in. The tray he'd been dipping his roller into had been overturned, and a thick, yellow stream of the stuff flowed into the grass and the dirt below five feet away from him.

"Uh, nope." I laughed. "Seriously, what were you tryin' to do?"

"Well," he said, sitting up and trying to wipe paint off his T-shirt, but all he managed to do was rub it in. "I thought I'd get a head start on paintin'. This place is a dump. I need to get it ready for when we open the cabins." He looked at the house, and that was when I realized the yellow paint dripping from Bax's entire body matched the faded color of his old siding.

"You wanted to paint your house... by yourself, even

though you know if you let go of your crutches, you'll fall over?"

"Maybe?"

"How'd you even get the paint bucket out here?" I shook my head. "I can't leave you alone for five seconds. Maybe I should've let those women have you. You probably could've convinced Felicity to paint your house."

Bax scoffed and rolled his eyes.

"You know that artist?" I asked. "What's his name? The guy who flicked paint onto the canvas?"

"Jackson Pollock?"

"Yeah, that's the guy. It looks like he got mad at you. You're an idiot. This couldn't have waited? You know your brother has equipment that will do this job in a nanosecond compared to how long it'll take you? And he has people on the payroll who can do the job. *I* could do it. There's no need to endanger your ability to walk for the rest of your life."

"Whatever," he grumbled. "I gotta do somethin'. I'm goin' out of my mind."

"Okay, well puzzles are just as fun and those you can do in a chair."

"A stupid puzzle? That's what you want me to do?" He rolled his eyes again, then swiped paint from his brow.

"For fuck's sake. Stop tryin' to wipe it off. You're just makin' things worse." Walking closer, I noticed the paint had landed in his hair on the crown of his head and had dripped beneath his shirt. It was probably in his pants too. His sweats had been coated with it. It was everywhere. "Alright, Michelangelo, let's get you cleaned up. That shit dries on your skin, you'll be scratchin' yourself bloody by the end of the day."

He looked down at the mess in his lap and on his arms, then rolled his shoulders. "Fine. If Rye gets back and sees me like this, I'll never hear the end of it. There's a hose around the side of the house."

I laughed. "As much as the idea of hosin' you down like a detainee in an Alabama prison amuses me, a hose isn't gonna do the trick, genius. We need warm water and soap. Lots of soap."

"I can't shower yet." Remarkably, it seemed not one speck of paint had landed on the part of his cast covering his foot and peeking out the right leg of his sweats.

"You have a tub, right, and I'm assumin' you have garbage bags? I've got duct tape in my truck."

With a good dose of apprehension in his voice, he asked, "What the hell you gonna do to me with duct tape?"

"Anything I want. Duct tape is magic. Just sit back and watch me work."

CHAPTER NINE

BAX

MORTIFICATION WAS my word of the day.

Out of everyone I knew, it had to be Bea who found me right as I was falling on my ass and dousing myself in paint the color of sunshine?

She was enjoying my humiliation and, for the second time today, stripping me bare and getting ready to help me with basic hygiene. It hadn't escaped my careful attention that had she not been on my farm, I wouldn't have been trying to paint my house in the first place.

Something about Bea made me want to at least try to act like a productive member of society. And then I felt guilty because poor Athena had been living in a dump, and it had taken a veritable stranger to push my ass into gear. Candy would've been on me ages ago to repaint the house, if she were still here.

In my bathroom, Bea smacked the back of my shoulder with her sticky hand. I heard the suction when she tried to pull it away from my skin. "Stop fidgetin'!"

"Stop ticklin' me," I spat back. I couldn't see her, but I felt her behind me, like a sexy, pint-sized shadow. Every time her skin brushed over mine, I shivered. "What're you doin'? You're givin' me goosechills."

When she snorted and bent over in a fit of laughter, her hair dusted my low back, and she caused even more chills. "What the hell are goosechills?"

I tried to turn to see the laughter in her eyes. I twisted but lost my balance and gripped the sink. "You know, when you break out in—"

"Goose*bumps*?"

Her puffs of giggles rushing over my skin had me smiling too. "Yeah, same thing."

"No, you made it up! Nobody says goosechills." She pushed me forward so I couldn't see her anymore and dragged a towel down my back, and I smiled. Her laughter was infectious. I couldn't help myself.

My bathroom really needed a makeover now. It was almost as annoyingly yellow as the outside of my house. Why had I never painted it a different fucking color? My mama had picked out the canary-cum shade when I was ten years old. It was ugly as sin, but I just kept repainting it.

I stood on my good leg, still braced against the sink, trying to see Bea in the mirror. After managing to wrangle me out of my shirt and sweats, she covered my cast with trash bags, which she'd patched together and sealed with duct tape. And now she was covered in paint too. While the bath water ran and warmed up, she wiped the excess paint off my shoulders and back with old, holey and threadbare bath towels I used to wipe Figs paws off when it rained. Luckily, Athena had recently washed them.

"You're a bossy little brat, ain't you?" As soon as the whisper left my lips, her head peeked around my arm and her eyes locked on mine in the mirror, and I clenched my jaw closed so nothing else ridiculous would come out of my mouth.

"Yeah, what of it? Now, stop movin'," she challenged, arching an eyebrow. "You're makin' a mess."

Her green eyes landed on the back of my neck, and she rolled her lip beneath her teeth again. She was always doing that, particularly when she looked at my body, and it was making me wild. I wanted to grip her jaw and smash those lips to mine.

The realization made the broken heart inside my chest jump and race like a jackrabbit.

"Can you get your underwear off by yourself, or do you need me to do it?"

"I think I can get 'em."

"I would tell you just to keep them on, but your ass is soaked in paint. Sit on the toilet, and when you get them off, use those strong arms and just slide over to the tub and sink in. I'll clean up later." She twisted and bent to shut off the tub faucet. "I'm gonna go find a big cup so I can wash your hair."

"Thanks." Technically, I could wash myself. My arms weren't broken, but if she wanted to run her fingers through my hair, I wasn't about to stop her.

She turned back to me before she walked out the bathroom door. "I put some of your body wash in the bath water." Swirling her hand in a circle over the deep vee between her legs, she said, "You know, so you can cover all your bits and baubles with bubbles."

A snort escaped my mouth when I saw the awkwardness all over her face. What was the big deal? She'd already seen my bits and baubles.

Bea gasped softly, watching my mouth as I laughed, and then slowly raised her eyes up to mine. She whispered, "Be right back," and she closed the door with a quiet *click* behind her.

Strong arms? I flexed my biceps and looked down at them. I mean, I supposed they were strong. I'd worked on a ranch my whole life, but why was Bea noticing my arms?

Oh, well duh, probably 'cause I'd stripped in front of her twice now.

Fuck. Could this get any worse?

Athena wasn't due home for hours. She had that drama-club thing after school, and then Abey called and said she'd have time to take Athena for new riding boots, so she'd pick her up after drama club. There was little danger of my kid walking in on this disaster in the middle of the day, but just what the hell did I think I was doing?

Brand would probably disown me if he knew I was about to be completely naked with his employee. Again. And she was important to him. As far as I knew, Brand and Bea had never had a thing for each other, but they were close friends. He relied on her a lot concerning Lee Construction. Besides me and Abey, there wasn't anyone my brother trusted more.

After nearly falling onto the toilet seat, I'd almost decided to dig through the bathroom drawer to root around for a pair of scissors, but I finally managed to get my boxers off, and I transferred myself into the bath. Going commando was getting more appealing by the day.

The urge to lean back and relax in the warm water was there, but it was only four or five inches deep. I raised my leg and rested my foot on the edge of the tub as I released the tension in my shoulders and pressed them back against the cold ceramic. More goosechills broke out over my neck and chest. My nipples hardened to two cold, tiny points of pain, and then Bea walked in, holding an empty thirty-two-ounce soda cup from the Stop and Go in town.

She'd found an apron in my kitchen covered in pink flamingos, though, I'd completely forgotten we even owned one, and when she saw me and my bare chest on display for her, she did the lip roll again, then pulled the apron's strings so tight, I worried they might cut off circulation to the lower part of her body. She tied them and then sat carefully on the closed toilet lid.

My bits and baubles were properly covered in bubbles, but I had an inkling that wouldn't last very long.

"Um, can you sit up?" she asked quietly. "I need to rinse your hair. You're gettin' paint all over the wall."

"Yeah," I said, and I used my core to propel me forward.

The laughter and teasing had gone from Bea's voice. "Fill this up."

She shoved the cup into my hand, then reached to turn the faucet back on, and I leaned forward and held the cup underneath the flow till it was full.

"Here." Handing the cup back to her, I risked a glance at her face. She blinked and moved her eyes to my hair. I closed mine but felt the warm rush of water when she tipped the cup over my head.

"I'm sorry I've put you in this position," I said.

It was emasculating, being bathed by a woman I barely knew. But the situation made me realize again that I had a bad habit of not accepting help when it was offered. As the oldest sibling in a big family, responsibility had always fallen to me, so maybe I'd internalized that and equated help to failure.

And then there was Candy. She'd always expected me to take charge, so maybe that had helped to fuel my need to control everything myself. I hadn't thought about it in a long time, but now I remembered arguments Candy and I'd had, and how I'd wanted her to weigh in on decisions we needed to make, but she rarely did. *"You're the head of this family,"* she used to say. *"You know what's best for us."*

I wished I'd realized back then what a load of bull that was.

"What position?" Bea asked.

"You know, the whole 'bathtime for a grown man' thing. You didn't come here to take care of your boss's brother, but thank you for doin' it anyway."

"No. I didn't. But it's fine."

"It's really not."

"I said it's fine, so it's fine. Quit whinin'." One of her eyebrows bowed in half, and she narrowed her eyes. "If I didn't wanna help you and your *sweet little ass*, I wouldn't. I'd call Abey or Devo or somebody."

A wavy, nauseating memory slammed me in the head of the night I'd met Bea, and of her getting right in my face to put me in my place after I'd drunkenly made a comment about her taut backside.

I winced. She was still pissed about that comment, but it seemed like the intimacy of our current situation had flipped her confidence on its ass. "Bea?"

She froze and stared at me.

"I'm sorry about that. I should've said sorry that night. It's no excuse, but I was way too drunk. I swear I don't make a habit out of gettin' shit-faced like that, but it was the first anniversary of— But what I said to you that night was inappropriate and probably demoralizin'. And I'm sorry."

"Thank you," she said, but she averted her eyes away from mine. "Now fill the cup again."

For the next ten minutes, I sat there in silence with my eyes closed, listening to her breathe, blindly refilling the cup again and again when she handed it back to me. She left the hot water running but pulled the plug so the yellow paint swill could drain. What the bubbles didn't cover, I hid with my hands.

I was freezing my ass off, but after she stoppered the tub again and added more body wash to the water, I endured the chill while the bath filled back up and she rinsed my hair one last time. And when she was done and she massaged in shampoo, my hands splayed wider and I leaned forward, because, *oh God.* I hadn't been touched like that in over three years.

The slow, soft strokes of her thin fingers over my scalp were like nothing I'd ever experienced. I never wanted her to stop touching me. I couldn't totally hide the erection that had grown hot and hard beneath the quickly dissolving bubbles, not in five inches of water, but when I looked at her, Bea's eyes were closed as she touched me.

The rhythmic caresses of her fingers became slower. She moved them gently over my hair, applying firm pressure occasionally and scrubbing with her fingernails to get the paint out.

"That feels good," I whispered.

"Mm-hm," she hummed, but her eyes stayed closed.

I had to try to start a conversation. If I didn't have the distraction, I was afraid I'd pull her into the tub with me, and then what? Bea didn't want that. Did *I* want that?

I did. Or I thought I did, but what would Candy—

Candy wouldn't say anything. Candy was dead. She'd been gone three years.

Mumbling, I asked the first question to enter my head, "So how'd you end up in Sheridan workin' with my little brother?"

Bea sucked in a breath, like I'd startled her. "Oh, um, I'd just moved there. I got lucky the day I walked into his office for my interview. He'd had one of his foremen at the time doin' interviews, but that guy had gone to lunch, and I'd gotten the time wrong, so Brand interviewed me himself. I guess we just hit it off. He offered me a job on the spot, and it was a good thing, too, 'cause if he hadn't, I probably would've ended up gettin' my meals from a soup kitchen."

"You were in a tight spot?"

"Yeah, you could say that. I left my ex-husband back in North Carolina. I'd been skippin' from town to town for a few years, lookin' for somethin' steady, but I didn't find it till I met Brand. He changed my life."

"You mean you *ran* away? Did he… Was your husband abusive?"

"No." She scoffed. "He wishes he had the balls. If anybody was gonna hurt anybody, it would've been me. He's a chauvinistic idiot. He knew I was through with him."

Her sometimes brusque nature was starting to make more sense to me now. "Good for you."

She nodded. "I haven't heard from him since I left, which was exactly one day after our divorce went into effect. Hit the road and never looked back. But I'd never been out of North Carolina, except to South Carolina once when I was little with my parents. We went to Myrtle Beach. My mama grew up around there. She always talked about takin' me there, but we only went the one time.

"Anyway, when I left, I didn't know where to go. I had a high school diploma and some construction certifications from when I worked for my dad, but most of those were out of date. I had a little money saved up, but that doesn't go far on the road.

"I tried out a few places: Nebraska, North Dakota, southeastern Wyoming, but nothin' fit. I'd never felt so alone in my life. So I kept goin'. I got a flat tire outside Sheridan and stopped there for the night. I saw elk the next day, grazin' next to my motel, and they were so beautiful. They seemed like a good sign, so I found a place to buy a new tire and stayed. I met your brother a week later."

"Wow. You've got guts. I don't know if I could leave my home like that."

"I needed to. All that's left there for me is heartache and misery."

"Your parents are gone? No brothers or sisters?"

"No. Only child, and my dad died when I was nineteen."

"Your mama?"

Bea paused, her fingers stilling in my hair at the back of my neck. "She passed when I was Athena's age."

I looked at her, and sympathy crossed over her features, but she smiled softly.

"You understand her," I whispered.

"I do."

CHAPTER TEN

BEA

"LEAN BACK," I said when I was convinced I'd gotten all the paint out of Bax's hair and had scrubbed the wall behind him so it wouldn't get dirty again.

He did as I asked, and I reached for the clean washcloths I'd brought from the laundry room. I set a pile of three on my thigh and grabbed the white one on top. When I leaned over the tub's edge and dipped the cloth into the soapy water between his spread thighs, Bax shifted away from me.

He was trying to be a gentleman, but deep down inside, I wanted his caveman tendencies to come out. I wanted him to drag me into the tub by my hair and get me wet in more ways than one.

Note to self: Don't go so long without human contact and sex next time, Bea. It turns you into a shameless, horny bitch.

The intimacy of the situation floored me. No man had ever let me be so close in such a vulnerable situation. Granted, I couldn't remember ever being in a situation this delicate, but it spoke volumes about Bax's character that he'd let me in so quickly. He barely knew me.

I didn't know him either.

Actually, maybe I did. I knew his grief and how it added shadows to his happiness no one else could see. And I knew his daughter because I'd been her in another life.

"Bea?"

"Hm?"

"You okay?"

His concern for me zapped me out of the trance I'd gone into, and craziness came out of my mouth when I looked in his eyes. "What would you do if I slid my hand beneath the water again? If I touched you, what would you do?"

He froze. "I'm not sure."

"Because of your wife?"

He nodded once. "Yes."

"And Athena?"

He relaxed and began to breathe again. "Yeah."

"I won't," I said. But oh, how I wanted to.

Athena had become a safety blanket for Bax. That was painfully plain to see, but I wasn't meant to be the one who stole that comfort away from him. I knew the cost too well.

But he whispered, "I want you to touch me."

I searched his nervous blue eyes, and he searched mine too. But did he really want that? Because I wanted to touch him so much, I ached inside.

One more slow dip of his head told me yes.

Could we allow ourselves a moment to give into this insane connection? Seriously, where had it come from? But any longer than that, and I would be risking ripping the blanket away forever.

Grabbing the bottle of body wash from the edge of the tub, I poured a little onto my washcloth, then dipped the cloth in the water again and worked up a lather in my hand. Bax watched like my fingers were little cobras ready to strike.

When I lifted the cloth to his clavicle and pressed it softly against his skin, his head tipped back against the wall, hands gripping the edges of the tub. His eyes rolled closed, and he drew in a breath slowly between his teeth. Out of the corner of my eye, I watched his cock twitch beneath the surface of the water, the useless bubbles long gone now.

The man was the definition of sexy. The way he didn't hide his sex from me, or his attraction to me, even though he had no clue what to do about it, was the most alluring thing I'd ever witnessed.

My mouth watered to taste his skin, but I knew that would be pushing things too far.

Most of the paint had run off his chest when I rinsed his hair, but I dragged the warm cloth over his skin slowly anyway, and he opened his eyes.

Somehow, seeing his unguarded vulnerability gave me courage, and my rag traveled lower. Molding the palm of my hand over his pec above the washcloth, I pressed gently with the tips of my fingers, and he moaned quietly.

Silently, I slid onto my knees between the john and the side of the tub. The extra washcloths fell to the floor, and I rubbed lower, letting the slippery fabric ride the ridges of his tightened abdomen, and Bax's breaths came faster.

"Bea?"

"Shh," I whispered. Dragging my eyes from his hard, wet chest, I looked right into his soul and admitted, "Don't talk. If you talk, I'll kiss you. The sound of your voice is makin' me insane right now, and I'm barely in control. I don't think you want me *out* of control."

"*Please*," he begged.

I froze. Did he want me to stop? "Please what?"

"Kiss me."

"You sure?"

"Yes."

The washcloth floated out of my hand, and I leaned further over him, bracing my hand next to his on the far lip of the tub, and moved closer. His fingers brushed against mine, and my hair fell between us, the yellow ends soaking up the water left from my cloth and plastering themselves to his chest.

I hovered above him, and his breath shook as it flowed jaggedly out of his mouth—the mouth that I was currently imagining on my body, with his warm lips and hot tongue doing things to me I hadn't felt in ages.

"Are *you* sure?" he asked.

"I think so."

"Then kiss me," he whispered, and he gripped my ribs, spread his hands wide over my shirt, and steadied me above him as I licked my lips and touched them to his.

He groaned, and heat pulsed between my legs when his tongue slid over mine.

But I was afraid. Afraid that I'd never wanted anyone as much as I wanted Bax Lee. Funny that, because not an hour ago, I still thought I hated him. But now that I'd realized I didn't, maybe all he wanted was my hand and my tongue. Maybe his wife was in the room with us. Maybe she was the one always on his mind and I was just a stand-in. I couldn't be special to him, not with her shadow pulling at my happiness too.

Besides, I'd only been here a day, for crying out loud. That in itself was enough to scare the crap out of me. I'd never been so attracted to someone I barely knew.

None of it mattered. Bax, no matter how alluring, was off limits to me.

But I moved my hand beneath the water again anyway.

When the smooth skin below his navel made way to coarse hair, I paused.

"Don't stop, Bea," he whispered into my mouth. "Make the ache go away."

I tilted my head and lifted my dry hand to his face, rubbing my fingertips over his scruffy cheek while his tongue, like wet velvet, soothed my own ache with every delve and dip into my mouth.

The pads of his fingers dug into my ribcage, raging desire rose deep inside me, and I slid my hand into his hair and gripped it so hard, my fingers hurt.

My other hand searched even lower beneath the water, and when his hard-on bobbed against my knuckles, I twisted my wrist and gripped his length in my palm.

He filled my hand completely, and he moaned and rolled his hips. The shallow water lapped at his skin in little waves, splashing quietly against the sides of the tub, and the black garbage bags covering his scratchy plaster cast rubbed and stuck to my arm beneath the hem of my T-shirt's sleeve.

"Feels so good to be touched by you," he breathed, and he pulled away from our kiss. His head lolled on the wall behind him, and he watched me, his eyes like a clear, cloudless sky.

"Are you *sure*?"

"Yes, Bea. More."

The warm bath water allowed my hand to pump smoothly while adrenaline pulsed through my bloodstream.

I wanted to give him more. Wanted to build him up and jump off this cliff with him. I wanted to feel his cum spill over my fingers, wanted to watch how the pleasure I gave him changed his face. Would he close his eyes when he came and clench his jaw? Or would his gaze stay on mine so that I could really see what he looked like when he let go?

Drawing the hardness of his cock through my closed fist over and again, I squeezed and pumped gently, then let his soft skin slide back down the palm of my hand.

I kissed him again, our tongues moving in rhythm with my hand working him, until I was moaning into his mouth and pressing my thighs together, but then we heard the kitchen door creak open and clap closed, and a familiar female voice called out.

"Bax? Son, where you at? I'm back from my retreat, and I brought chicken."

RUSHING to dress a man twice my size with wet skin and only one leg to stand on was a skill I never knew I'd need.

"It's my mom," Bax whispered. "Jesus, how embarrassin'." But then he raised his voice and aimed it at the bathroom door. "Yeah, Mama. I'm in the bathroom. Be out in a sec."

Whispering back, I said, "Yeah, I got that. I met her last year." I'd never forget Mervella Lee's gruff smoker's voice, but Brand had told me she'd recently quit.

Still, the sound of her bustling around Bax's kitchen was an unwelcome interruption.

"Want me to hide in here?" I asked as I reached up on my tiptoes to towel-dry the droplets of water dripping down the back of his neck from his hair.

"No way," Bax said, watching my eyes as I placed my hand on his chest for leverage so I could rub faster. "If you go out there with me, she'll leave sooner. If you hide, she'll be here all night."

The non-paint-covered Wile E. Coyote pajama pants I'd snagged from his laundry basket when I went to find the cup and washcloths fit over his cast easily, and when he was fully dressed in them and a clean black T-shirt, I opened the bathroom door and walked ahead of him into the kitchen.

Bax's mom's eyes flared when she turned from the open fridge and saw us together, but she didn't address me directly. To Bax, she asked, "Who's this?"

"Mama," he said as he lowered himself into a kitchen chair at the table and set his crutches against it, "this is Bea. She works for Brand."

"Oh, that's nice," she said and she walked over to kiss his cheek. "Your brother sent you a nurse? How are you, honey?" She looked at me when she said it, at the apron I'd found hanging on the back of the laundry room door, which fell to my knees and was now covered in wet, yellow splotches, but then she focused solely on Bax, like I wasn't even in the room. "I'm sorry I wasn't here when you hurt yourself. I would've come sooner if someone would've called me. I had to hear it from your sister this mornin' when she stopped by the trailer to make sure I'd gotten home from Montana."

Bax tried to hide a guilty grin, and I laughed right out loud at her fawning over him like a five-year-old with a skinned knee.

"Uh no, Mrs. Lee," I said, "Brand didn't send a nurse. I'm the forewoman at Lee Construction. We met last year when you visited."

Finally, her full scrutiny landed on me. With her hands on her hips, she looked me over, seeming to question something about me, possibly why I'd just been in the bathroom with her son who was *not* my boss. She must've come to an answer, because then she forced a smile and turned to close the refrigerator.

"Oh, that's right. Your name's Sweetie, ain't it? I do remember a woman who worked for my son." Under her breath, it sounded like she said, "Seems my *other* son has a sweet tooth when it comes to women."

Did she think we couldn't hear her?

"*Mama*," Bax warned.

"My name is Bea," I reminded her, but I had a hunch she hadn't actually forgotten that fact. "And I'm the person in charge of makin' sure your house gets built."

She didn't like that. She scowled. Did the woman ever smile? "What happened to the man who did that job before?"

"Man?"

"Zach or Zeke or somebody."

I sat in the chair next to Bax's, watching his mom carefully and how she tried so hard to hold on to the way things used to be. "You mean the guy who quit and started up a rival company and then tried to steal Brand's crew? His name is Zach Brinley, and he's the reason the position was open when I applied… two years ago."

"Oh," she said.

Yeah, oh. I was picking up what she was putting down. I was a woman, so surely I couldn't do the job, right? I remembered getting that gist from her when she and Abey visited, and I distinctly remembered how much it had pissed Abey off. Brand told me his mom changed her tune somewhat after she and Abey had a "come to Jesus" moment, but seeing her now, I wasn't so sure how much she'd changed. But for Athena's sake, I hoped I was wrong.

Maybe her prickly disposition didn't have anything to do with sexism or bigotry. Maybe it was about seeing Bax with a woman who was not his wife. It wasn't like we were making out right in front of her or even touching, but the undercurrent from what we'd just been about to do hung heavily in the air between us.

My attraction to Bax was like a live wire, zapping and buzzing around me. I thought I could even hear it crackling until I realized the sound was coming from an old box fan in a living room window, blowing cool fall air into the house.

"Well, I guess I'd better go," I said, untying the apron and pulling it off. I hung it over the back of my chair when I stood. "It was nice to see you again, Mrs. Lee."

"Oh, mm, you too." Yeah, that had sounded like the equivalent of "oh, bless your little heart" when it oozed like rancid honey out of a southern woman's mouth.

"Wait, you're goin'?" Bax asked with a faint hint of panic. He leaned forward, like he wanted to reach out for me, and the pleading look in his eyes begged me to stay.

I smiled, mischief lifting the corners of my mouth even when I ordered them to stay down. "Your mom's here, so you don't need my help anymore. Besides, I have a lot of work to do before the crews get here in the mornin'." I flashed a toothy grin before I said, "If you need help later tonight, you know where I'll be."

My unspoken invitation had Bax reaching beneath his kitchen table, probably to adjust the hard truth inside his pajama pants, but then his eyes slid over to his mom, and he flopped back against his chair in defeat.

CHAPTER ELEVEN

BAX

MY MAMA HAD an immutable knack for overstaying her welcome where Athena and I were concerned.

She flitted around my house, apologizing over and over for "abandoning" me in my time of need, tending to me, cleaning, fluffing pillows, and washing and folding laundry for hours, like I was five years old and couldn't possibly lift a finger for myself.

Okay, fine. Admittedly, I'd fallen behind on laundry. I wasn't ungrateful, and all that shit needed to be done, but my mother had always had a way of inserting herself into our lives when Athena and I were probably best left to figure things out on our own.

When Abey brought Athena home with her new riding boots, Mama started dinner and then sat with us while it cooked in the oven, sipping decaf in the living room while Athena chattered away about drama club and how she'd been chosen to play the Ghost of Christmas Past in the school holiday show.

Mama didn't like that. Oh, she was glowingly proud of Athena for getting the part, but she seemed to be bothered by the fact that she thought Christmas Past was a boy's part, and she wanted Athena to have a girl's part so she could fix her hair and make her a pretty costume.

It put my Road Trip right over the edge. She stood, and with waving hands and indignant scoffs, told her Grandma to get with the times, that girls could be boys, and boys could be girls if they wanted to.

Devo joined us after her meeting. She showed up in the middle of the rant and sat on the couch next to Abey, fully enthralled by Athena's performance. My sister and her fiancée had a knack, too, for showing up when food was ready. They ate roasted chicken and wild rice with us when it was done, then hung out after Mama left. Who cared about the extra food when their presence was the reason my mama didn't stay? She may've gotten on board with Abey's and Devo's relationship, but her big toe was the only part of her body on the boat, and she sure as shit wasn't comfortable with it.

"You guys cool if I run an errand?" I asked as I reached for my crutches on the floor beside my chair and pushed up.

Devo snorted a laugh, snuggling back into Abey's side on my couch. Abey slipped her arm over Devo's shoulder and asked, "An errand? Where you gonna go?"

"Uh, I need to… to talk to Sweet—or I mean Bea about somethin'."

"You need to talk to her?" Devo taunted. "Or you need to *talk* to her?" She wiggled her dark eyebrows.

"Shut up. It's about the cabins. We were havin' a conversation about it earlier before Merv showed up."

Calling our mama Merv still made us giggle like twelve-year-olds, and Mama hated it with a passion, which was why we still did it.

"Go ahead," Abey said, chuckling. "We'll hang out for a

bit. You have satellite, so that works out for us, and Athena said she's got a lot of homework so she'll be upstairs for a while."

"Thanks. Is it cold out tonight? Should I grab a flannel?"

"No, it's not too— Wait a minute," Devo said, those eyebrows now furrowing in perplexion. "Just how are you plannin' on gettin' to Bea's cabin? You might've been able to cheat with the brace, but with that bulky cast in your way, I'd pay good money to watch you try to drive. You can't."

"I was gonna take the skid steer."

She laughed, and Abey said, "If Rye finds out you drove his Bobcat, he'll kill you."

"He lets Athena drive it."

"Yeah," Abey said, "'cause she's a better driver than you."

"C'mon, gimpy." Devo popped up off the couch. "I'll drive you." She grabbed her keys from the kitchen table on our way out the door.

Devo held my crutches while I slid into the cab of her truck, which, now that I was thinking about it, seemed like the same make and model of Bea's truck. Different years probably, but it was a heck of a coincidence that they drove the same POS Chevy when there were perfectly good Fords all over the place. Man, I missed driving my own damn truck.

I looked at my blue beast longingly as Devo pulled away from my house and asked, "You got condoms?"

I choked on spit. "What?"

"Rubbers, contraception, raincoat, dick wrapper, etcetera."

"Why would I need that to go to a business meetin'?"

Devo snorted. "Business meetin'. Right." The silence after her acknowledgement of my true intentions was awkward as fuck, but finally, she said, "I like Bea. She's pretty cool."

"Mm."

Yeah, I agreed with that statement. What other woman would show up at her boss's brother's house and start helping out like she'd lived there her whole life? Especially if that brother had made a seriously rude comment about her ass when he was drunk two years ago.

"Abey says you haven't dated since Candy passed."

"I haven't."

"How come?"

"Dunno."

She looked at me as she took the turn onto the dirt road that, in the near future, would be called Bear Lane. We even had street signs made and ready to go up.

"If you wanted to start now, no one would judge you."

Right. My mama would. Brand would.

Athena might.

I'd judge me.

When I didn't respond, she shrugged. "All I'm sayin' is you could do worse. That's all."

"Thanks for the ride," I said when she pulled up outside Bea's cabin, next to her truck. I was right; they both drove old Chevy Colorados.

"Welcome. Want me to come back for you later?"

"Naw. I'll figure it out."

"'Kay."

After Devo had driven further down the lane and turned around in the mini roundabout Rye plowed clear for us, I made my way to the cabin's porch and opened the door. It then occurred to me I should've knocked, but I'd already gotten used to going in and out of the cabins to check their progress.

Inside, a small fire had been lit in the fireplace, loud pop music played from Bea's phone on the small kitchen table, and I saw piles of papers and rolls of blueprints stacked next to it. I smelled food cooking, but Bea was hidden behind the refrigerator.

Suddenly, she jumped around the fridge door with a cordless nail gun in her hands. "Ha!" she hollered as she stuck her landing, her bare feet shoulder-width apart and planted on the floor.

My hands jerked up to cover my face, my crutches fell out from under my armpits and clacked loudly on the hardwood floor a second later, and I crumpled like a dropped accordion right after. "Don't fuckin' shoot me! Goddamn, girl."

My ass hit the ground, and pain shot up my tailbone.

"Sorry! I thought you were a bear." She grabbed her phone and rushed to me, hands flapping in front of her, trying to find a way to help. "I'm makin' soup, and I thought the delicious aroma of roasted butternut squash had lured him in."

She turned off the music as I lay flat on my back on the cold floor, looking up at her and thinking, *She keeps a nail gun in the kitchen?* And *didn't Brand install radiant floor heaters?*

I also had the thought that maybe Devo and Rye were right. Maybe I could... date. Would that be such a bad thing? I mean, it wasn't like I was contemplating marrying anyone.

Would it hurt?

"You okay?" Bea asked. "You didn't break any other bones, did you?"

"I'm okay. Although, I'm no spring chicken. That's probably gonna leave a bruise."

"Here." She held out her hands, but I didn't try to get up. Instead, I reached up and held them.

I wanted to stay like that. I liked my view of her thick, dark hair falling wild and messy over her shoulders and the blush on her cheeks 'cause she was embarrassed she'd almost nailed me to the wall.

"Come down here with me," I said, and I tugged.

"What? On the floor?"

"Why not?"

"Whatever," she said, shrugging, and she sat next to me. "How'd you even get here?"

"A good Samaritan dropped me off."

She'd changed from the jeans she'd worn earlier in the day, which were no doubt some shade of yellow now, into a long, flowing purple skirt and another oversized sweatshirt. This one was gray. Its neck had been cut out so that it slid over the top of her shoulder, showing a thin, black bra strap and her tanned skin, and it had the orange and black logo of a popular tool company on the front.

"Soup?" I asked.

"Yeah," she said. "Remember? It's the whole reason we went to the store this mornin'. Your sister left me a bunch of fresh veggies, so I thought I'd make soup to keep in the fridge while I'm here. I was gonna bring some up to your house after it cools."

"Thanks."

"Why are you here, Bax?"

"I thought you wanted me to come."

"No, I did. I do. It's just… What were we thinkin'?"

"I'm not sure," I admitted.

She moved to get up, but I let go of her hands, grabbed her wrist, and leaned up on an elbow. "But don't leave. Don't walk away and act like today didn't happen."

"I don't wanna put you in a weird situation. I work for your brother, and you have Athena. Candy. I-I don't want…"

"Don't want what?"

"I don't wanna bulldoze into your life and interfere."

I thought about that. I didn't want that either. But that wasn't who she was. "You wouldn't. I don't think you're that kinda person."

"Still. It wouldn't be right."

"Hey," I said quietly. "Why don't you let me choose what's right for me, huh? I'm a big boy. I can decide for myself."

"I mean, what did you think would happen though?" she asked. "I can't have sex with you."

"That's not what I wanted."

Her eyes lowered to the floor and she breathed, "Liar," but then she lifted those sultry emeralds and dipped her chin.

"Okay, yeah, I do want that. I'm a guy, and you're beautiful and funny and I got a feelin' you'd be amazin' in bed. But it's not why I came here tonight."

"For the record, I'm dynamite in bed," she said with a coy smile, "but why did you?"

"I'm not sure. I guess I like bein' around you. I like the sound of your voice too."

And also, suddenly I'm starved for human connection.

It felt like I'd been starving for *her*.

She blushed, her cheeks pinking to a deep rose color. "I can't believe I said that to you."

"I'm glad you did. I felt the same way. I feel that way now, but you're right. Sex… It's not— I can't. But I want you." *Fuck.* I couldn't believe that had just come out of my mouth.

She bit into her lower lip. "It's crazy, right? We don't even really know each other."

"I've never felt like this. It's like you're a drug, and I need you."

"But you were married. You were in love with your wife."

"Yeah, but this is different."

She rolled her eyes. "How's it different?"

"It's a… a physical pull. I can't explain it."

I'd never felt so confused in my life. It was like my sunny, happy past was in a boxing match with this new, sexy, darker present. But both were strong and beautiful, and now, in real time, parts of that past seemed to be fading away, like Candy in my dreams.

Being with Bea *would* feel like flipping the TV channel, and I realized quickly that I could easily become addicted to her and to the easy, relaxed way she made me feel. I'd spent the last three years feeling the opposite of relaxed or easy.

She laughed. Maybe she didn't believe me? But then she nodded. "I understand."

"So maybe sex is off the table," I said cautiously, "but I'm open to… alternatives."

"Like?"

"C'mere." I patted my chest. "Come closer. Kiss me again."

She leaned down. Her hair fell around me, hiding us together inside its dark halo. It felt safe in there, and when her lips touched mine, I responded.

My hands lifted up to cradle the sides of her face so I could pull her even closer. She got up on her knees and climbed over me, straddling me and settling her warm center over my stomach, and the beast inside me wanted to push her lower. I wanted her to rub herself to ecstasy on my dick. If she'd just lift her skirt a little, she'd get a good ride because I was hard enough to make her come through my pants.

Pulling back, she gasped for a breath and looked in my

eyes, and in hers I saw desire. Hot, wild desire. Man, it felt good to be wanted again.

Desire was what she saw in my eyes too. It was the only sure thing I knew in the moment. All thoughts of loss and sadness and the resignation I'd begun to feel about the expectation of spending the rest of my life alone—all of it fled from my mind.

"More," I whispered.

She planted her hands above my shoulders on the floor and opened her mouth over mine. I licked at her tongue, moving and molding my mouth to hers, breathing into her and stealing all that desire so I could thrust it right back inside her.

She tilted her head, moaned, and rolled her hips. The movement lifted my shirt up a couple inches, and she pulled the fabric of her skirt out from between us, bringing the heat between her thighs flush with my bare stomach.

"Shit. The floor's killin' my knees," she whispered.

"Here." I whipped my shirt over my head and handed it to her and she tucked it under her knee. Tilting my head back, I located the blanket on the couch, grabbed the corner and dragged it down, then tucked it under her other knee.

"Much better," she said, and she smiled, but then her gaze moved to my chest. "Oh God, Bax. Why do you have to be so sexy?"

The better to tempt you with, my dear.

She attacked my chest with her mouth, her tongue sneaking out to taste my nipple, all the while humming her approval in heated moans and eager breath. And when she sucked it into her mouth and her hair tickled my chin, I almost came. The sweet smell of her skin and the herbal scent lingering in her hair from her shower didn't help *at all*.

Shit. I hadn't told her, but she could probably guess that I hadn't had sex in more than three years, and she was moving her body lower with every lick, until she was so close to dry humping me over my stupid pajama pants that I knew with the first press of her heat to my hard dick, I'd explode for sure.

Gripping her ribs, I lifted her.

She gasped and raised her head. The loss of her pussy so close to my cock, even covered in clothing, ached so bad that I thought the pain pills the hospital had given me after surgery couldn't even make it better.

Bea's body was my only cure.

"What are you doin'?" she said. "Did I go too far?"

"Not fuckin' far enough," I gritted through clenched teeth, trying to control the release that wanted to erupt out of my body. "Lift up your skirt."

She moaned and complied a lot faster than I thought she would.

"Sit on my face, Bea. Come in my mouth. I wanna taste you."

CHAPTER TWELVE

BEA

A TALL, sexy man with a filthy mouth?

Sign me up.

"Are you sure about this?" I asked. "Am I hurtin' you?"

"You're not hurtin' me, sweetheart," Bax said, the endearment like a caress. How many times had I been called Sweetie? But sweet*heart*? Not nearly enough. From his mouth, it made me feel warm and beautiful. Not at all like a gloppy, too-sweet Cinnabon. "Besides, I do my best work flat on my back."

Oh God, yes. This wouldn't turn out like the last time I'd been with a man. If Bax thought for a second I was unsatisfied after this—whatever *this* was we were doing—I felt certain he wouldn't leave my cabin until I screamed his name.

"Good. I like orgasms as much as the next girl. If you can make me lose my mind on the floor in full light, you will have earned yourself a steak dinner."

"I already had dinner."

"So eat me for dessert."

"Fuck," he breathed. "But I'm sorry the floor's kinda dirty."

"I don't care about dirt, Bax." I cocked an eyebrow above him, daring him.

Using the edge of the couch, I braced for stability and felt his hand slip beneath my skirt. He held me in place, his fingers clutching the skin above my hips, and then I lifted the skirt and exposed myself to him again.

I wanted him, and the wild look in his eyes, like a mustang who'd just gotten the scent of a mare in heat, made me moan and roll my hips.

Being seen as one of the guys at work or as a little girl because I was so short didn't do much to enforce the belief that men found me sexy, but the appreciative hum in the back of Bax's throat and his tongue peeking out of his mouth as he examined my body, was trying to convince me. He looked at my underwear like they were nothing more than pink skin on a peach, and he was about to tear them off with his teeth.

"C'mon now," he said as I lifted higher on my knees. "Get these things off. Let me taste you. I want you to ride my tongue till you scream."

Oh yeah, that sounds so good. He may not have been ready for sex, but *damn*. The dirty talker had come out to play!

"Rip them off," I ordered.

He winced. "They look expensive."

"Do I seem like the kind of woman who spends hard-earned money on underwear, Bax? I bought 'em at Walmart."

He hesitated. Had he changed his mind? Insecurity tried to derail me. "If you can't show me you want me, what are we even—"

Riiiiiiip.

With a handful of cheap lace, he molded his warm fingers to my ass cheeks, and he pulled my body to his mouth.

Breath hitched in my chest when he made his first pass

between my pussy lips, testing me with the flat of his tongue, and I moaned when he swallowed. Relaxation flowed through my every nerve ending. My head fell back and breath escaped me in a long, quiet sigh.

His mouth felt amazing, but I was still afraid to do something that might hurt him. I barely allowed my body to touch his lips.

"Don't hold back. Suffocate me with this pretty pussy."

"Oh my God," I groaned, but I obeyed and pressed my core to his waiting mouth. "Are you sure you can handle this? It can't be comfortable for y—"

He grumbled. "Quit babyin' me, Bea. That ain't who you are. Use me. Who the fuck gives a shit about comfort when there's a goddess above them, gettin' off and using their face to do it?"

"You don't even know m—" He lapped at my clit and sucked it into his mouth, and the hoarse grunt that traveled up from the depths of my gut would've been embarrassing, but then he groaned and drank from my body again, and I began to grind my business *all* over his face.

When in Rome.

My skirt fell from my hands, and I gripped the couch cushion. The fabric pooled around Bax's head and cut off my view of his eyes, but the darkness beneath seemed to help him concentrate. He fucked me with his mouth, just like he'd promised, using his chin and nose to rub. His hand sneaked beneath my skirt, and he slipped two fingers inside me.

Yes! Baby, it ain't gonna take much more than that.

I rode him, and he moved his body to my rhythm, bending his good knee and humping air beneath me.

I couldn't see him, but I could hear him, the wet suction of his mouth, his low moans, and his quickened breath suggesting that he quite liked what he was doing to me.

But it wasn't enough.

I craved his cock deep inside, and I wanted to fuck him until we were drowning in a pool of sticky sweat.

Too far, Bea. This is just a little bit of fun. There will be no fucking. There will be no falling. There will be no nothing.

I increased my pace, chasing release now, and rode his mouth like it was the stiff ridge of a saddle's pommel. The short hair above his lip scraped against my clit, and I felt my cum flowing down over his chin. The sound of his lips smacking and his tongue lavishing my body filled up the cabin. The only other noise I could hear was the quiet crackling of the fire.

I rolled my hips again and again in smooth strokes, but when he slipped another finger inside me and pumped, flicking at my clit with his tongue like he was trying to win a contest, my eyes fell shut and my body locked in place as hot pleasure rushed through me like wildfire.

When I lifted my skirt, he tried to erase the smile from his lips, but I caught it. I moved down to straddle his chest again and slid my hand between my legs, feeling how wet he'd made me, and I couldn't help myself; I smiled too.

I dragged two fingers through the slick slowly and held them above Bax's mouth. He opened for me, and I slipped them between his lips. Looking into my eyes, he sucked them clean and moaned. His eyes closed as he sucked harder, and I leaned down and kissed him, licking around my fingers, our saliva mixing with my cum. But then I pulled them out and slid my wet hand between us, reaching beneath his pants to return the favor he'd just given me.

He ate at my mouth like it was a melting ice cream cone and he didn't want any of me to go to waste, and I dipped my hand below the waistband of his boxers, but what I found there was better than any ice cream I'd ever tasted.

"Did you have a little party in your PJs, Bax?" I asked, feeling extremely proud of myself for making him come without even touching his cock, but heat filled my cheeks as our eyes met again. No man had ever admitted to giving me that kind of power.

"Yeah," he breathed, "just now, when you fed me your cum with your fingers."

He chased after my mouth with his until I gave it to him again, and I released his softening hard-on. I got to my feet, letting my skirt fall to the dusty floor, and held my hands out for him. He took them as he dragged his tongue and teeth over his bottom lip, scraping and licking the remnants of my pleasure onto his tongue.

"For a dad, you have a downright filthy mouth," I said. "I approve. And next time, I'll make you come with mine."

"WHO'S YOUR FAVORITE FOOTBALL TEAM?" I asked Bax as I settled next to him on the loveseat and tucked my bare feet under my butt.

He was still shirtless, and his chest and the dark-brown hair dusting it was so very distracting.

I covered us both with Athena's fuzzy blanket, careful not to spill on it. My soup was still at tastebud-burning levels, but I blew on each spoonful before I fed it to him. He totally could've fed himself, but we were sharing a small bowl full of my butternut squash concoction, and it was more fun this way. He stared at my mouth every time I sucked the broth from the spoon.

"Wait. Are you comfortable?" I asked as he shifted on the cushion next to mine. His broken leg stuck out into the middle of the cabin's tiny living room, and his good leg was bent at the knee and touching mine. Bax manspreading was kind of hot, and it wasn't like I could blame him. He really did look uncomfortable.

"I haven't been comfortable since I broke this fuckin' leg. After surgery, they put me in a special brace 'cause I had stitches and they didn't want to risk infection the first few days. But as soon as this cast was in place, I was miserable.

"And to answer your previous question, I have no idea. I don't watch much football these days. Hockey's where it's at, and my favorite hockey team is whoever Mack Goddrick plays for. He's magic on the ice. In one game, he got four teeth knocked out. Blood everywhere. They pulled him off the ice and took him to the locker room to make sure he was okay, but then he came back, and in, like, one minute, he scored on the guy who slapped that puck at his mouth. It was miraculous.

"When I started followin' him, he played for Chicago, then he went to Dallas, and then Toronto. But I grew up around local hockey, so that's what I really love to watch."

"Ehhh," I buzzed. "Wrong answer."

"S'cuse me? What you got against Mack Goddrick?"

"Nothin'," I said. "I have no clue who that is. My problem is that you think hockey is better than football."

He laughed. "Oh really? So then, if I say hockey players are infinitely more skilled and athletic than football players, you would disagree?"

"Violently," I replied, deadpan and steadfast in my conviction.

"It's true," he argued. "Have you ever watched hockey? Those guys are like wizards on their feet. The speed and the way they turn and pivot and slap the puck to the net at a hundred miles an hour? It's the definition of athleticism."

Bax gasped when I admitted I'd never watched a hockey

game. "That's a damn shame," he said. But now, hearing him defend the sport like I did football, I was a little curious.

"Football players are beasts on the field. They're much stronger than hockey players."

"Oh yeah?" He wiggled his eyebrows. "I used to play football. You're lookin' at the former Wisper High quarterback. How you like me now?"

Slapping my hand to my chest, the soup in the bowl slopped around a bit, and I swooned. "Oh, Bax, the things you say to a girl."

He chuckled. "But hockey's still better."

Dropping my hand, I rolled my eyes.

"This is a fundamental difference between the two of us then, huh? Insurmountable?"

"Yes, although I do condone your love of a Chicago team. Chicago football is my favorite."

"Oh, the 'Superbowl Shuffle,'" he said. "Is that your theme song?"

"Yes! That's what I grew up on. It was before my time, of course, but my dad used to sing it and dance around the house."

"Did you live in Chicago? I thought you said you grew up in North Carolina."

"No," I said, trying not to let memories of my dad overwhelm me. I tried not to think about him at all if I could help it. "I've never lived there, but my dad's family came from Chicago. He lived there as a boy, so Chicago was his team too."

"That's why I love hockey. My dad loved it. My best childhood memories are with us all around the TV, watchin' a game. That was before the farm started failin' and before he and Abey had a fallin' out."

"They did?"

"Yeah. He basically disowned her when he found out she was gay."

"That's awful," I said as I fed him another spoonful. "How did she handle that?"

"Mm." He swallowed, and just like the first night we'd met up in Sheridan, I found myself fixating on his Adam's apple as it bobbed. He needed a shave, but my body heated and I blushed when I realized it, because the stubble covering his upper lip, chin, and cheeks had helped to give me the best orgasm I'd had in a long time. "She might not agree, but I think she handled it with grace. She worked her ass off in school and then at her job as a deputy. The whole town of Wisper loves her, and they're proud of her. I hope she knows that. I hope it gives her back some of the love our dad took away.

"Every mornin' when I wake up, I make a conscious decision to be a better man than he was."

I smiled at that. I knew a little something about bad family legacies. It was the reason I never touched alcohol or medication.

"What about your mom?"

"Ah. Mervella Lee." He tsked his tongue. "She was brought up to obey and defend her husband no matter what. I don't think she wanted to cut Abey out of her life, but while my dad was still alive, things between them were… difficult. After he died, our mama tried everything she could to avoid the subject, but Abey finally forced her to face it last year."

"Brand mentioned that."

He scoffed. "Does my brother spill all our family secrets? What a gossip."

"No, he doesn't. It's just that when he found out Abey stood up to your mom, he was really proud of her. I think he just needed to tell someone."

"Well anyway, Abey and Devo got together and fell in love, and everything changed for Abey then." He looked at me. "You know? She couldn't accept the status quo anymore because Devo deserved better, and Abey finally decided she did too. Merv put up her usual fight, but I guess she decided learnin' to live with Abey's sexuality was a better option than losin' her only daughter forever."

"Wait. You call your mama Merv?"

He chuckled. "Yeah, but only when we wanna piss her off. Make sure you do it too."

"Okay." I laughed. "Like she doesn't already hate me, but she seems to favor you."

"You noticed her icy reception earlier?" He huffed a laugh. "I don't think she favors me. She loves all her sons the same, even though Dixon doesn't deserve it most of the time. But she defers to me 'cause I'm the oldest male in the family."

"Seriously?"

"Yeah, like I said, it's how she was raised, but it's pretty fucked up. If she was smart, she'd look to Brand for answers. He's the one who has life all figured out."

"Is that why she barely looked at me earlier today?"

"Probably. Plus, you're a woman in a"—he imitated quotations with two fingers up in the air, then dropped his hand into his lap—"man's job. You should hear the shit she still says to Abey about her job as the deputy sheriff." He opened his mouth for the next spoonful as I held it to his lips. He swallowed, then smiled and said, "This is really good, Bea."

"Thanks." Why was one little compliment from him making butterflies erupt in my stomach like they'd just snorted cocaine?

"Who taught you to cook?"

"My mama, I guess, before she died. But honestly, I don't know if I even remember any of that. My dad was hopeless after she passed, so things like laundry and cookin' fell to me."

"That wasn't fair. You were just a girl."

"Fair or not, it's what happened. By the way," I said, "I admire how you care for Athena."

He rolled his eyes. "Don't."

"Don't what?"

"Don't admire me for that. I'm a shit dad."

"You are not. You two are so close. You know her so well. I loved my dad. Worshipped him, really, but if you'd asked him what my favorite color was or what classes I loved in school, he couldn't have answered. He was too wrapped up in his grief until the day he died."

"I'm sorry, sweetheart," he said softly, reaching over to sweep a lock of hair behind my ear so he could see me better. "Tell *me* your favorite color."

"No, I shan't," I teased. "Before I leave to go back to Sheridan, you tell me. Let's see if you can figure it out."

He smiled and said, "Okay, challenge accepted. And just to be clear, I think it's hot."

"What, the soup?" I asked around a mouthful, which *was* really good. I'd have to remember to write down all the spices I'd added.

My little cabin kitchen had been stocked surprisingly well, with a few pots and pans and the olive oil, rosemary, and ginger I'd needed, but when we'd stopped at the store to get chicken stock, I grabbed veggie stock instead, sage, and garlic. The soup was creamy and rich and perfect for a cool fall night.

"No," Bax said, "your job and the fact that you're really damn good at it."

CHAPTER THIRTEEN

BEA

THE NEXT MORNING when I stepped outside my cabin, crisp October mountain air slapped me in the face.

I'd dressed in my Carhartt overalls with a moisture-wicking thermal turtleneck underneath, thermal socks, my steel-toe boots, a black beanie, and fingerless gloves. Steam rose from my nose and mouth as I breathed, preparing to address the crews gathering in the unpaved roundabout.

There were ten guys for each house and a crew of twenty to finish the cabins, plus a few specialty guys who'd be stopping by throughout the job to do whatever they'd been contracted for. Brand had hired a masonry guy to come out and add some stone features to the cabins' porches, just to pretty them up a bit, and he'd add fire pits to each lot. Electricians had already roughed in, but they and the HVAC guys would be out in the next week to do final checks and tests.

My cabin had been finished ahead of time, minus the stone façade, but all the rest were still in varying stages of completion, all without appliances and finishing touches, so as soon as roofs and walls were up, that would all be delivered and finished too. And then furniture would be delivered along with things like blinds and curtains, pots and pans, bedding, but I'd probably be back in Sheridan by then.

Guilt kept washing through me, making my stomach burn, because of what Bax and I had done last night. Although, after I drove him back to his house, I crawled into my bed and slept like a damn baby.

It wasn't that I thought what we'd done was wrong in a general sense, but fooling around with him wasn't the smartest idea I'd ever had because I knew I'd be leaving in a few weeks. One-night stands weren't a foreign concept for me, but this guy had a family. He had a history of heartbreak, and I didn't want to do anything to add to it.

So why was I already trying to find reasons to see him again?

But I had a job to do, so, gathering up all my girl power, I tried to forget the warm, chestnutty smell of Bax's skin and bellowed into the morning, "Listen up!"

Some of the guys kept talking amongst themselves. There were always a few in every crew, guys who didn't automatically defer to a woman in charge. But they were about to.

Lifting two fingers to my lips, the earsplitting whistle I let out seemed to bounce off the trunks of the trees surrounding the clearing we were congregating in. All eyes finally landed on me standing on the bed of my truck. It was the only way they'd all see me.

"Mornin'. I'm Bea. If you work for Brand Lee and Lee Construction, you work for me." A couple men snickered, but there were a few women in the sea of faces beneath me, and they nodded in solidarity. "Yeah, yeah, I know. I'm a woman. I'm short, and maybe you think I don't look like I know what I'm doin'. You'd be wrong. I do. I can do any job on this site, and probably faster than you. So don't fuck around. Let's get these jobs done and quick, before winter hits and we all have to go home underpaid."

More nods. People were starting to gear up. They were ready to work. *Good.*

"Alright, house crews, you should already know your jobs since you've been at this a while, but the new assignments are in your inboxes.

"Also, Brand wanted me to apologize again for the delay, and you should've received the bonus he set up for y'all. If you have any questions about the new crew configurations, my number's in the email. You can call, but I probably won't answer unless you blow up my phone. Text is better.

"And cabin crew"—I pointed to the southwest, to a small, unfinished structure Bax and his family would be using as a picnic area and community building for guests—"meet me by the rec building. We've got a few things to go over before I let you loose. I'll be there in five.

"Giddyup, people," I said, clutching my clipboard under my arm. "Let's get to work."

Everybody milled around for a minute, saying hello to their coworkers, but they all headed to their assignments quickly. In construction, the faster you got on the job, the faster you got off. If the sun was still up and high in the sky when your day was done, then it was a good day.

A stocky guy with a bushy mustache and a beer belly hung back by himself, away from the groups getting in the parked trucks on their way to their designations. He had a clipboard in one hand, too, and a huge Thermos tucked under his arm.

"You must be Clay Marveaux."

"Yup, in the flesh."

"Nice to meet you," I said, jumping down from my perch

and extending my hand for a shake. "I'm glad to have you here to help me rein in the chaos."

"You were pretty good with the guys. They respond to a firm hand."

Whoa. Could it be true that Brand had found a nice guy for me to work with, one who didn't try to step all over me and prove his manly dominance? Still, history would keep me appropriately skeptical until Clay proved me wrong.

"Thanks. Yeah, I'm used to it. It's kinda my superpower. Should we head to the rec hall? We've got a lot to get to."

"Lead the way, miss Bea," he said. "By the by, you got a crew name?"

"A nickname?" I tried not to laugh. "Nope, sure don't."

With his black cowboy hat, brown suede jacket, rodeo belt buckle, and the toothpick stuck out the side of his mouth, I had a feeling this cowboy-turned-builder, Clay, and I had about zero things in common in our personal lives, but on the job, we'd get along just fine.

BY THE TIME lunch rolled around, a symphony filled my ears: hammers hitting wood, saws buzzing, people lifting and hauling and climbing. The cabin crew called out to each other, asking for help, acknowledging the help given, checking measurements and dimensions, their voices singing lyrics to a song that sounded like home. I was in my happy place.

"Bea!"

I turned to the sound of my name from one voice that didn't belong and saw Athena running toward me.

"Athena, what are you doin' out here? You can't be here. Not without a hard hat and your dad's permission."

She stopped in front of me, and her face fell. "Oh, I'm sorry."

"No, you haven't done anything wrong, but this isn't the safest place for a kid."

"I'm almost fourteen, Bea." She rolled her eyes. "I'm not a kid."

I laughed. *Oh, the naivety of children.* "Still, Athena, just to be safe."

"Okay, I hear you." She shrugged. "I like your outfit."

"Thanks," I said, scanning the dirt on my overalls.

I'd shed my gloves and beanie once the sun rose high enough to chase the chill out of the air, but my hard hat had surely left an ugly bump in my hair. Athena confirmed it as I removed the hat and she looked at my hair and giggled. I held the hat out to her, and she hugged it to her chest while I pulled my scraggly hat hair into a pile on my head and wrapped the scrunchie permanently attached to my wrist around it to hold it up.

"I like yours too." I pointed to her light-purple puffer vest. I found a paint chip once that had the color listed as Old Dusty Lavender. "That's my favorite color."

Her lips lifted into the biggest smile, and she was so cute with her braid pulled over her shoulder and her adorable but semi-buck teeth gleaming in the sun. She'd worn some serious-looking work boots. The kid really knew her way around a farm.

"Really? Mine too!"

She looked around my work site and the future of her family's new business venture, watching as my merry music makers paused their song and packed their tools away for the lunch break. "You're really in charge of all these people?"

"Yep." I cupped my hand around my mouth, hiding my

lips from onlookers. "Don't tell 'em I said this, but I'm like a female version of Gru, and they're my Minions."

I winked, and she laughed.

And then, just to prove my point, one of the crew walked up. From the scowl on his face, I got the feeling I wouldn't like what he had to say.

He glanced at Athena but focused on me. His coveralls were cleaner than mine, his hair barely mussed from the hard hat I'd noticed he rarely wore. I'd learned his name earlier in the day, but now it wasn't coming to mind. Wait, was it Jensen something? I only remembered his first name because one of the other guys had called him Jen, and he clearly had not liked that. And, it seemed, he didn't like to actually work. I wasn't surprised by that. It happened with new crews; they spent the first day feeling me out, seeing what they could get away with.

Jensen Linney? Loony? Lovey?

He didn't start off in my good graces now. "You scheduled HVAC for Friday?" he said. "That's a mistake. Cabins nine and ten are nowhere near ready. You're gonna cost the boss unnecessary money when they have to come out again next week." He looked me up and down, at the fountain of hair on the top of my head, like it wasn't possible for little ol' female me to know what the hell I was doing.

Here we go. "It's Jensen, right?"

A curt nod was his only answer, and he fixed his hands over his hips. He was attractive in a tattle-tale kind of way. He had a young face. It was tanned from the sun, but his cheeks were pink from the cold, and his hair was too long, but not like a sexy guitar-player or a surfer. The ends frayed around his neck and ears and hinted at an impending mullet. I knew they'd come back in style, but on Jensen, it wasn't a pleasing look. It made me want to find some clippers and go at him like I was trimming a hedge.

A few of the guys had gathered behind him, maybe to cheer him on when he challenged me, or maybe they were waiting to see how I'd handle him.

"Well, thanks for sharing your concern, Jensen. I appreciate it, but they *will* be ready." Where did this guy get off? I had more information than he did.

His eyes narrowed infinitesimally. "It's a mistake," he repeated. "You're doin' things all wrong. Does Mr. Lee know about the changes you've made to the crew? This job was fine before you got here and fucked it all up." He glanced at Athena again, probably regretting his choice of words. "S'cuse me," he said to her.

Athena scowled. She didn't like this joker any more than I did.

"Mr. Lee is well aware," I said. "And since he put *me* in charge, I know that you don't work on HVAC. You're a drywaller, right? So how is it you think you can tell me I'm wrong?"

He lifted a finger in the air. "I am, but—"

"Listen, Jen, lemme just stop you right there. It's lunchtime. I'm hungry. I'm sure you're a little peckish. I'm gonna give you the benefit of the doubt and guess that your current mood can be attributed to hunger, so go to lunch. Have a sandwich."

I looked at Athena. "Cover your ears."

She did, loosely, but I knew she could hear every word I said.

To Jensen, I continued with, "Grab a Snickers or replenish your chakras or whatever the fuck you need to do to adjust your attitude. I don't give a crap what you put in your mouth, but make sure you wash it out before you clock back in. I don't need you to tell me how to do my job. The cabins *will* be ready for HVAC on Friday. If they're not, I'll owe you a beer. But if you can't manage to do what you've been hired to without whinin' like a baby, feel free not to come back at all. Capisce?"

Athena's mouth popped open, and she clapped both hands over it.

Jensen glanced at Athena again, but then he shook his head silently and stormed away, back to his girlfriends. One of them actually winked at me.

Inhaling deeply, I turned away and faced Athena again. I smiled. "Where were we?"

"What a jerk," she whispered conspiratorially.

"Nah. He just forgot to put on his manners when he got dressed this mornin'. So what's up?"

She laughed. "I just came to invite you up to the house for lunch. I had a half day at school today, so we're havin' tamales. Devo's mama showed me how to make them. They're really good." She smirked, and there was a little sparkle in her eye. "Daddy helped me fry plantains, and there's rice, and he made the verde sauce. It's good too."

"Oh. Thank you. It's really nice of you to offer."

Shit. Did she know what her dad and I had done last night? No, she couldn't know, but why was she grinning at me like that? Would Bax want me to come for lunch? He probably didn't want anyone to know we'd been together or, like, that he'd had his mouth between my legs. Although, tamales did sound way better than soup. I mean, the soup was good, but was there ever a time tamales wouldn't be better?

"Pork, beef, or chicken?" I asked.

"Chicken and pork. Take your pick."

"It's a date. Thanks, Athena."

"Yay!" she squeaked. "Okay, head up when you're ready."

"Give me ten or fifteen minutes and I'll be there."

She skipped off to Rye's big, black RAM, idling where the crews had parked this morning. Rye waved out his open window as Athena climbed into his front seat, but his keen eye was focused on the retreating group of blowhards and their ringleader, Jensen. Rye should've known better than to bring Athena onto a construction site, but no matter. I'd scold him about it over tamales.

After packing away my own tools and checking on the rest of the cabin crew to make sure everybody had something to eat, I called Clay on my drive up to the house. The house crews had broken for lunch, too, and Clay said all was good. I'd need to check in on them and get visual confirmation. I made a mental note to drive to each house site after lunch, but right now, my blood sugar was on the floor, and tamales were calling my name.

I stepped out of my truck in Bax's driveway and almost fell on my face when something came up behind me and stuck its cold, wet nose up the butt of my coveralls.

"What the hell!"

I caught myself on the hood of my truck. My hands slapped the metal so hard that I would've bet anyone in the house heard it.

As I turned to locate the perv, I heard the hum of a small engine and Bax's voice.

"Are you okay?"

"I'm fine," I said, looking down at the young German Shepherd behind me, chasing his tail, and an all-black lamb, who stared up at me like he'd just found his long-lost mama.

"Sorry!" Athena said as she parked a small, white and red

Bobcat behind my truck. She jumped out and ran around to help her dad.

"Who are these evil doers?"

"They're not evil," Athena said. "That's Figaro, and the lamb is Pekoe."

"Here. Let me help," I offered, stepping around the mongrels toward the tractor. "You wrangle the inappropriate farm animals."

Bax handed me his crutches, and I moved closer so he could lean on my shoulder if he needed it.

"Fig," Athena called as she began jogging backward toward the barn. "Pekoe! C'mon!" She turned and they followed, and I listened to the glittering sound of her laughter in the noon sun as they chased her and jumped, trying to catch her.

"I hope you're hungry," Bax said. He did lean on my shoulder, though I wasn't sure he really needed the support. "No joke, Athena and Devo's mama made a hundred tamales last week. Rye put away about fifty by himself, but there's still a ton left."

"I can't eat fifty," I said, "but I can probably put you back four or five. I'm starvin'."

Bax smiled as he crutched his way to his front porch, and I followed. He didn't say anything more as we made our way up the stairs, me with my arms out in case he fell backward, but what the hell would I do if he did? Cushion his fall with my ass, that was what.

He glanced back at me, and the memory of what we'd done last night in my cabin looked all sultry and secret spread across his lips. When I thought about his mouth on me, his fingers pumping inside me, and him swallowing my cum, my whole body pulsed and heated in waves.

"You don't have anything to say to me today?" I asked.

I moved around him and held the door for him, and he hobbled into his kitchen.

"Yeah, you want red sauce or green?" he asked as he leaned against the counter by the sink. "Also, you look hot in those britches."

"Ha. My britches are not what I meant."

Setting his crutches against the counter, he reached out for my arm and pulled me to his chest.

"Athena will see," I said.

He shook his head. "Nope. She already ate. She's gone to help Rye in the barn."

That little… fixer-upper. My hands gripped his biceps. "Does she know? She can't know!"

"She doesn't know anything. I didn't come home last night and sit her down to tell her how you fucked my face and came in my mouth."

"Bax!"

"It's just us here, Beatrice Baker. Just you and me."

He stole a quick kiss, and the smile dawning on his face as he pulled back was like the sun coming out to shine after a brutal thunderstorm. It was like he'd just realized he'd given himself permission to kiss me, and that realization freed him somehow.

"Sit and I'll make you a plate," he said, but he looked to the right, where a big Mexican spread sat waiting beneath his dated, dark-walnut cupboards, complete with plantains, rice, and sour cream, and his smile faded into perplexion. "Or how 'bout I sit and you make our plates? I don't think I can carry all that."

I rolled my eyes. "Sit your ass down."

CHAPTER FOURTEEN

BAX

BEA GOT TO WORK, loading up two plates with both chicken and pork tamales still wrapped in their steaming cornhusk casings with all the delicious fixings that Athena had prepared and set out for us, and I sat at the table and listened to the calming sound of Bea's voice as she talked.

"I love tamales. I've never tried to make them on my own, but I ate them a lot as a kid 'cause our neighbor made them all the time, and she knew how much my dad loved 'em. We traded with her. My mama wasn't as good a cook as Mrs. Ortiz, but she made really good greens and fried mushrooms, and she could whip up a mean Tater-Tot casserole when she wanted to. And soup."

She smirked, reminding me of the night we'd shared, and set a plate in front of me, slid into the chair next to mine with her own plate, and then asked, "Why would Athena invite me to lunch but then not eat with me?"

Raising an eyebrow, I unwrapped my first tamale and dug into it with my fork. "I think you may have fallen victim to Rye and Athena's matchmakin' services."

"But... Really? I didn't think she'd want that. I mean, the

other day when I said I didn't like my nickname, she jumped down my throat a little about her mom's name."

"I haven't said anything to her about you. I'm not sure what I'd even say. She can be protective of Candy, but she also worries about me. Maybe she saw you and thought one plus one could equal two."

"It can't," she said. "I work for your brother."

I nodded, all too aware of that fact.

"And I live seven hours away."

"Athena's just a kid," I said. "She doesn't get it." I tried not to let the disappointment I was feeling show in my eyes hearing her say it, but I had my own reasons Bax and Bea sitting in a tree wasn't a good idea.

But maybe Athena wasn't the only one guilty of doing a little first-grade math. It seemed I'd gotten the answer wrong, too, because I found myself wishing Bea could stay after the cabins were done.

Maybe we could… What? She'd only been here a few days. What exactly did I want from her?

Sex for one thing. Good God, tasting her wasn't enough. I wanted to fuck her.

Hard.

It was like that one little taste and the smooth rolling of her body over my mouth had awoken the man I used to be. Before life happened and broke me down.

"Where'd you go?" she asked, and I looked at her before I realized what I was doing.

"Huh?"

"You got quiet all of a sudden."

"Nowhere. I'm here."

She saw the confusion on my face. That was easy to deduce from the way her eyes got big and she looked down at her plate intently, like the answer to time travel lay tucked inside a tamale, and if she paid close enough attention, she could go back to when we hadn't complicated the fuck out of everything. We hadn't had actual sex, but not having sex was just as complicated as having it.

Was I desperately attracted to Bea? Yes.

Was she attracted to me? I thought she was. *I mean, you don't sit on a guy's face and let him eat you out if you're not, right?*

But Bea was right that the circumstances were far from ideal.

Still, knowing that didn't make me want her any less.

Neither of us said another word as she stuffed her face, and I sat there, watching her dip bites of tamale into sour cream and verde sauce and then shovel them into her mouth, and I kept thinking about how absolutely absurd it was that I'd finally moved on from Candy's death and her loss enough to want another woman, but now that I had, the woman I'd found myself wanting was so unavailable, it wasn't even funny.

BEA WENT BACK TO WORK, and I spent the afternoon trying to distract Athena from getting even more curious about Bea than she already was. She came to drive me back to the barn after lunch, and that was when the questions started, and they didn't stop for at least a half an hour.

"Where's Bea, Daddy?"

"She went back to work."

"Oh. I thought she might hang out and keep you company. Do you think she'd like to go muddin' with me? She could ride Aunt Abey's ATV."

"I dunno, Road Trip. Ask her."

"You should've seen her earlier. One of the men workin' on the cabins questioned her, and she handed him his a— She put him in his place. She's so cool, and I think she's pretty, Daddy. Do *you* think she's pretty?"

"Sure."

She drove over a big bump on the dirt path and winced as it jostled and tossed me around on the seat. "But, like, *really* pretty or just normal pretty?"

"I don't know what that means, Athena."

"Like, when you look at her, do you think 'she's beautiful'? Or do you just go, 'meh'?"

The question made me laugh. "The first one."

If anybody looked at Beatrice Baker and thought anything other than, "She's fuckin' gorgeous," they were nuts. And when I pictured her handing her crew member his ass, I had to hold back a laugh. I would've paid money to see it.

Bea Baker was breathtaking.

Her skin glowed under the light of the sun, and she had these faint freckles across the bridge of her nose.

Her green eyes were the oddest color, kind of hunter green, kind of teal green, depending on the light, but absolutely mesmerizing either way, especially when she was speaking her mind.

She had these bangs that drove me wild. I'd never noticed much about women's hairstyles, but dang. Athena had told me they were "curtain bangs," but whatever she called them, they were sexy, the way they swopped down and framed her face like a painting, drawing my eyes to her high cheekbones.

She was on my mind so much that I had a hard time looking at anything else when she was around. I'd been sketching her in my down time, which was pretty much all the time lately, as long as no one was around to see the goddess I'd scribbled onto my sketchpad in graphite lines.

And her body? Fuck my life. Tight ass, tiny tits, and toned arms. I wasn't used to a woman built like Bea. It kind of surprised me that I'd be into it since the only other woman I'd ever been with had been tall and soft.

And the warm, succulent space between Bea's legs? *Goddamn, I wanna fill that ho—*

"I think so too," Athena said, completely oblivious to my horny daydreams. "Does she want kids? I mean, like, do you think she'd be a good mom?"

Shit.

I made it to the barn answering the rest of Athena's questions with a copy-and-paste answer of "I dunno," and when we got there, Rye grabbed my crutches and helped me out of the skid steer. He listened to Athena's interrogation, trying discreetly to hear my answers, but finally, he stepped in and showed me a little mercy.

"Athena, can you saddle Tulsa for me, please?"

"Sure," she said in a chipper voice, and she skipped into the barn to do what he'd asked.

"What's this about?" he asked me, nodding after my precocious kid. Was that a guilty grin on his face? He'd been trying to conceal it, but it was plain to see. He was in on the matchmaking thing with my daughter. I knew it now like I knew my own name.

"I'm not sure," I said.

Yeah, Athena and Rye were in on it together, but Athena's reasoning was still a mystery to me. Was it just that she liked having a woman around? Had I fucked up the single-parent thing so much that my kid was desperate for another adult to tag in?

Rye's distraction had worked, but Athena was quick, and as soon as she led the buckskin mare I'd bought for her out of the barn, she started up with the questions again.

Rye threw me an apologetic smile, took the lead from Athena's hand, shrugged, and then she and I watched from the fence as he exercised Tulsa in our ring and got her ready to ride. He'd been working with her for weeks, but it looked like the horse was finally ready.

"Are you gonna ask Bea on a date?" Athena asked, peering up at me with her hand shading her eyes from the sun.

The sip of water I'd just taken from the plastic bottle hanging from a lanyard around my neck spewed from my mouth as I coughed. My resourceful daughter was worried about me getting dehydrated, and if I didn't drain the bottle, its weight gave me a nasty ache in my shoulders.

"What? I bet you'd have fun."

Taking the hat off my head, I dropped it onto Athena's. "Where's your hat?" She shrugged and adjusted mine to shade her eyes better. The light-colored straw material brought out the highlights in her hair that reminded me of Candy. Soon the weather would demand my felt hat, and the smooth, dark-gray color didn't remind me of my dead wife at all.

"Athena, I'm not really in a position to take a woman out on a date right now," I said, trying to swipe the water off my shirt and not fall over, but even if I wasn't reliant on crutches, her questions still would've made me unsteady.

"Why not? Bea could drive. I get that your manly, misogynistic view of the world makes you want to drive, but Bea's a strong lady. She won't mind. And then y'all could go get dinner or see a movie or somethin'."

"Did you just call me a misogynist?" I asked, and Athena cocked an eyebrow. "Seriously? I just let my not-yet-fourteen-year-old daughter drive me in a tractor. How's that misogynistic?"

"Good point," she said. "I take it back. But I stand firm on the manly comment."

"Road Trip, where's this comin' from? You and me, we're doin' okay on our own, right?"

She sighed and turned her head to watch Rye lunge Tulsa around the ring. "Sure, Daddy. We are."

"Talk to me, baby. What's goin' on in that head of yours?"

She tossed her shoulders again. "It's nothin'."

"Athena."

Taking a deep breath, she chewed on her lip and turned back my way. "I dunno. I just thought… I thought maybe, if you had a girlfriend, you'd smile more. You used to smile a lot before Mama died."

Here it was—proof of the weight of my happiness.

"I'm sorry I've made you worry about me," I said. "But I'm okay. You're right that I smiled more when Mama was alive, but I'm not *un*happy. How could I be with you around?"

"It's not the same thing," she argued.

"No, you're right. It's not."

"Everybody needs someone to hug and kiss and love. Even me."

My heart stuttered to a stop in my chest. "'Scuse me?"

Rye stopped fast in the middle of the pen, and Tulsa reared at his sudden movement. As soon as he had her back down on all four hooves, he called over to me, "What the hell did she just say?"

Athena rolled her eyes and took a step backward, out of the path of my oncoming dad tantrum.

"So, I kinda have a boyfriend," she said, looking back and forth between Rye and me.

"This is, like, a ceremonial position, right, Athena?" Rye

said. "You're not gonna go on dates, are you? 'Cause I dunno if I can handle that."

"Uncle Rye, cut it out," she said with a good dose of exasperation lacing her tone.

I was speechless. My little girl going on dates?

Oh God. I can't handle that.

I'm not ready!

"Daddy? Are you okay? You look kinda green."

I couldn't focus on much, but I thought I heard Rye curse and then the sound of Tulsa's lead slapping dirt when he dropped it. Out of the corner of my eye, I caught him hurdling the fence, and next thing I knew, he was behind me, his arms out and ready to catch me if I decided to fall on my ass.

"I'm fine," I said. "I got this. I can handle it."

Yeah, sure, you got this. No problem.

I looked at my daughter and said, "You're grounded till you're thirty-five."

Athena sighed for the 107th time today, rolling her eyes again.

"I gotta go," I mumbled. "The physical therapist will be here in fifteen minutes."

I turned and hobbled back to my house, trying desperately not to panic, but I had no fucking clue how to navigate teenage dating!

I MADE it through the evening by imbibing two shots of really cheap whiskey and by pretending the boyfriend conversation hadn't happened.

Linda dropped off no less than five casseroles when she delivered our order later in the day, so I threw the tuna-noodle casserole in the oven and stuffed the rest in my deep freezer in the garage, which still held casseroles from three years ago, when every single unmarried woman in the county and even some that *were* married dropped one off. They were probably freezer burned, but I'd never thrown them out because I figured, in a pinch, we might need them.

Which, now that I'd really thought about it, I realized was disgusting, so that's what I did after dinner, cleaned out my deep freezer. Rye carried four garbage bags of old food and its containers to our bear-proof cans on the side of the house, but then he brought them into the garage. They'd probably end up stinking up the place, but it might help to keep scavengers away till garbage day.

As I supervised Rye, Athena followed us in and out of the garage, trying to bring up the boy subject at least four more times, stating passionately that Logan Jacobs's parents were fine with them dating, so why couldn't I be?

And every time, all I could do was shake my head and try not to picture the daughter I still imagined to be four years old in the throes of passion with some snot-nosed, fourteen-year-old sex addict.

It gave me the fucking ick!

She went up to her bedroom disappointed. I popped two ibuprofen, which maybe wasn't the best idea after the whiskey, brushed my teeth, and for the first time since I broke my leg, made the dangerous trek up the stairs.

The physical therapy I'd started and would continue three times a week for the foreseeable future wiped my sorry ass out, which made no sense to me because I'd spent my entire life on this farm, doing much harder labor than lifting my leg two inches off the floor from a seated position in sets of ten for five minutes. Jordan, the PT guy, said my muscles had spent the last couple weeks guarding my broken bone, so they needed to relax and get back to their regularly scheduled programming, which was why I was utterly exhausted.

When I was in the safety of my bedroom, I peeled off my T-shirt, dropped it to the floor, fell face first onto my bed, and at 8:07 pm, passed the fuck out.

At one in the morning, a knock on my door woke me.

"Athena, please go back to sleep. We can talk about it tomorrow."

She didn't say anything, but my door opened and shut quietly, and then the covers rustled next to me in the darkness.

"Athena?"

"Shh," Bea shushed me. "Go back to sleep."

CHAPTER FIFTEEN

BEA

BAX SAT UP, and his boxsprings squeaked. "What's goin' on? Are you okay?"

"Yeah," I said. "You said I could stay here if I was more comfortable, and tonight, I'm more comfortable."

His room was pitch dark, but the moon shone in the window just enough for me to see his outline.

"Okay…" he said, twisting and reaching for the light on his bedside table.

As a warm yellow glow filled the room, I scooted down and laid my head on a pillow, tugging the edge of Bax's blanket over my hip, and I tucked my hands beneath my cheek. "I'm sorry I woke you, but I'm pretty sure there's at least one bear out by the cabins. I kept hearing a noise. I have no clue what it was, but it scared the crap out of me."

"Uh, just for future reference, if you think you hear a bear, stay in your cabin! Are you nuts?" He shook his head. "Dammit, I should've given you bear spray. I can't believe I forgot. I'll get you some tomorrow."

Rising up onto my elbow, I asked, "Is this not okay?"

Shit. You're a dick, Bea. Why didn't it occur to you that maybe he's not ready for another woman to be in his room?

But I really was freaked out by the noises I kept hearing outside my cabin. At first, I'd thought it was a person. In fact, my very first thought had been that maybe Bax had come back for round two, but then I swore I'd heard someone fumbling with the doorknob. Bax had another key, so I knew then it wasn't him.

"No, it's fine," he said, lying back down and resting his head on his pillow. He turned to look at me. "But I almost had a heart attack just now when I imagined you tryin' to run from a grizzly."

"Oh, okay." I closed my eyes and snuggled into his covers. "Well, that didn't happen, so calm down. Go back to sleep."

"I'm calm, but I'm not sure about the sleepin' part."

I yawned. "Turn out the light, and don't make a big deal out of this."

He snorted. "There's a woman in my bed. It's kind of a big deal."

"You have a kid. It's not like it's the first time. Wait." My eyes popped open again. "So should I not run if I come across a bear?"

Still looking at me, he arched a sexy brow. "You ever hear the sayin', 'if it's brown, lay down. If it's black, fight back, and if it's white, say goodnight'?"

I snorted. "No." *Seriously? That's the best bear advice you can give me?*

"Words of wisdom."

"You want me to lie down in the dirt and let the bear eat me?"

"You are delicious," he said with a smirk, and I blushed

from head to toe. "But he won't. Bears don't see us as food, but if you get in their personal space or for whatever reason they feel threatened, they will fuck you up proper. If you can walk away slowly, do that—you can't outrun a bear—but if it's too late for that, it's best practice to stay as calm as you can. In other words, don't go berserk, try not to make eye contact, and most likely, he'll leave. But if the worst happens and he attacks, cover your head and play dead.

"And if it's a mama with cubs, just pray."

I rolled onto my back and stared up at the ceiling, trying hard not to imagine the worst happening. "I'm more freaked out than I was five minutes ago. I think I made the right decision to come to your house."

"Didn't you ever see a bear in North Carolina? Y'all have black bears, right?"

"Yeah, and yes, I have seen them, but from afar. We had one goin' through our garbage cans once. My mama and daddy got up in arms, but he wasn't there long and he never came back." I shrugged. "I guess we were lucky considerin' where we lived was pretty rural."

When I turned my head to look at him, I caught him staring at my profile.

"We should go to sleep," I said cautiously, as opposed to fucking each other's brains out, which was what I really wanted to do as my eyes wandered down the wide expanse of his bare chest above the blanket tucked around his hips.

"There's another bedroom or I can sleep on the couch," he said. "I mean, if you want privacy."

"Rye's on the couch. At least, that's who I think the big boulder was under a pink blanket with red hearts all over it. Whoever it is, they're sawin' some serious logs."

Bax chuckled.

"But I thought for sure your dog would bark at me and wake the whole house."

"He's Rye's dog, really, but Fig stays out with the herd most of the time."

"Oh. Good to know," I said. "But the third bedroom is the room next to yours, right?"

"Yeah."

"The door's locked." I really had tried to find somewhere to sleep that wasn't occupied by the one person I couldn't seem to stay away from but absolutely should have.

I couldn't bring myself to wake Athena; she had cross country and school in the morning. And I assumed the locked third bedroom had been Bax's and Candy's before she died.

The room he'd been sleeping in before I woke him couldn't have been a married couple's room. It looked pretty barren and undecorated. Besides the bed and the side table, there was a hardback dining chair in one corner with a pair of dirty cowboy boots set on the seat, a dresser with three open drawers and clothes falling out, and not one picture on the wall or any kind of personal decoration.

"Bax?"

"Sorry," he said, shaking his head like he was trying to shake away a thought. "It's uh, the room's not... There's a lot of junk in there and it's not really set up for guests. I forgot."

"Okay. Then I'll sleep in here with you tonight. Tomorrow, I'll get that bear spray, and do you have a shotgun around here I can keep at the cabin?"

"Bear spray's a better bet, but yeah, I'll show you how to use the gun tomorrow in case of emergency."

I scoffed. "I know how to use a shotgun, Bax. You can't be surprised by that, and I wouldn't aim to actually shoot the bear. I'd fire into the air or nearby or whatever. But if it comes down to me versus a grizzly, the grumbly bitch is goin' down."

He laughed. "You're right. I'm not surprised. It's in a locked safe in my closet. I'll get it out in the mornin'."

"Thanks."

"But I mean, you're welcome to stay here, too, not just tonight… if you want to."

"I do want to. The cabin's nice, but yeah, I'm kinda freaked out. I can't really sleep with all the nature noises. But I don't know if it's a good idea. Athena's down the hall, and—"

And if I stay, I might take advantage of you. I'll try not to, but the heat comin' off your body right now might just lure me in. I can't make any promises.

"I want you to try," he whispered.

"What?"

He rolled onto his side, pushed up on an elbow, and propped his head in his hand. "You said you'll try not to take advantage of me, but I want you to."

"I thought I said that in my head."

"You do that a lot," he murmured. "Say things out loud that you mean to leave unsaid."

"I do?"

"Yeah. It's cute. Plus, I kinda like knowin' what you're really thinkin'."

How long had I been doing that? Dozens of inappropriate inner thoughts ran through my head, and I winced when I realized I had no clue if I'd actually said them out loud.

His gaze burned the side of my face, but I was actively trying to avoid it. This time, I made sure my inner diatribe didn't leak out: *You work for his brother. Get a grip, dammit!*

"Athena asked me today if I was plannin' to take you on a date."

Whoa. "She did?" I pushed up on my elbow, too, and we were face to face. "What'd you say?"

"I didn't really answer."

Pulling Bax's blanket up higher to cover my chest because I suddenly felt exposed even though I was fully dressed in leggings and a sweatshirt, I said. "I'm not much of a dater."

"You and me both," he said. "But this"—he lifted his hand to my hip and slid it down the outside of my thigh, then tugged the blanket down and slipped that hand between my legs—"this I can do."

My hand reached out slowly—of its own volition, thank you very much—and I watched with fascination as it slid over his hip where his sweats had dipped a bit, and then lower over his smooth abs. They tensed when I touched. Bax held his breath, and my mouth watered. All it would take was one slip of a finger beneath his waistband, and the night could take a turn. "If I didn't work for your brother—"

"You do, I know."

"Yeah, but if I didn't and if I didn't live a whole day's drive away, *would* you ask me out?" Searching the burning blue of his eyes, my hand moved in slow motion over his skin. "I mean, like, are you… available for that?"

"Available? I'm not seein' anybody." He moved closer, inching his hand slowly up my inner thigh, slipping closer to the wetness his nearness, the sound of his voice, and the heat from his skin had caused.

I moaned softly, the anticipation of getting naked with this man making it impossible not to. For such a rough, grumpy guy, his touch felt delicate and soft.

"But I meant are you in a place to do that?"

"'In a place?'"

"Are you *ready*, Bax?"

His eyes rose to mine, and thank God 'cause if he stared any harder at my body, I might've internally combusted.

"I don't know," he stated simply, "but I want you."

One simple sentence, but there was so much contained within those seven words.

I thought about how to respond, but I rolled my lip beneath my teeth, and he groaned and leaned closer to kiss me. I moved onto my back and pulled him with me, and his hand finally found its way to my pussy over my leggings.

He rubbed and I gasped into his mouth.

"Ride me, Bea. It's all I can offer, but I promise, as soon as my leg will cooperate, I'll repay the favor and fuck you into the next week."

Could I make any other noise besides moans? But I did it again loudly. "But what about Athena?"

"Lock the door and don't scream."

Gently, I pushed him away, and I rolled off the side of the bed and jumped over to lock us in his bedroom. "Please, *you'll* be the one screamin'." I lifted my sweatshirt over my head, and my hair fell and swayed down my bare back.

It didn't escape my notice how quickly I'd abandoned my "I work for your brother" excuse, but I would analyze my lack of propriety later. *Lack of loyalty?* But surely Brand could see that making his brother smile was a kind of loyalty… Wasn't it?

Bax stared at my breasts as I walked around to his side of the bed, pulling the blanket off his legs and letting it slip down to the floor. "I don't doubt that," he said when I climbed over him carefully and straddled his hips. Beneath his sweatpants, he was hard as stone.

Scooting lower, I moaned again when his cock made contact with the heat throbbing between my legs.

"Condom?" I asked.

He nodded to the side table. "Drawer. Foreplay?"

"Don't need it. I'm already turned on."

"Yeah," he said, "so am I, which is why foreplay's probably a good idea. It's been a while for me." He paused but then commanded, "Get up on your hands and knees."

CHAPTER SIXTEEN

BAX

BEA ARCHED AN EYEBROW, but she did what I'd told her to.

She hovered over me, her hot hands planted on my shoulders and her knees digging into the bed next to my hips, and I slipped my hand beneath her soft, tight-fitting leggings, my fingers gliding slowly lower over her smooth belly until I reached shaved-short pubic hair. She hadn't worn underwear or a bra, and I had no idea why, but that fact excited me more than it probably should've.

My other hand wound its way through her hair, and I pulled her lower and kissed her again.

She was right; she was ready. Wet heat coated my middle finger as I slipped it inside her, and her eyes rolled closed as she rocked her body over mine slowly, riding my hand and kissing me like I couldn't ever remember being kissed.

Her mouth was hot, too, and she tasted like possibility.

Before she'd arrived in Wisper, I hadn't really thought about what it would mean to kiss someone again, or how soul bearing a kiss could be, but with Bea, it was intense. The kiss was deep, like she was searching inside me with her tongue for answers to questions she hadn't yet asked, and I was just searching her. I wanted to know who she was. Why she'd grown up to be the strong, independent woman she was now.

I wanted to know why she seemed to want me, a depressed dad, a widower, a man whose life had gone completely off the rails.

Granted, two of my fingers were now buried inside her body, pumping and curling to bring her the most intimate pleasure a person could give another, so maybe that was the reason she was kissing me with everything she had.

Her lips tasted sweet, her breath even sweeter, and she played with my mouth, pulling at my lips with hers, her tongue dueling smoothly with mine, but then she'd relent and let me kiss her harder—a sexy push and pull. She rolled her hips over my arm in slow and determined waves, moaning and arching, then she tore her mouth away and leaned her forehead against mine.

"More," she whispered.

I lowered my thumb and placed soft pressure on her clit.

"Yes," she breathed.

My heart raced inside my chest as I watched the pleasure I gave play across her face. I rubbed round and round, pumping my fingers deep inside her, and I closed my eyes and focused on her breath rushing over my lips as it sped and she rocked harder on my hand.

She smelled kind of like cinnamon, spicy and warm, but sweet too, and it surprised me since she so emphatically denied being sweet.

She was though. It was easy to see the way she cared about my kid. The way she'd cared for me.

I couldn't help imagining burying my cock deep inside her and feeling her body squeeze mine if we came together. She hadn't even touched me yet, and I was nearly already there. The sound of her soft moans as her body climbed closer to release was enough to do me in.

She panted and begged, "Kiss me," and I felt her body grasping my fingers tightly.

When I pressed my lips to hers again and slipped my tongue inside her mouth, she gasped, her body froze above mine, and she came as soon as my eyes locked on hers.

She held me there, in the cradle of her surrender, but finally, I slid my fingers out of her, and she blinked slowly, like she was disappointed at the loss of me inside her. But she leaned over to reach for my beside drawer, and she pulled a condom from the box my brother, Dixon, had thrown at me one day when he'd gotten fed up with my wallowing and told me, "Go get your dick wet. Nothin' else is gonna pull you outta this slump."

Like finding some random stranger on the street to fuck would've cured the pain caused by losing my—

"Bax?"

"Huh?"

"Where'd you go?"

"I-I'm not sure I can do this."

"It's just sex."

I had no response to that, at least not one I was ready to admit.

It wasn't *just* sex. There was a connection between Bea and me. I had no idea what kind of connection, and I had no clue what it meant or if I should be denying it. I didn't want to, but there was a part of me screaming that I should. That I wasn't ready, maybe I'd never be, and that I didn't deserve it.

Maybe I hadn't deserved it the first time around, and that was why Candy and the baby had been taken from me.

"Bax?"

When I focused on Bea's face, there was no pity etched there. All I saw was understanding.

"I'm sorry."

"There's nothin' to be sorry for," she said quietly. "If you're not ready, you're not ready. It's okay." She lowered her body over mine, sitting astride my thighs. My cock jerked between us, still raring to go even though my mind had screeched to a sudden stop. "But… may I?" she asked, and she looked between my legs, at the hard-on tenting my sweats. "It wouldn't be sex. It would only be release."

Relief was what it would be. To have Bea's hand or her mouth around my cock? Sweet fucking relief.

I nodded, and she smiled, her green eyes warm with acceptance. She really was okay with my unreadiness to have sex.

"Should I not kiss you?" she asked. "Does that make it too personal for you?"

"Oh, God no, Bea. I love when you kiss me. You're really good at it. I want you to get personal with me. I have a feelin' you don't do that with a lot of people."

She shook her head.

"It's just that sharin' my body with someone again, actual sex… It scares me."

"Why?"

I shrugged. "Dunno."

But I did know. If I had sex with her, I already knew I could fall in love with her, at the very least with the way she made me feel. And if I loved her and lost her?

She watched my face, and she seemed to accept that I couldn't tell her my reasons. She slid down my body carefully and then moved so that her legs straddled my good one. I spread for her, moving my cast out of the way. My leg didn't hurt much anymore; it was just a heavy, useless weight.

Bea's hand lingered on my thigh. She trailed her fingers higher and dipped them below my waistband, swirling them through the coarse hair there, and when she lowered the front of my sweats with one hand and grasped my dick in her other, I moaned so loudly, I worried I'd woken the rest of the house.

Bea smiled softly, pumping gently, and I watched as she scooted lower, leaned down, and opened her mouth.

Her small tits brushed over my leg, nipples hard and begging for my attention, but the warm, wet suction of her mouth around my cock felt like Christmas and the Fourth of July and New Year's Eve all in one second and I couldn't concentrate on anything else. It felt like freedom, and it released something inside me. Adrenaline coursed through my bloodstream.

"Stop," I said.

She froze, and my cock fell from her lips. She sat up, wiping the side of her mouth with the pads of two fingers. "Too much?"

I shook my head against my pillow. "Fuck me, Bea. I want you. I'm ready."

"No, Bax. You just said you *weren't* ready."

"I was wrong. You showed me that. I am ready." I was the head of my family. The owner of a goddamn business for Christ's sake, and the father of a teenager. If I couldn't handle getting my rocks off with a beautiful woman, it didn't bode well for the rest of my life.

Grabbing the forgotten condom on the bed, I ripped open the package and rolled it over my steel-hard erection. When it was in place, she licked her lips, rolled them, and scooted forward on her knees.

"Are you sure?" she asked, slipping her leggings down one leg, and she pulled some yoga move, stretching back while she leaned on her other leg.

"Yes."

She pulled at the other leg of her pants, her opposite hand planted on my shoulder for stability, and then the tight leggings disappeared, but I had no clue where they'd gone because she centered her body over mine, descended slowly, and took my body inside hers.

I cried.

All that silent bravado leaked from the sides of my eyes as I realized how much I'd missed connecting with another person this closely. I cried because of what I was leaving behind by being with a woman who wasn't Candy. I cried because, finally, I had moved on and it felt fucking monumental.

I felt free from the sadness and the despair, from the guilt and desperate hope that I'd ever feel this way again.

Bea had just released me from the belief that I never would.

She brushed my tears away with tender fingertips, and she rolled her hips, taking me deeper inside her body. Desire and euphoria rushed through me. I wanted to flip her. I wanted to take her and fuck her and give her everything I never thought I'd have to give again.

I couldn't, so I held it all inside and let her set the pace.

For a woman who acted so tough, she was light and soft and perfect, and she handled my roiling emotions with care. She lifted my hand and placed it over her breast, and when she reached for my other hand, I didn't need her guidance to know she wanted me to hold her while she gave me what I so desperately needed.

Every movement and action she took showed that she was doing this for me. This was all about me and letting me use her to get over my dead wife, but I hadn't forgotten that she had things she needed to get over too. A shitty marriage, the life she'd been mourning with her family, and her home.

"Kiss me," I said. "Take me and let me take you too. We both got no place else to be."

A soft moan was her only response, but her own sadness flashed across her face. She leaned down and took my mouth with hers, and she watched me as she placed kisses on my lips and cheeks and my nose as she rode me slowly.

My hands slid to her hips, and I grasped them tightly, holding on for the ride. She rose above me, reveling in the way I made her feel, and fuck if I wasn't proud of that. I was just happy to find myself capable of causing her to feel pleasure at all. If she'd been in my bedroom a year ago, I wouldn't have been able to.

Shit, a year ago, I couldn't even jack off without intense guilt about feeling pleasure when the person I'd loved practically my whole life couldn't anymore.

But I wasn't feeling guilty now.

And I didn't feel lost anymore, like I was stuck between home and a strange place I'd never been.

I felt whole again. And I felt found.

"Yeah, sweetheart," I whispered when Bea whimpered above me, and she arched her back. "Take me with you."

Her hair fell like rain down her back, swaying and swinging with her body, and a rose flush bloomed on her chest. I watched her, wanting her more and more with each passing second, and when I licked two fingers and slid my hand between the apex of her thighs and rubbed her clit, she jolted and called my name.

I came with the sound of her pleasure caressing me in the warm, yellow glow from my lamp, and she collapsed on top of me, kissing my neck and leading me down from Heaven with her lips.

CHAPTER SEVENTEEN

BEA

"I FEEL BAD I'M KEEPIN'" you up," Bax said while I snuggled closer to his chest.

I'd insisted on getting redressed just in case Athena came into the room, but now I remembered I'd locked the door so that wouldn't happen. But still, I didn't want a repeat of hurrying to help him get dressed while someone waited on the other side of the door.

"You probably have an early start in the mornin'."

"Yeah." I yawned. "But it's fine. I'll take a micro nap at lunch."

He laughed softly. "What the hell is a micro nap?"

Assuming he could figure that out on his own, instead of answering, I blurted, "What was Candy like?"

I couldn't help asking. Athena was such an amazing kid, and I wanted to know if she took after her mom. But really, what I wanted to know was if Candy and I were anything alike. If that was why Bax was attracted to me. Candy and I certainly didn't look anything alike. And if we weren't simi-lar, then why *was* he attracted to me? From the pictures hanging in his living room and the one I'd seen in his brother's office, I knew Candy had been all tall, soft, curvy mom, and I was hard, short, and worn.

He wasn't my type *at all*. He didn't have a motorcycle or tattoos, he actually cared about his fellow human beings, and he was somebody's father. Maybe it was because he had a broken femur, but he was kind of a homebody. I couldn't figure out why I wanted him as much as I did, and even more now we'd slept together.

But I did want more. More sex. More cuddles and kisses. More everything.

The way his deft fingers stroked leisurely through the length of my hair was intoxicating, and if he leaned down one more time to kiss the top of my head, I was going to go insane and jump his bones again. At least the ones that weren't broken.

He cleared his throat.

"It's okay if you don't wanna talk about her. I was just curious."

"No," he said. "No, I don't mind, actually. It's funny; I was just thinkin' about what she'd think of you."

"She probably wouldn't like me."

"I think she would've. She was sweet and kind-hearted and really smart, but she didn't want to be in charge. She always wanted me to lead. But she didn't like that about herself, you know? She always said she wished she had a stronger backbone.

"She deferred to me in practically all situations. She wouldn't make a decision if she didn't know what my opinion on an issue or a problem was. It didn't matter what we were talkin' about: finances, business decisions, family decisions. Even a lot of things about Athena. I guess I'd just assumed that when she became a mom, Candy would have that mama-bear thing. You know? I mean, she did in some ways, but if there was a problem, she expected me to handle it."

"That's a lot of pressure on you."

"Yeah," he said quietly, thinking. "We got together when we were still in high school, and back then, I didn't know what I wanted. I just knew I loved her. But now, if you asked me what I wanted in a partner, I'd say an actual *partner*. Someone to help me make those decisions, to hash 'em out with me. Weigh the pros and cons. Someone who brings strength to the relationship.

"Candy would've thought you were a badass 'cause you're so strong and sure of yourself."

"Hm." It hit me as I thought about how he'd described Candy that it felt like he was hinting at something here. Was I elated he was describing me when he listed all the things he wanted in a woman?

Or did it terrify me?

"What?" he asked, anchoring his hand loosely around the back of my neck.

"It's just that I think I'm this way because I got tired of havin' no backbone. So maybe she and I were alike. But I got so fed up with men tryin' to run my life and tell me what to do. Honestly, that's probably why I'm the way I am.

"Growin' up, I was a daddy's girl, through and through. But as much as I loved him, my dad seemed to think me bein' his princess meant I wasn't strong or smart or that I could make decisions, and I didn't do a very good job of convincin' him because I did whatever he thought I should. I didn't go to college because he said he needed me and wanted me to work with him at his construction company.

"It's one of the things I wish now I could go back and tell him. I want him to know that, while I miss him and wish I could have him back in my life, I don't *need* him."

"He knows."

I snorted. "What, are you about to tell me you believe in ghosts?"

"Naw. Not ghosts. But I think the people we lose stay with us, you know? In the background. In our dreams. They see us."

I pushed up off his chest, spearing him with a doubtful look. "I never would've guessed you'd be into woo-woo nonsense."

He shrugged, and his eyes drifted from mine. Was he embarrassed? "Maybe it's what I need to believe."

"I'm sorry," I said, instantly feeling like the biggest ass. "I shouldn't judge."

"It's okay." He shrugged and his eyes found mine again. "It does sound kinda nonsensical when I say it out loud. Now come back down here. I like snugglin' you."

He pulled on my arm gently, and I cuddled against his chest again, tucking myself into the crook of his arm and laying my head right where I'd wanted to since I'd first seen him without a shirt, like his chest was my very own nest. I kissed below his clavicle, and he sighed.

"How did she die? I started workin' for your brother after she'd already passed, and Brand rarely mentions her."

Bax stiffened beneath me. "Aneurysm."

Suddenly, I felt like that young, unsure teenager again who wanted my daddy to talk about my mama. Oh, how I'd missed her, but I saw in my dad's eyes that just the mention of my mama's name made him ache. It had made my dad angry because he couldn't have her.

Sometimes I wondered if it was my fault, if me wanting to keep my mama's memory alive had been the reason I lost my dad to hydrocodone. After he broke his back, he'd needed the pills at first, but very quickly it became easy to see that he felt more than physical relief when he took them. They allowed him to be numb. To forget all he'd lost.

"I'm sorry. Forgive me. I shouldn't have asked."

"It's okay, really. It's good practice for me. Athena tries to talk to me about her mama, but it's…"

"Painful," I said, finishing his sentence.

He was quiet and still for a minute, but then he went on. "It's easier now to talk about her. After it happened, I couldn't say her name without imaginin' what she went through that day, you know? If it hurt. If she was scared. If she thought about the b—"

He cut himself off, and that rigid feeling was back in his muscles.

"Thought about what?"

"… Athena. If she thought about Athena in her last moment."

"I'm sure she did," I said, yawning. I covered my mouth, and Bax kissed my hair again. "He couldn't talk about her, but my dad told me once that after my mama's car accident, before she died in the hospital, I was the only person she talked about. Honestly, he loved her so much that I wondered if it made him jealous.

"But Candy knew Athena was in good hands. She knew you'd be the best dad, even if you had to do it without her."

The silence between us after that was a little uncomfortable. Bax's body never really relaxed. I wanted to talk more, but I couldn't keep my eyes open much longer.

"Go to sleep now, sweetheart," he whispered, kissing my head once more and caressing my hair. "You're tired, and you got mountains to conquer tomorrow."

WITH MY YETI FULL of hot coffee, I managed to sneak out of the house before Athena woke.

Rye had already showered and left before I came tiptoeing down the stairs, and Bax still lay in peaceful dreams upstairs. When I left him, his arm lay spread across the bed where I'd slept all night. Maybe in his dreams, he was still holding me.

Steamy breath punched out in front of me when I snorted at myself as I stepped onto Bax's porch into the cold air. *What a sappy fuckin' thing to think, Bea.*

Darkness lingered outside, but morning light clawed at its edges on the eastern horizon, so I wasn't super freaked out about bears anymore. And besides, the closer I drove to my cabin, the more I could hear other trucks and the crews arriving for work, so I wouldn't be caught alone. And if a bear wanted to hang out with a bunch of construction dudes, more power to him. At least they were all bigger than me, so the bear would probably eat them first and I'd have time to grab my nail gun.

"Mornin'," Clay said when I parked and got out of my truck.

Lo and behold, Jensen hadn't quit, and he hadn't complained after our first little run-in, but he wasn't super chatty with me either. I didn't expect we'd skip hand in hand to go get manicures together, but he could see that cabins nine and ten were much closer to the HVAC stage than they were yesterday morning, so he knew I was right. His silence was as close to hearing him say "I was wrong" as I was going to get. And I was fine with that. I'd never been under the false impression that I could change men's ideas about women with words. It was action that made people like Jensen believers.

"Mornin'," I responded to Clay, stifling a yawn. "I just

ran up to the main house for coffee." *Lie.* "Let me grab the plans in my cabin. I need to change real quick," I said, looking down at the leggings and sweatshirt I still wore, "and then I'll meet you back out here."

If he had any suspicions about my tawdry nighttime activities, Clay didn't let on. "Good deal," he said, and he leaned back against his tailgate as steam rose from the top of his Thermos when he screwed off the lid and took a tentative sip of his own brew. "I'll be here."

Once I'd changed and chugged as much of my coffee as I could before I brushed my teeth, I flossed and rushed back outside. It wasn't like me to arrive after my crew. If I wasn't fifteen minutes earlier than everybody else, I felt late and rushed for the rest of the day. I wasn't mad about it today, though, because for the first time in a long time, I woke up feeling… happy.

Sure, orgasms had a little something to do with that, but it was more about the guy who'd given them to me.

It seemed absolutely hilarious to me that I'd come down to Wisper expecting to hate Bax Lee, but I hadn't felt connected to a man like I did to Bax in forever. I'd felt that way with my ex in the beginning, but the feeling quickly died when I realized I wasn't much more to him than arm candy, which had never made sense to me because I'd always found my reflection in the mirror a little plain. But Lincoln had never cared about the things I'd loved or my dreams.

Bax seemed to, and he talked to me even when the subject was painful for him. He listened when I talked about my parents and childhood.

That wasn't nothing.

And the way he touched me? Just the way he looked at my body— It seemed Bax didn't find me plain at all.

The nagging doubt in the back of my mind kept trying to

convince me that it was because he was still mourning his wife. Maybe right now, different was the thing getting him through the day, but he'd probably end up with some other buxom blonde in the future, like Felicity from the grocery store, and I'd go back to my lonely little life, with my plain hair and plain, barely there curves.

Was it so bad to enjoy his attention now, when it was fixed on me and made me feel truly beautiful?

Outside, the chatter of the cabin crew preparing for the day filled the air, but Clay wasn't where I'd left him. I spotted him by the woods north of cabin three and headed that way as I tugged on my hard hat and gloves.

"What is it?" I asked when I saw the faint look of concern marring his features while he stared between two tall pines into the dark forest. The trees were so dense on this part of the property that I didn't imagine he could see much. Yellow leaves fell like confetti all day long, but the aspens were still covered in them, and the firs and pines had grown in thick clusters between the aspens.

"Not sure," he said.

"Did you see a bear?"

He laughed. "You'd know if I had. No, I saw a man standin' over here. I turned to grab my phone off the bed of the truck, and when I turned back, he was gone. He's not on any of the crews. He wasn't familiar." He shrugged. "Maybe he was lookin' for work?"

"Yeah, maybe, but then why the hell did he take off into the woods?"

"Got me stumped," Clay said. "I'll keep an eye open for him with the house crews and you do the same here. He has brown hair down to his shoulders, kinda medium dark. Looked scraggly. He's pretty tall, six-three or -four. He had on a canvas Carhartt coat and a dark beanie."

"Okay. Thanks. I will," I said, but besides the long hair, he'd just described half my crew and Bax and Rye too. How the hell was I supposed to find that needle in my haystack while simultaneously running four crews and overseeing so many builds that they'd all started blurring into one in my mind?

I hoped if the guy needed a job, he'd come back and ask. I could find a shit-ton of things for him to do. It wouldn't be the first time I'd paid a guy under the table who'd been a little down on his luck. As long as I didn't have them performing jobs that they could be injured doing, Brand provided petty cash for things like that. Our deal was that I had to attempt to get the guy to provide his social security number so we could pay him properly. Most people worked a few days and collected the cash when they could, and then they took off, but there were two guys on my home crew who'd started at Lee Construction under the table but were now high above board and providing for their families easily.

My day flew by. Lunch came and went so fast, I forgot to eat. We were supposed to have received a delivery of sinks, tubs and bathroom fixtures, but it never showed up so I spent two hours on the phone trying to locate it. I lost my voice for a while after cussing out the idiot at the warehouse for five minutes. He finally found my load and said it would be delivered the next business day, but it was costing my guys half a day and they were pissed. I was too. We couldn't afford any more delays.

On the plus side, Devo's and Abey's roof and exterior siding had been installed, and the drywall would go up today while the roofers got started on Rye's house. This stage of the builds always made me happy because it meant the end was in sight. It also meant that once the three houses were done, I could allocate the house crews to the cabins, which would allow for everything to be finished before our deadline.

The chill in the air today had me feeling glad for that. Winter could come crashing down any time, and that would suck a big, fat dick. If we got a lot of snow, we'd be screwed, and the crews would have to leave the job with lighter pockets than they were expecting.

The holidays would be here before we knew it, and I hated the thought of any of my guys struggling through Christmas. I made a note in my phone to get my hands on some free turkey and ham vouchers from the Food Mart or a market in Jackson that I could pass out to everyone when the job was done.

All of that had me worrying that the mysterious lurker from this morning might be going hungry too. Been there, done that, and I tried every day to repay the kindness I'd been shown.

CHAPTER EIGHTEEN

BAX

"IT'S A GOOD SHOW," *Candy said, sitting next to me on the edge of my bed.*

Not our *bed; I'd burned the mattress in the back yard during a fit of sleep-deprived rage at God after the funeral. Abey had to threaten to arrest me to stop me from dousing my fire with more lighter fluid before I set the whole forest ablaze.*

It was weird, but somehow, I felt Candy next to me, even though I knew she was in my head and not really here.

This time, my dream was full of bubbles, like the kind I'd made as a kid with soapy dishwater and plastic rings. They kept popping in front of my face and splashing me.

"What is it with you and TV shows?" I asked her in a sleepy voice, batting at the bubbles with a lazy swipe of my hand. "I can't figure out why you'd go to all the trouble to visit my dreams and then talk about television."

"A pretty show," she said. "I like it. It's strong. It's got good bones."

Pretty? A show was pretty? Were we still talking about

Sons of Anarchy, because it sounded now like she was talking about a house.

Wait. Pretty? Was she talking about Bea?

My face heated with shame and embarrassment.

"No," Candy said. She reached out and let her fingers hover over my forearm. She didn't make contact, but I felt her touch anyway, like she'd dragged a feather across my skin. "It's a good show. Don't change the channel this time."

"Are you talkin' about... Bea? The woman I"—my head rolled to the side, my eyes focused on the spot next to me on my bed where Bea had slept, cuddled up next to me all night —"You know?"

Of course Candy didn't answer. Instead, as she began to fade away, she said, "He's comin'. Say hi for me?"

And she was gone.

Another bubble burst next to my cheek, and then it dripped up my face, which was physically impossible, but it was also itchy, and it whined.

When I opened my eyes, my hand still searching Bea's empty spot, two big, brown, glassy orbs stared at me with happy expectation. Figaro's tongue lapped at thin air, trying to reach my face again, and I heard Athena's voice in my bedroom doorway.

"Mornin', sleepy head. Fig needs to go out, but I'm late for cross country. Aunt Abey's waitin' for me."

Fig barked in my face to confirm that he indeed did need to pee. So did I, come to think of it.

"Mornin'. On it. Have a good day. Sorry I overslept."

"It's okay, Daddy. You must've needed the sleep. See you later."

She whirled around, my Road Trip off on yet another adventure. Fig lunged after her and followed, and I dragged my ass out of bed. My daughter didn't need to know the reason I'd slept through two alarms was that I was up all night fucking Bea, and then I dreamt of Athena's dead mama again.

But I felt like a shit dad for both reasons.

If I really had moved on, why was I still seeing Candy in my dreams? And what had she meant, "He's comin'"?

Was this, like, some Jesus thing? Candy had barely tolerated church the whole twenty years we were together. Her parents weren't religious at all. She only went to keep the peace between her and Merv. But as the thought left my head, all I could remember from the dream were the bubbles popping and she kept talking about TV.

And where the hell was Bea? I looked at my phone. *Oh, duh. She's already at work.* But why hadn't she woken me?

Before the conversation about Candy, Bea had been so cute as she scrambled around my room, trying to find her leggings tangled up in my bed sheets. I told her she didn't have to sleep in her clothes; I'd wanted to fall asleep with the feel of her soft skin against mine, but the anxiety she'd felt about Athena finding us naked pinched up her face, and it was so contradictory to the confident hard-ass I'd come to know.

I tugged on a T-shirt, found my slippers and stuffed my foot into one, and then hobbled down the stairs, listening to the kitchen door slam shut behind Athena when she left and to the sound of Fig yipping and running in circles by the same door while he waited for my geriatric ass. When Rye had first brought him to the ranch, Fig hadn't left Rye's side, but since I'd broken my leg, he seemed to want to stay closer to the house, unless Rye had him working the cows.

"I'm comin', I'm comin'. Jeez. Hold on, would ya?" It occurred to me then that Athena could've let him out when she left, but she'd probably used Fig as an excuse to wake my butt up. She'd gotten creative over the last few years with ways to force me to face the days when I'd had a hard time seeing the point.

Fig zipped out the door when I opened it, and I shivered. Dang. Fall would give way to winter soon, if this morning's temperature was any indication, but the westbound sunrise brought a warm, blanketing glow to my family's land, and I watched as it traveled right to my porch.

The dog ran to the barn to see what Rye had gotten up to. I could hear horses and cows causing trouble out there, so I slathered peanut butter on two pieces of toast and poured myself a cup of coffee. I burned my tongue when I chugged it, but thankfully Bea or Rye had brewed it, 'cause I needed the caffeine today.

After the seriously frustrating effort of trying to get the only clean pair of pants I had left in my laundry basket over my cast, I pulled on a sweater I hadn't worn in probably ten years and muck boots, which were the only shoes I could fit over the bottom of the cast, and I grabbed my warmer felt hat from a hook by the kitchen door. I fixed it on my head, gripped my crutches tight, and followed slowly after Fig.

"Why didn't you call?" Rye asked when he saw me sweating and breathing hard after my dangerous hobble to the barn. He'd cleared the path like he'd promised, but I still found two rocks to trip over and almost pitched myself forward both times and fell on my face. "I would've come to get you."

"Sounded like you had your hands full."

He nodded. "Yeah. Blue decided he wanted to dip his wick when he saw Tulsa this mornin', even though he hasn't been the proud owner of balls for a long time. And then this damn bull decided to kick off again. He's got the rest of the herd in a tizzy."

When Red Pepper and I made eye contact through the fencing around the solitary pen Rye had him in, I shot daggers at the animal, but if a bull could smirk, he was, and he tossed his head, like he was saying, "Oh yeah, I remember you. And I know that you know that I'll kick your sorry ass to Hell and back if I want to."

"Dick," I said under my breath, and Pepper huffed and trotted off to the opposite side of his pen. "So, Tulsa and Blue, huh? Should we plan a horse weddin'?"

Rye laughed. "I'm sure Athena would have a ball with that, but maybe the celebration should be for somebody else?" He speared me with a look, and I knew right then that he knew what I'd been up to last night with Bea.

"Don't start, and I know you and Athena are in cahoots. Don't you even try to deny it."

He slapped a hand to his chest in a surprised, "who, me?" gesture. He said, "I'm happy for you, man."

"It's not— She's not— Just mind your business."

"Okay, okay," he said, chuckling.

"How'd you know? Shit. You don't think Athena knows, do you?"

"Naw. Don't stress. Your bedroom's right above the livin' room, and I was up. Had a weird dream at one thirty last night. I popped in my earbuds, but it still took me a good twenty minutes to get back to sleep. Man, I can't wait to get into the new house. Sleepin' in the barn ain't the picnic you might imagine, and it's a pain goin' back and forth between here and Aubrey's place, but listenin' to you havin' sex is *so* not my idea of a good night's rest."

My face had to be red and hot enough to start a fire. "Can we change the subject, please?"

"Yup, but here's another whopper. My dream was about Candy."

Seriously? "We both dreamt about Candy then," I said. "What'd she say to you?"

"You ask that like you think I had a conversation with a dead person in my dream."

"I did. I always do. It feels like it's really her."

"Yeah, it's weird you say that 'cause that's how I felt too. All she said was 'Help him,' and she told me she likes the barn and Tulsa. Oh, and she brought up the time we all got drunk and I ran through one of my dad's barns naked and got bit on the ass by a mare." Rye let out a throaty chuckle, but then he pursed his lips, pausing. He stared at me, and I knew there was some kind of bromance check-in coming. "There somethin' you need help with, buddy?"

"I don't think so. I mean, besides, you know, cookin', workin', and child rearin'."

"You're doin' just fine with all that stuff on your own. Maybe a little bit slower than usual." He eyed me. "This is a weird conversation."

"Agreed," I said. "I'm changin' the subject. So I was lookin' at the plans last night for the cabins and outbuildings. What do you think about addin' a boat house in the spring? Guests will want lake activities. Fishin' and maybe paddle-boats? The lake's not huge. Not big enough for speedboats, but we can definitely do kayaks and canoes. Maybe a big party pontoon boat?"

"Great idea."

"And Athena thinks we should have a little concession stand in the rec hall to sell, like, ice cream cones and chips and stuff in the summer, and trail mix and hot chocolate in the fall. She said, 'Think summer camp but posh and less invasive.'"

He laughed. "Boy, your kid sure is smart."

Yeah." I nodded, looking past my house to where Lee

Lake lay. I missed my early morning swims, but the water would be too cold now anyhow.

Fall was in full bloom. The Aspens stood up tall, like yellow crayons in a box. Against the backdrop of the blue morning sky, the tree line and mountains beyond looked more like a painting than they did real life.

"I like it," I said. "We're not gonna be all-inclusive, and the guests will probably make the majority of their food in their cabin kitchens or they'll eat in town, but just to have somethin' extra, especially during the peak seasons. And remember we talked about offerin' guided horseback tours and hikin'?"

"Yeah. I talked to Presley about it," Rye said, referring to his friend and his dad's former cattle boss. "Obviously, he won't be doin' the horseback tours. We'd get sued if we unleashed him on guests, but he said he knows a guy who could handle that operation. He's a seasonal cowboy, travels around to different ranches, but Pres thinks he might settle down for the right job."

"Cool. You know, we've got the barn and the cow shed, but we're gonna need another barn and a bunkhouse. My dad's old barn is good for equipment storage, but not much else. If this little cattle endeavor of yours pans out, we're gonna need a lot of things."

"Yeah, and your inn idea wasn't a bad one either. Maybe that's somethin' we can add later. We've got the land for it, for people who do want all-inclusive getaways."

"I was thinkin' about that too. I'll ask Bea about it. She'll have an idea about how long somethin' like that would take to build."

Rye tapped his chin. "And if she were the one in charge of that build..."

"What?"

"She'd have to be here to oversee it all."

Hm. He had a point, and I kind of liked it. Endless days and nights spent with Bea, building shit when the sun was up and breaking each other down under the glow from the moon shining in my bedroom window every night?

I could get used to that.

"You stayin' here again tonight?" I asked my best friend.

"Nope. Got a date with my girl."

"You sure? I was thinkin' I might cook out."

"Am I sure if I wanna spend the night with the woman I love? Damn sure. You're really gonna cook?"

I scoffed. "Yeah. I cook every night. What's the big deal?"

"You used to. Now, how you gonna juggle steaks and potatoes with those crutches?"

"Oh." I looked down at the annoying wooden sticks. "Good point. I'll need help."

He winked. "And I know just the contractor for the job. Bet she'll be hungry after a hard day's work."

I rolled my eyes. "Oh, shut up." But I couldn't hide my smile.

CHAPTER NINETEEN

BEA

AFTER EVERYONE WENT HOME for the day, I spent an hour inspecting the work and wandering the area.

I never saw the mysterious guy, but I still had a high sun and daylight left, and I wanted to check out the lake Brand had told me about. He'd described whole summers spent on Lee Lake, having picnics, barbeques, and rock-skipping competitions. He said his dad used to dig a hole in the earth and pack hot coals into it, and then his mom would put veggies and meat into a Dutch oven and bury it to cook.

Growing up an only child was lonely sometimes, so I could imagine how fun that must've been, the adventures Bax and Brand and their siblings must've had when they were young.

I found the little trail that Brand had marked on a map for me and followed it to the lake, and boy, what a view. The dark, green-blue water glistened in the afternoon sun, reflecting the mountain behind it. It looked like one of those oil paintings by the guy from the eighties, with his fabulous hair and happy little trees.

A hollowed log floated near the bank, stuck to the edges

of weeds and lily pads. As I followed the trail around the lake, I kept my eye on it so I'd remember where the trailhead was, and when I looked over my shoulder to locate it, a turtle popped onto the log. Deer drank from the little creek that ran down the mountain and fed the lake, and fish swam by as I meandered, rising to the surface of the water to gulp air, making little *blip* noises in the still afternoon.

Invisible birds sang to me, and peace descended over my body. Taking a deep breath, I sat in the tall grasses lining the lake, patting down a spot with my butt and staring across the glassy surface of the water. I looked up at the blue sky, wondering what Mother Nature had in store for me. Would she cooperate and hold back her snow, or was she getting ready to rage? I hoped for the former, but I knew there would be no negotiating with her. Best just to focus on the work still left to do instead of worrying about all the what ifs.

Bax was never far from my mind. I saw him changing right in front of my eyes, from the closed-off widower he'd been when I got here to the bold, brave single father he was turning out to be. He certainly had more courage than me. I'd stayed in a marriage I knew was no good because I'd been too afraid to admit that I'd failed or that I deserved better. Bax hadn't failed at anything, but he deserved better than the sadness and pain he'd barricaded himself behind.

My own dad had shown me that losing love was a recipe for the end of a life, but maybe he'd been wrong.

An hour later when I got back to my cabin, I was so utterly relaxed that I didn't even notice the guy from this morning. He moved out of my line of sight as I approached the front door, and I caught him in the periphery, dressed exactly as Clay had described. He stood on the far side of my truck, trying, I thought, not to get too close. When we made eye contact, he took two steps further away.

"Hi." I tried to sound friendly and casual, though the hair at the back of my neck stood on end because the primal part of me knew he shouldn't have been there and I shouldn't have been alone with some unknown guy, who truthfully seemed a bit sketchy.

The guy didn't answer. He looked back and forth between me and the cabin door. Had he been about to rob me? But I realized I didn't fear him. All I felt as I looked at his ratty clothes and his dirty hair was… sorrow.

The day he promoted me, Brand had made me sign up for a self-defense class at a local martial arts studio up in Sheridan. He'd said it was non-negotiable since I'd be alone on job sites a lot of the time, with only men. He also bought me a bulk box of pepper spray to carry with me at all times that had some kind of UV identifying dye so if I ever was attacked, the cops would know who did it. It had never come to that. The majority of the guys I worked with were respectful, and if they weren't, they mostly kept their distance, but I was glad for the skills now.

I didn't have my pepper spray on me. Stupidly, I'd left it lying useless beneath my seat in my truck, but I didn't think I needed it this time, and if it came down to it, I could break his nose with one thrust of my hand to his face and flip him onto his back using one arm and his own body weight for momentum. Thank you, Hapkido.

Errantly, I wondered if pepper spray worked on bears. Did it have the same ingredients bear spray had?

But I also tried to remember that asking a stranger for a job wasn't easy, if that was the reason he'd shown back up. "Can I help you with somethin'? Are you lookin' for work?"

"No," the guy said roughly.

"Oh. Okay, then what're you doin' here? This is private property."

He scoffed. "I know that."

"So then…?"

"Never mind," he mumbled, and he turned to go.

Something made me try to stop him. I wasn't sure why, but it just felt like he needed… *something.* He looked familiar somehow, but I couldn't pinpoint the reason. I felt sure we'd never met, and we stood too far apart for me to really see his features.

"Do you need help?" I had to ask.

I knew this guy. I didn't *know him,* know him, not his name, but I'd met plenty of guys like him before. Down on his luck, maybe he'd lost a job, or he was on drugs. Or both. Maybe he had a kid to feed but couldn't. A man like that could absolutely be a threat to me, especially a tall guy like him. Maybe I should've felt fear, but I didn't.

He seemed surprised by my question. He stopped, but he didn't turn. I thought he might say something else, but then he picked up his pace and rushed to get out of there. It was then I noticed something big and bulky dangling from one of his hands by his leg. He gripped some kind of handle tightly, and I could tell whatever he was holding had some weight to it, but he'd covered the whole thing with a small plastic tarp.

Parked in the dark shade of a big tree off to the side of the dirt lane, a car waited for him. I couldn't tell if anyone else was in the car, but I thought he was most likely alone when he placed the covered object on his front passenger seat and then jogged around and slid into the driver's side of a dirty, beat-up four-door sedan. The next thing I knew, he had started the car. Its muffler cracked loudly, and the tires spit rocks back my way as he took off.

Um. Okay?

"BEA!" Athena greeted me when I showed up at the house, with my backpack and suitcase packed into the passenger seat of my truck. She reached in to hug me through my open window and spotted the suitcase, and a smile spread across her cute face. "Are you stayin' here with Daddy and me?"

"Yeah," I said, pushing with my shoulder on my door when she backed away. I yanked the suitcase across my seat and set it on the gravel, then slung my backpack over my shoulder. "There's bears by the cabins, I think."

"Oh, well yay!"

"Yay?"

"Yeah," she said, and she grabbed the suitcase by the handle and dragged me by her other hand to the porch stairs. "I mean, I'm not happy you're scared, but I'm happy we'll see you more."

"Oh. Thanks. Yeah, I was gonna borrow a shotgun, but there's a lot of people comin' and goin' all the time. It's probably best if I, you know, stay with other humans."

She laughed. "Good thinkin'."

In the kitchen, Athena parked my suitcase next to the laundry-room door and introduced me to her "best friend in the whole wide world," Shaylene, who had an elfin face and white-blond hair with raspberry-colored highlights streaked throughout. It hung down nearly to her waist. Shaylene had been preparing graham crackers, pieces of broken-up chocolate bars, and huge marshmallows, situating them in a decided order on a baking tray, but she paused to wave at me.

"S'mores after dinner?" I asked, and both girls grinned and nodded. "Nice to meet you, Shaylene. Athena, where's your dad?"

"He's out back. Don't laugh when you see him. He made Uncle Rye drag his recliner out there before he left to go see Aunt

Aubrey 'cause Daddy said his back hurt sittin' in the lawn chair. And he's wearin' these funny, plastic-y pants 'cause they're the only clean ones he could find that will fit over his cast."

The girls giggled and tee-hee'd, and I tried not to laugh.

"I threw his laundry in the wash. Oh, here," Athena said, walking to the fridge. She opened it and grabbed a big, ceramic serving plate holding six fat beef steaks. "Can you take these to him, please? The veggies and potatoes are in the oven, but we'll bring 'em out when they're done."

"Sure."

The novelty of my presence wore off quickly, and Athena turned to Shaylene. "So anyway, Logan asked if I wanted to go to the dance with him. It's on my birthday. Can you believe that? It's like a fairy tale…"

Dropping my backpack by my suitcase, I took the heavy plate from her hands and pushed the kitchen's screen door open with my boot, then carried the steaks out behind the house.

Sure enough, Bax was there, relaxing in his La-Z-Boy in front of a huge grill, wearing the plastic-y, maroon pants, which seemed to be some kind of track pants, a brick-red and hunter-green plaid sweater that looked like it could win an ugly Christmas sweater contest, and no shoes or socks.

"Well, ain't you dashin' tonight?" I said, holding back laughter. "This outfit is just weird enough to start a trend."

Bax whipped his head in my direction. "Don't you start too," he complained. "I'm cold and these are the only pants I had clean that would fit over this damn cast."

"Then why aren't you wearin' socks and shoes? Or *a* shoe."

"'Cause my foot's swollen again, and the sock made it itchy. Then, only wearin' one sock irritated me, so I took the other one off." He shrugged, like that made complete sense, and wiggled his toes in the grass.

He'd tried to hide it, but I'd seen the big pad of paper he'd dropped over the far side of the recliner when he heard my voice.

I set the steaks on the little prep table attached to the side of the grill, then turned and pointed to the paper. "What's that?"

"Nothin'."

Whatever it was, it was clear he didn't want me to see, so I closed my eyes and tipped my face up to the sky, appreciating the warmth from the setting sun on my skin. It had just begun its slow descent to the west, and the golden light it cast over Bax's backyard felt magical. The mountains surrounding it weren't so bad either, and they had me imagining wood nymphs and fairies emerging from the forest to join the barbeque.

The solar lights I'd bought at Bob's Feed and Tack would be glowing around the edge of Bax's huge yard and in front of his house within the hour.

"What about bears?" I asked with my eyes still closed. "Won't they smell the steaks?"

"They might, but we have electric fences back here. You can't see 'em from the house, but they're there. It's not a bear-free guarantee, though," he said, "but I've got the bear spray too." He paused, and I could feel him watching me. "You stayin' for supper?"

I opened my eyes and focused on the tight set of his shoulders beneath his sweater while he awaited my answer. "I'm invited?"

"'Course. Abey and Devo are droppin' by, too, and we've got s'mores *and* apple pie for dessert. Courtesy of Rye's girlfriend, Aubrey."

My mouth watered. "Thank you. I accept your invitation."

He nodded once, and his shoulders released their tension. He'd tried to hide a small smile, but his dimple gave him away. So did his eyes. They flashed in the evening light, like sunshine reflecting off a clear, aqua ocean. "How was your day?"

"Good. The crew finished Abey's roof and siding. They've already started on the drywall, and Rye's house is almost at the same stage. Oh, hey, do you know anyone with long hair?"

Bax's eyebrows dipped. "Uh, yeah. Lots of people."

"I meant a guy. He has hair down to his shoulders. It's brown."

"No, not that I can think of. It's not to say someone I haven't seen in a while hasn't grown their hair out, but nobody comes to mind. Why?"

"Have you met Clay yet?" I asked as I sat in the lawn chair next to Bax's recliner. He nodded. "Well, this mornin', Clay saw some guy by cabin three. He took off before Clay could talk to him. I thought he might be lookin' for a job on the crew, but after work, I went for a walk by the lake, and when I got back, he was there again."

Bax sat forward. "What? Somebody was fuckin' around by your cabin?"

"Yeah. I mean, he wasn't doin' anything. It felt like he was lookin' for somethin' or someone. I asked him if he needed help, but he said no, and then he drove away."

"What kinda car?"

"An old gray or silver sedan, or maybe it was white and just really dirty. Not sure what make or model. He parked down the lane so I couldn't tell. It looked kinda rusty and banged up."

"Was he alone?"

"Yeah, as far as I could tell. Though, he had somethin' with him. Some big thing he was carryin'." I shrugged. "I'll keep my eye out, but I really don't think he was there to cause trouble. I thought you might know him because when I pointed out that this was private property, he seemed a little… indignant? I dunno. But he said he already knew that."

"I'll let Rye know. If you or Clay see him again, I wanna know about it."

I nodded.

Bax relaxed back in his chair and turned his head toward me. "I want you to stay here with us… until your job's done."

"I'm way ahead of you. I brought my suitcase with me."

"Good." He nodded, and some kind of look of satisfaction flooded his eyes. He hadn't mentioned what he'd tell Athena about where I'd be sleeping, but we could work that out later. Maybe it wouldn't be a big deal to her if I slept in her dad's room, but then again, it might be a *huge* deal. Teenage emotions were so hard to predict, but I hoped she'd be okay with it since she'd been playing matchmaker extraordinaire.

Smoke rose and heat wavered above the grill, and it drew my attention away from Bax's face. "Think your grill's ready."

"Huh?" he said, and he blinked, but then he followed my gaze. "Oh, yeah. Okay."

He pushed himself up on the arms of his chair, trying to stand, but I laid my hand on his shoulder.

"Sit. You can direct me if you feel it's necessary, but I know how to put steaks on a grill rack."

Bax smirked. "Thanks," he said, and he sank back down into his chair. "The physical therapist says it's good for me to do stuff for myself, but I gotta watch out for *how* I do it. Apparently, I've gotten pretty good at usin' other muscles to protect the broken bone, but they aren't the muscles I *should* be usin'."

Huh. If that wasn't a perfect metaphor for love after loss, I didn't know what was.

"You can flip the steaks when they're ready."

"Deal," he said, and he smiled easily. "Um, I didn't have time today to clean out the extra bedroom. That'll take me a while. So you're gonna have to sleep… you know, with me again."

Showing judge-like restraint as I dropped the first steak onto the rack, I shrugged and said, "I'm fine with that." But I couldn't wait to get back up to Bax's bedroom.

"Rye will probably stay at Aubrey's house tonight. I could sleep on the couch if you—"

Without turning to face him, I asked, "Didn't you like spendin' the night with me?"

"I did," he said. "Did you… like it too?"

"Yeah." I dropped another steak on the grill. It sizzled loudly when meat met hot metal. "So I'll stay with you again tonight," I said, but then joked, "but don't get used to havin' me in your bed, Bax Lee, 'cause I still haven't decided if I like you yet."

CHAPTER TWENTY

BAX

"OUR HOUSE IS DONE!"

"Whoa, whoa, whoa," Bea rushed to say when Devo jumped up and down next to the grill like a little kid. "I didn't say 'done.' I said 'almost done.'"

Abey and Devo arrived shortly after Bea, and they dragged more lawn chairs from the garage to the back yard.

Athena and Shaylene lay on a blanket by the edge of the tree line, bundled up in fleece hoodies, gossiping and looking up at the stars starting to pop in the early evening sky. The way Athena's hands painted pictures in the air, I was sure they were talking about boys. Or girls. But definitely about the dance she'd been begging me to let her go to with this shady Logan character.

I'd tried to start a fire in the firepit, but Bea was too scared I'd fall in, so she did it herself. It raged now, throwing off heat and sparks and lighting up our little gathering. She'd run into the house to find my slippers so my feet wouldn't freeze.

How sweet was that?

"Bea," Devo said, "I distinctly remember the word 'drywall.'"

Bea laughed. "I did say 'drywall.'"

"That means practically done." Devo squealed, and she wrapped her arms around my sister's waist and squeezed.

"Thank you," Abey told Bea, slinging her arm over Devo's shoulder. "Really. We can't wait to get in there."

"I haven't done much," Bea said. "But you're welcome."

"Babe," Devo said, looking up at Abey with pitiful puppy dog eyes. "I need the credit card. I've been makin' those lists on my phone, and now I gotta order all the stuff! We need curtains and rugs and cleanin' supplies. Oh, we could pick up that couch you liked and store it at the rental."

"The rental is smaller than a garage. It won't fit in there."

"You're right. Okay, well, we could store it at the community center."

"Or, and just hear me out, but why don't we wait till the house is *actually* ready and buy the couch then?"

Devo tsked, her excitement waning just a little. "Fine. Aren't you excited at all?"

"'Course I am," Abey said. "I can't wait to live with you in *our* house on my family's land. C'mere." She pulled Devo closer. Devo pushed up on her toes, and they kissed.

Bea looked at the grass, her cheeks pinking softly.

"How do you like your steak?" I asked her.

She looked up at me, and the longing I saw in her eyes for the kind of love and connection my sister and her fiancée had with each other was suddenly plain to see.

"Medium rare."

"Me too," I said and smiled.

"Bax, you know we like ours medium, right?" Devo asked.

"Yep."

"Thanks. Abey, come in the house with me. The Wi-Fi sucks back here and I wanna show you the coffee table I found."

They skipped off toward my house and left me and Bea alone again. She rose from her chair and lifted the grill's hood, then grabbed the tongs and began to flip the steaks. The melted fat dripped from the rack and sizzled on the charcoal briquettes below.

When I was standing behind her, I reminded her, "You said I could flip."

My breath rushed over her shoulder and little wisps of her hair played in the air. I tucked them behind her ear, and she shivered.

Without turning to face me, she held the tongs up and snapped them together twice. "Here."

Letting my right crutch fall to the grass next to the grill, I put tentative weight on my bad leg. It held up, but my left leg and crutch supported most of my bulk. I took the tongs from Bea's fingers, and she stepped to my side and let me flip the steaks.

"You got quiet," I said.

"I did?"

"Yeah, when my sister kissed Devo."

"Oh. It's just that it was such an intimate moment, you know? Private."

"Yeah, but they don't mind. They've had to fight a lot of bigotry in their lives, separately and together, so now they like showin' affection in public. Plus, it helps that this is our family land.

"This is where Abey feels the most comfortable. Which is kinda weird when I think about it since my house is the same house she grew up in, the same house in which my dad treated her like a second-class citizen because she was gay.

But I guess she knows I don't hold the same opinion. Athena certainly doesn't, so I hope she feels at ease here."

Bea smiled softly. "That's really sweet, Bax."

I shrugged. I didn't mean for it to be sweet. It was just how things were.

Bea said, "I've never had love like that."

"No? Not with your ex?"

"No." She shook her head. "We were young. It wasn't love. It was infatuation on his part. And I was just lookin' for… I dunno. Attention? I felt so alone when my dad died. I *was* alone. I just wanted someone to care about me. I wanted to know there was one person in the world who cared if I was late after work or who'd listen if I had a bad day. Or a good day.

"It didn't take long for me to realize I'd chosen the wrong person."

"I'm sorry, sweetheart, sorry you felt alone."

She shrugged one shoulder, twisting her lips. If I wasn't wrong about the little flash I'd seen in her eyes before she turned her head away, there were tears glistening there. I balanced on my good leg and switched my crutch to my right side, then leaned on it, and I wrapped my arm around her shoulder and pulled her closer.

"I care."

She tucked her head against my chest, still hiding her face from me. "Thank you. Even if your care only lasts five minutes, it feels good."

"BEST S'MORE I've ever eaten," Abey told the girls, and they responded with "Mm-hm," both their mouths full of the gooey treats.

Athena had a glob of marshmallow stuck to the edge of her lip, and she held her hands up in the air so she wouldn't get the sticky mess on her clothes while she chewed.

"Aubrey's apple pie was pretty good too," I said. "She could win competitions with that stuff."

Everybody nodded, and Athena licked the marshmallow off her bottom lip. "I'm gonna ask her to teach me her recipe so I can make it for Logan. He loves apple pie."

I had to try really hard not to groan out loud.

Athena's light brown hair was a mix between Candy's blond and my brown, but right now, she looked so much like her mama. Memories swirled in my head of Athena as a care-free four-year-old, running around this farm, chasing animals, getting dirty, and being happy. But my reality was that she was more like Candy had been in high school. God, that really smarted. Why couldn't she stay my little girl forever?

Bea watched Athena, too, and I wondered what was going through her head.

"Best steak I've ever eaten too," Bea said.

"Damn straight," I replied, and I dropped my empty plate in my lap so I could flex my biceps. "Man make steak. Man eat steak."

Devo laughed. "Man fall on his butt like a toddler."

"Hey," I said. "Man has a broken leg. He can't help it."

"Yeah," Abey added with a chuckle, "because man tripped over his own foot."

I laughed and relaxed back into my recliner. "Who wants to help me carry this chair back into the house?"

Athena had been watching me. All night, I'd felt her quizzical gaze. She had to be registering the difference in the energy between Bea and me. At the very least, she'd noticed how I couldn't tear my eyes away from Bea most of the evening, but I'd just said the magic words, and at the same time, both girls yelped, "Not it!" They scrambled to their feet, grabbed the blanket they'd been sitting on and the empty baking tray, and took off toward the house, giggling the whole way.

"Lemme translate that," Abey said. "What you meant was who wants to carry that old, heavy POS back into the house, 'cause you sure as hell ain't gonna do it." She rolled her eyes. "We'll do it, and then we've gotta head out. I have to be at the station early tomorrow."

"Really?" Devo whined. "Tomorrow's Saturday."

"Yep." Abey stood and folded her lawn chair. "Frank's coachin' football practice, and Dan's out sick with the flu. Roxi, Shelley, and I have our work cut out for us."

"Dang it. I was hopin' for some snuggle time with my woman." A guilty grin grew on Devo's lips. "Plus, you're more susceptible to shoppin' propaganda when you first wake up."

Abey rolled her eyes again, but laughed. "Fine," she said. "If it's cool with Theo, buy the damn couch and have it delivered to the center."

"Eeeee!" Devo jumped in place. "Thank you."

Bea stood and folded her chair too.

"Help," I said, holding my hands out to her. "I'm old and I can't get up."

She laughed. "C'mon, old timer." She grabbed hold of my hands, planted her boots in the grass, and tugged.

God, her *laugh*.

The sound was gritty and sexy, and it made goosechills rise on the back of my neck. It felt like I knew her when she laughed like that. Like I'd heard it before and her happiness had been ingrained deep inside my soul.

Feeling the inexplicable connection we seemed to share when my skin touched Bea's, a beat of anticipation shot through my body, and I stood and grabbed my crutches leaning against the side of the chair. My sister and Devo picked up my recliner and lumbered with it toward the house, grunting and arguing with each other about who was going to drop their side on whose foot.

Bea had been gracious about the sketchpad I'd been trying to hide from her all night. She hadn't peeked once, but when they lifted the chair, it fell open on the grass by my feet.

She bent to pick it up, but when she saw the drawing of the house I'd sketched, she gasped. "Bax, you drew this?"

"Yeah," I shrugged as best I could with the crutches. "It's not a big deal. I'm not that good. It's just somethin' I do to pass the time."

"'Not that good'? This is beautiful. It's so realistic." She looked up at me, and the awe I saw in her eyes nearly knocked me back down on my ass.

"Thank you."

"Seriously," she said, trailing her finger over the roof of the house in the picture, "it's like I could walk onto the page, open the door, and step right into your house. How did you learn how to do this?" She looked up at me, her green eyes almost gray in the growing dark.

"Dunno. I've just always scribbled, you know? I never really had time to focus on it. When I was younger, we had the sheep farm, and our dad never let us relax. There was always somethin' that needed to be done. And then when he passed and I took over, it was worse 'cause it was all on my shoulders.

"Lately though, I've had time."

"What else have you drawn?" she asked, and she balanced the sketchpad over her arm so she could flip the page with her finger.

"No! Don't look at that."

CHAPTER TWENTY-ONE

BEA

BAX THREW out his arm to take the sketchbook away from me as I flipped to the next page, but the swift movement stole his balance, and he toppled to the ground like an old tele-phone pole in a stiff wind.

I dropped the book. "Shit! Are you okay?"

He groaned on the ground. "I'm fine. My ego's just a little bruised." He rolled onto his back in the grass and looked beside him, to where his sketchpad had fallen. It lay open to the drawing I'd been trying to see.

A drawing of me.

"Whoa," I breathed, and I lowered myself to the grass, too, and crossed my legs in front of me.

In the mostly black-and-white sketch, Bax had captured an image of me standing in the dark next to my truck, dressed in the same clothes I'd been wearing when I first arrived at his house after my harrowing encounter with Wooly Wally. My hair was as dark as the night, and it flowed over my shoulder like silk. The only color on the page was the purple hue of my oversized RedHead sweatshirt.

The expression he'd given me in the drawing looked kind

and warm, even though I'd felt tension between us that night. I'd still thought he was an asshole.

I'd never seen myself look so… pretty.

I picked up the sketchpad, securing the previous page underneath. "Can I have this?"

"No!" he said, and he sat up. "Sorry, I meant, if you don't mind, I wanna keep that one. It's not done."

"Okay, but will you draw somethin' for me?"

"Like what?"

"Dunno. I don't have an artistic bone in my body. Whatever inspires you." I stood, brushing dirt off my butt.

He cocked his head and reached for my hands again. I closed the sketchbook and secured it under my arm, then grasped Bax's hands and held steady while he pulled himself up and balanced on one foot.

"Where are your pencils?"

"There," he said, and he looked at the ground as I bent to grab his fallen crutches and handed them to him. A few feet away in the grass lay a plastic baggie with twenty or thirty different graphite pencils contained within.

"Will you draw somethin' for me now?"

"Okay." He blushed. It was hidden a bit in the dark, but the fire behind us and the white moon above us, slipping through slow-moving clouds, lit his face a little so I could see. "Come to my room."

"GRAB THAT CHAIR," Bax said when we were in the safety of his bedroom. He nodded to the hardback chair in the corner and the mud-crusted Tecovas on top as he sat on the edge of his bed. "Bring the boots too."

Athena and Shaylene were in the middle of a *Friends*

marathon in Athena's bedroom, but I locked Bax's door just in case. A sly light glinted in his eyes. I wasn't a hundred percent sure what that meant, but I had a hope and a guess.

"Where do you want 'em?"

"At the end of the bed."

I dragged the chair to the end of Bax's unmade bed, set the boots on the floor next to the chair's leg, and then stood there, waiting for further instruction.

He looked at me, tilting his head this way and that, and when he found whatever light or angle he'd been looking for, he scooted backward and stuffed a pillow behind his back. He bent his good knee and rested the sketchpad on top.

"Take off your clothes."

I snorted. "'Scuse me? What did you just say?"

"Get naked and sit backward in the chair so the wood slats hide your bits and bobbles." He winked, and then he showed his hand—his tongue peeked out and slipped over his lip and he scraped it with his teeth, like two years ago, when I'd dealt him a royal flush. Only, that night, he'd been too drunk to know the power of his hand.

Tonight, he'd figured it out.

Two can play at your game, bucko.

Facing him, I sat in the chair to remove my boots and socks, and then I stood. I kicked them away and turned, and my hair cascaded down my back when I lifted my sweatshirt over my head. I tossed it next to my boots, noticing the dried mud on the soles and vowing silently to sweep and mop for him tomorrow.

With one hand, I spun the chair away from the bed. It scraped over the old hardwood, and I watched Bax over my shoulder while I unhooked my bra and let it fall down my arms to the floor. I kicked it away and unbuttoned my jeans.

His Adam's apple bobbed as I pushed the denim over my

hips, but I lost my view of his face when I bent in front of the bed, dragging my jeans to the floor, giving him an unobstructed view of my ass. I left my undies on, though, 'cause no way was I sitting on that rough wood with no barrier. I straightened slowly, stepped out of the jeans, and walked behind the chair.

Slowly I turned, looking right in his eyes, and gripped the chairback with both hands, then spread my legs over the seat.

He groaned while I used the power of my thighs to lower myself inch by inch until the cold wood bit at my ass cheeks, and then I sat and rolled my hips to get semi-comfortable.

"Now let your legs fall open. Sit up straight."

I steeled my spine, and his hand moved to hover over the bulge beneath his ridiculous maroon track pants. He adjusted his hard-on, but then he picked up his baggie of pencils and searched through it till he found the one he wanted.

His eyes rose to mine. "Mess up your hair a little."

Dragging a hand through my hair, I rustled it and let it fall where it wanted.

"Fuck, Bea. Yeah, that's it." He sat forward and pulled his phone from his pocket, then snapped three pictures of me.

"What's that for?"

He smirked. "Just for reference."

The girls' giggles danced down the hall and through the air every now and then, but silence ruled the moment. Bax began to draw, and I sat there, still as stone, loving how his eyes lifted every few seconds to capture me. They caressed and slipped all over my skin, and I'd never felt more beautiful.

His soft gaze landed on mine, and the desire I saw painted across his face had my body heating up. I rolled my hips again, trying to squeeze my thighs to ease some of the ache building between them.

He lifted his baggie again and found a different pencil. After a few strokes, it wasn't working for him, so he tossed it onto the bed, then reached back in and dug out a broken piece of charcoal.

Sketching with it, he used his index and middle fingers occasionally to smudge what he'd drawn. He was into it, working furiously, his fingers trying to move as fast as his eyes. I didn't mind him being so distracted since the thing distracting him was my body.

He'd been at it for at least twenty minutes, and it had begun to feel like my muscles would ossify. I arched my back and stretched my arms up in the air, laced my fingers together, and my breasts pushed out in front of me.

Bax looked up when the chair creaked, and he froze, his gaze traveling frantically all over my body, but finally, it landed on my face. "Yeah, sweetheart. That's it. Stay like that. Don't fuckin' move."

Charcoal dust covered his hands and fingers. He reached up to scratch beside his nose and left streaks and black smudges on his cheek. He bent his neck, concentrating on some detail, but then he pushed his sketchpad away. It fell onto the bedcovers, and he scooted to the side.

"Is it done?"

"No," he said as he stood and grabbed his crutches leaning against the wall. He opened his bedside drawer, and my heart kicked into overdrive. Was he getting what I thought he was?

I stayed perfectly unmoving, arms still raised, back still arched, legs spread wide and propped up on the tips of my toes. My nipples were as hard as ice, but the wetness his eyes on my body had caused warmed the insides of my thighs.

Bax came to the end of the bed. He sat, set his crutches

on the mattress behind him, and then he straightened, crooked his finger at me, and spread his legs. "Come to me."

I stood and lowered my arms, but I rolled my shoulders and my neck from side to side. Bax growled softly and scooted a few inches backward.

As I began to step toward him, he said, "Slow now. I need to watch you move. *All* of you."

I stalked forward as slowly as I could, and his eyes ate me up. He didn't miss one movement I made.

Standing in front of him, I let my eyes eat him, too, as he tugged his T-shirt over his head. Anticipation danced inside me. I wanted to jump him and lick his skin, but I denied myself, and the denial made my body ache even harder. The sweet pain blooming low in my belly throbbed, and moisture welled between my thighs.

He slipped his hands beneath the waistband of his pants and pushed them down with his boxers to the tops of his thighs, and his hard cock sprang free from its confines. His broken leg stuck out to the side, but he bent his other knee and braced his foot on the floor.

I replied to his invitation by sliding my fingers over my hips, beneath my underwear, and I slipped them down my legs. His low moan told me he liked seeing me completely naked.

No man had ever looked at me the way Bax looked at me, like if he blinked, he'd lose me forever, and in the moment, holding onto me was all he knew.

I took two steps closer, feeling the heat radiating off his chest as he held the condom out for me. His hands were filthy, and I wanted them all over me.

Leaning over him, I bent at the waist and grabbed the condom wrapper between my teeth.

Bax groaned, and his bare cock twitched in the empty space between us. "Fuck," he whispered.

Straightening, I gripped the wrapper between my fingers and pulled. It ripped open as he slipped his hand between my legs, sliding his fingers through the slick mess between my thighs.

I gasped and shivered, and he cupped my pussy with his hand and pulled me closer as I rolled the condom on. His dick was burning hot and as hard as concrete. Wrapping my fingers around it, I pumped twice, needing to feel the hardness in the palm of my hand that would soon be inside me, but then let him fall from my grasp.

His tight and rock-hard shoulders were my anchors, and I climbed up and let my knees straddle his hips on the bed.

Leaning back on his elbows, he watched me, and I used the strength in my thighs again to control my slow descent, taking him inch by thicker inch. When I held him fully seated inside me, he fell back on the bed and moaned loudly. I covered his mouth with my hand to remind him to be quiet, and then I began to move.

The knowledge that there were other people in the house with us, and that they were fully awake and just down the hall, should've stopped us. It was wrong. What if they heard? What if they saw?

But the perverseness of that knowledge made every touch of my skin on Bax's hotter. It drove my desire higher, made my heart race, and soon I was fucking myself on his body, riding him hard and wet, grasping for his arms and chest, making us both sweat and clutch at each other like we'd cease to exist if we didn't.

His abs flexed, and I felt his thighs harden beneath me as he sat up. The base of his dick and his pubic hair ground against my clit with every roll of my hips. He filled me completely, and I gasped and arched as he wrapped his arms around me.

Holding me close, he watched pleasure play over my face, and then he lifted his hands and cupped my breasts inside them. He leaned down and laved one with his tongue slowly while his fingers pinched and caressed the other one. Streaks of charcoal colored my skin, shading the still-building desire I felt for him in grays and black.

Up and down I moved over him, taking him deeper inside with each descent, feeling his hard length stroke me from the inside out, the pressure building.

His fingertips dug into my ass cheeks, his big hands pulling me closer, not letting me escape what he was giving me. He closed his eyes, and his head lolled on his shoulders as he allowed himself to feel me, to feel the pleasure I gave right back to him.

Dragging my fingers lazily over his hips, his obliques, and his ribcage, I watched as goosebumps rose all over his chest. It reminded me that he'd called them "goosechills," and I laughed.

He froze. His eyes popped open, and he began to buck up into me fast and hard. "Do that again," he begged.

"What?"

"Laugh." He buried his face in the crook of my neck, licking and sucking, and his hands roamed my ribs until he found the spot he wanted, and then he dug his fingers in and tickled me.

I threw my head back, trying not to make noise, but I giggled and laughed and let myself drown in his attention.

Even if it only lasted a couple weeks, being with him like this made me feel amazing. He made me feel special, like I mattered to someone in this harsh world, and I never wanted the moment to end.

When I looked in his eyes, he was all business. His body hardened and tightened with every thrust inside me, and he latched onto my breast with his mouth again, this time rougher, his teeth caging my nipple. He gazed up at me, and then he reached between us, coated two fingers in the mess we'd made together and rubbed my clit. Round and round he rubbed, over and again, giving pressure exactly where I—

His sketch on the bed behind us drew my eye, and I stared at the sexiest image I'd ever seen of myself as an orgasm crashed over me, like angry waves battering the edges of a distant sea.

My body clutched at his, and his cock throbbed inside me. It pulsed and jerked as he came, too, making me crave him all over again because the vulnerability he kept offering to me took my breath away and made me desperate for more.

CHAPTER TWENTY-TWO

BAX

"IT'S JUST A SCRIBBLE," I said, watching Bea next to me on my bed, naked and flat on her back.

Her knees were bent and knocking together while she stared at the picture I'd drawn of her. She held it in her hand, and her dark, chocolate hair lay wild and disheveled beneath her shoulders, the wispy ends curling up and licking her arms. I traced a lock with my finger, watching how my skin next to hers made hers look darker.

"You're beautiful," I said. "I don't think I could ever do you justice."

She ignored my compliment, focusing harder on my sketch. "It's not just scribbles. This is art."

"Barely."

"Bax, you made me look sexy. Only an artist can do that."

"Then you're an artist, too," I said, feeling kind of shy and silly, coiling a lock of her hair around my finger now, "'cause you're sexy every day."

She blushed. "I don't see myself that way."

"Why not?"

She rolled and set my sketchpad on the bedside table, flashing me the perfect view of her ass. Reaching out, I slid my hand between her legs, gripped her thigh, and pulled, and she rolled back toward me and tucked her hands beneath her cheek.

"Dunno," she said. "I guess I've always been a little different. You know? On the outside, all I see is short and chubby."

"Chubby? You're nuts. You're perfect."

The blush darkened. In the smallest voice, she said, "Thank you." After a minute, she shivered and shook her head, finally interrupting the eye contact we couldn't seem to break. "I'm not overweight. I know that. I'm more like a string bean—curve-*less*—but it's just this thing in my head.

"When I was little, my daddy called me Belly. Apparently, I had a habit of runnin' around without a shirt. My mama said I hated them, and I'd take mine off in the most inappropriate places. Church, the grocery store, when they pulled up to a drive-through window. And I had a pot belly, so my dad would pat my stomach and call me Belly, like an old man after Thanksgiving dinner.

"I guess it stuck with me."

Caressing my hand over her stomach, I leaned down to kiss it. "No old-man resemblance here. You are beautiful and perfect just the way you are." I dragged my lips over her soft skin and taut muscle, and she shivered and laughed. "God, I love when you laugh. If we could bottle it, we could sell happiness to the masses."

"Shouldn't we get dressed?" she asked. "What if Athena and Shaylene wake up?"

Bea had fucked me long into the night. She was well sated now, three orgasms later. One I'd given her with my cock, another with my mouth when she rode my face again, and the other with both. The girls were fast asleep. Bea had checked to make sure, and my door was still locked.

"No. I told you I want you naked."

"And I told you I think we should sleep fully dressed with our winter coats, socks, and boots on. That way, if Athena does see us, she won't think anything's goin' on."

"Would it be so bad if she did?"

"It wouldn't be the end of the world, no. But I don't wanna hurt her, Bax. I've only been here a week, and I'm leavin' here once the job is done. Remember? The job in which I work for your brother?"

"Yeah. I remember, but if I told him I really want you, he'd accept it."

What I'd said gave her pause. Her green eyes roamed my face.

"Would he? I'm not so sure. And besides, how are we gonna have a relationship seven hours away?" She blushed again. Roses appeared on her cheeks like two full harvest moons, and I rubbed my thumb over the warmth. "I mean, you didn't say the word 'relationship,' but I'm assumin' that's what you meant. But if you just meant sex—"

"Actually, I wanted to talk to you about that, about the distance."

"What about it? If you're about to ask me to give up my job this soon, I'm sorry to tell you, my answer will be no."

"I wouldn't do that. And we're not there anyway, but what if there was a reason for you to stay? A new job?"

"What new job?"

"The guys and Abey and I have talked about buildin' an inn. We need a boathouse, concession stand, and other buildings. A bunkhouse for the seasonal employees. At least one more barn."

"And Brand has agreed to build it all?"

"No. I mean, I mentioned the inn idea to him, and he liked it, but no, there's no official plans yet."

She swiped at the hair curling against her cheek a little aggressively. "Okay well, when he signs on, you let me know, but until then, my job is in Sheridan. Seven hours away."

I felt a little bit of a cold front washing over my skin, but the bedroom was burning hot. "Have I made you angry?"

All emotion dissolved from her face. "I'm not angry."

"You seem a little defensive."

"Yeah, well maybe 'cause my job is the only thing I have that's good in my life. And because you have a daughter whose life I don't wanna fuck up. And maybe 'cause you're—"

"I'm what?"

"Still married. At least in your heart."

Ouch. Bea watched as I collapsed onto my back, and breath escaped my mouth in a huff.

"I'm sorry," she said, leaning up on her elbow. "But it's true, isn't it?"

"It's actually not. And you're the reason."

She scoffed quietly. "How can I be the reason? You barely know me."

Rolling back on my side, I draped my chest over her hip to grab the sketchpad and flipped it back to the first drawing I'd done of her and turned it so she could see. Her finger trailed down the image but landed and then hovered over the purple sweatshirt I'd drawn her wearing. Which was her favorite color, I already knew. A little lavender piece of braided rope hung from her keychain, and the background image on her phone's home screen was a photograph of purple wildflowers.

"When you showed up here and I realized I was attracted to you, it hit me. My marriage has been over for a long time. I had no choice in the matter, and because Candy's dead, I thought that meant I couldn't move on. Like, it wouldn't be right for me to 'cause she didn't get a choice either.

"But now I know the reason she's not here doesn't matter. She's just gone. I'm not, and I can't keep livin' like I am. It's not fair to Athena. It sure as shit ain't fair to me, and it's not fair to you."

Bea stayed quiet for a few minutes, and I watched her processing what I'd said. It was true. It may have taken years too long for me to admit out loud, but it had been true a long time.

Her voice was soft and quiet when she finally spoke. "I admire you. Maybe it took you a few years to figure things out, but you did. I didn't. I stayed in a marriage just 'cause I was afraid not to. You didn't get to choose how your marriage ended, but I did, and I didn't have the guts to end it. Not for a long time.

"What if I make a mistake again? What if the choices I'm makin' now are mistakes? What if I get stuck again? I don't think I have it in me to pick up and leave a second time. I'm not sure I'd survive that."

"You think this is a mistake? You and me?"

"No, I-I didn't say that."

"Sounded like you did."

I rolled on my back, feeling confused and a little defeated. Maybe I was alone in this. Maybe the feelings I'd been having for Bea were one-sided. She was right; it had only been a week, and I'd been out of the game a long time. I'd probably been reading the signals wrong.

"Bax," she whispered. "This is good, right? This thing between us?"

Why did Bea's question sound exactly like the one I'd

asked my daughter when I was still trying to dissuade her from asking me to change?

"Yeah, really good," I said. "You have no idea how relieved I am to know I'm capable of feelin' this way again."

Apprehensively, she asked, "What way?"

"Attraction. Desire. That I could want someone the way I want you."

She moved closer and rested her leg over mine. I gripped her thigh and yanked it higher. When I felt her soft skin against my stomach, I grew hard again instantly. To be fair, though, I'd been hard since she stepped foot in my bedroom.

With the palm of her hand, she touched my cheek and turned my head, and we stared at each other for the longest time, just considering the words between us. But when she leaned in to kiss me, I gave in. The confusion didn't go away, but it fell to the wayside as need filled me back up.

"I want you too," she whispered into my mouth. "Can't that be enough for now?"

I didn't have the answer. *Was* it enough? I wasn't a man who had affairs. I'd been built for the long haul, but she was right that we barely knew each other. There were still a lot of things I hadn't told her, things she'd probably need to know if we did decide to start a relationship.

And some of those things were too fucking hard for me to say.

"Get on your back, sweetheart," I said. "Spread those thighs for me."

I flipped her and pinned her wrists to the bed. Sliding down to the end, I dropped my legs over and put all my weight on my left foot, then yanked her ass to the bed's edge.

Opening her thighs as far apart as they would go, I bent over her, pressing my mouth to the mess we'd made between her legs. She gasped when I licked her cum onto my tongue and slid two fingers inside her, and she moaned loudly. This time I covered her mouth with my hand, and then I fucked her, using the end of the bed as my crutch.

Damn my leg and damn the pain. It was just another thing in my life stopping me from doing what I wanted, what I *needed*. And right now, I needed Bea on her back. I needed to be deep inside her, so deep she'd have no choice but to feel for me.

So deep, she'd scream my name and it would be written on her soul in charcoal.

So deep that when she left, she'd take me with her.

IN THE MORNING, Bea jumped in the shower, and I went downstairs for coffee.

The privacy my bedroom afforded was very much worth it, but the stairs were still a bitch for me to navigate. The PT guy had said I needed to get used to them again anyway, and knowing a closed-door haven for Bea and me existed up there, I wasn't all that mad at the stairs anymore. Although, it still took me a year and a half to get to the bottom or climb up.

Athena and Shaylene sat sleepy-eyed on the couch, seemingly oblivious and covered in fuzzy blankets. They'd moved their marathon to the living-room TV, but they barely noticed when I bumbled down the steps.

"Mornin', Daddy," Athena said, her mouth open in a yawn, but she didn't look away from the TV.

"Mornin', Road Trip. How'd y'all sleep?"

"Good," both girls said in unison.

"Pancakes okay?" I asked on my way into the kitchen.

"Yeah," Athena said. "I'll make 'em after this episode."

"No, baby, relax. I got it."

Finally, she looked at me. *"You're* gonna cook? You sure?"

"I think I can manage breakfast today, but get 911 ready on your phone, just in case." I winked, and she smiled.

Bea had set the coffee to brew late last night since she had to head to the cabins to work today, so while the machine gurgled and percolated, I got two mugs ready and pulled out the milk.

In the sing-song voice Athena usually reserved for when she really wanted me to buy her something, she said, "Oh, Daddy?"

"Oh, Athena?" I sang back.

"Is Bea havin' breakfast with us too?"

"Uh, yeah," I said, feeling my cheeks heat and redden. "Think so."

When I peeked at her, Athena arched an eyebrow at me. She gave me a thumbs-up and smiled, then went back to her show.

Guess that told me what I needed to know about how my daughter felt about the new woman in my life.

Now, I just needed to figure out how *I* felt about the new woman in my life, and that woman needed to figure it out too.

CHAPTER TWENTY-THREE

BEA

THE SMELL of impending cold and snow hit my nose the second I stepped onto Bax's front porch, and my anxiety about finishing the builds hit the roof.

Breathing deeply, inhaling the earthy scents of pine and spruce warming in the morning sun, I calculated in my head the tasks the crew and I could get done with only half a workday. Saturdays weren't mandatory, thanks to Brand, but most guys chose to work them for the extra hours and overtime. I'd have a nearly full cabin crew today, but only for five hours.

The guys wouldn't start till nine this morning, so I'd had time to eat chocolate-chip pancakes with Bax, Athena, and Shaylene. The girls snarfed down their breakfast in record time and had gone back up to Athena's room to talk boys and clothes before Shaylene's mom came to pick her up.

Bax had managed to make the pancakes without falling over, but he was covered in flour and batter, and the kitchen was a disaster. I told him I'd come back after work to help him clean up. He said he could do it, but I was betting the cooking and all the mischief we'd gotten up to last night had worn him out, and I had a feeling when I got back, he'd be asleep on the couch.

It felt really nice to know I had a warm home to come back to after work. Even if the kitchen was still a dusty pancake disaster and the floors needed the kiss of a mop, Bax's house would be filled with silly laughter and family, and I realized I hadn't had that since I was Athena's age. The house itself was nothing special, but it was what it held within that made me feel safe and… hopeful.

Athena had asked if I'd help her shop for a dress for her dance, the one she would be attending with her *boyfriend*, who, if the look on Bax's face told me anything, he wanted to murder.

I'd agreed to help after work. Although, I wasn't sure what kind of assistance I could provide. I'd never been to a town dance before. But I'd been a friend, and something told me that was what Athena really needed.

TURNED out what Athena had actually needed was a buffer and a wingwoman.

After I'd finished my half day and had sent Brand a text to fill him in on the crews' progress, I stuffed a microwaved and lukewarm tamale in my mouth and chewed as I drove Bax and Athena along the western edge of Wisper till we hit the highway and then to Jackson.

Tourists were out in droves on every road, trying to force themselves to enjoy time away from their busy lives in the mountains. All the businesses' parking lots were filled to the brim, no matter what they sold: western hats and boots, scenic helicopter rides, hiking and horseback tours through Grand Teton.

Closer to Jackson, traffic was a bitch, congested and annoying. The day was warm enough for sweatshirts, but snow showed on the tips of the mountains surrounding us when they peeked in and out of the low clouds. In a few weeks, we'd need winter coats.

Sitting tucked between Bax and me, Athena chittered away the whole drive about her boyfriend and how perfect she thought it was that the dance fell on her fourteenth birthday. It had to be fate, she'd said. "Written in the stars."

Bax hadn't said a word except to grunt at me when I needed to turn. I couldn't tell exactly what he was thinking, but I had a good guess. He sulked as Athena and I walked and he hobbled behind us from my truck to the second dress store after we'd parked near Town Square.

The antler arches surrounding the square were weird as shit, but kind of beautiful beneath the colorful cottonwoods and aspens, which I'd recently learned the locals called quakies after their scientific name, Populus tremuloides, meaning "poplar that trembles." The common name, Quaking Aspen, had grown popular in the area, and it was fitting. The aspens' yellow fall leaves shivered in the wind as if an earthquake shook the ground beneath.

"How 'bout this one?" Athena said, pulling the skirt of a floor-length aqua-colored dress out from a rack stuffed with fancy silks and lace.

Bax had insisted on accompanying us, though I was sure Athena had hoped for a girls' day of shopping. We'd found a cute little boutique dress shop, but Bax was right when he complained that the store seemed geared more toward women than it did young teenage girls. But the formal shop we'd tried first only had plain, satin getups, and Athena hated every single one.

"It looks like somethin' a mermaid would wear," Bax

said, his eyes wandering the small store and landing on a menagerie of sequins and high stiletto heels displayed on clear shelves bolted to the wall behind us. Again, I couldn't decipher the look on his face; it was either fear or dismay at the thought of Athena going on a date. Or both.

Athena frowned. "Okay," she said, dropping the blue fabric and pulling a different dress from the rack. She held it up in front of her. "This one?"

The sleeveless, deep-red, formfitting dress had a thin sheath of lace covering what looked like silk underneath. It was a little skimpy for a not-yet-fourteen-year old, but it was pretty, and I had just been about to suggest Athena wear a sweater over it or a pashmina or something, until Bax opened his dad mouth.

"Are you twenty-seven?" he asked her.

"No," Athena said, confused.

"Are you Ariana Grande?"

Athena and I both rolled our eyes.

"No, Daddy."

"Are you Taylor Swift?"

Athena huffed her annoyance.

Bax crossed his arms over his chest and shrugged one shoulder indifferently. "Then no."

"Well then," she said, exasperated, "you pick! You've shot down seven dresses. Do you want me to wear jeans to the dance?"

"Yeah," Bax said, sitting up straighter in the chair the saleswoman had dragged from the office in the back for him to sit on. She'd done it with a flirty smile and shy laugh. For the love of Pete, the man got hit on everywhere he went! "Or better yet, don't go at all. Why don't you stay home? We could do movie night instead. Invite all your friends. I'll order pizza and get some of those gooey chocolate-donut things you love from the new French bakery in Wisper. That sounds like fun, right?"

Athena's face was quickly becoming the color of a tomato. "They're called éclairs, Daddy. And all my friends are going to the dance. It's on my birthday. I'm goin' to the dang dance on my dang birthday!" She turned toward me. "Help?"

Okeedokee then.

Fixing my hands over my hips, I took control of the quickly spiraling shopping trip. After all, on the Bea-Baker personality scale, I was a #1 Man Bosser. "Bax, how about you pull that hat down low over your eyes and take a nap? That's what dads are supposed to do in these situations. Nobody wants your opinion."

He grumbled something under his breath, but then did as I'd asked. He tightened his arms over his chest, and his biceps stretched the sleeves of his gray T-shirt, his fingers digging into his skin as he clenched his jaw and fought the urge to say more. Miss Flirty behind the counter looked like she might melt into a puddle of drool. She licked her lips like a hungry coyote, but finally, she emerged and tried to help us.

She pulled five more dresses for Athena to try. Three were knee-length cocktail dresses, and two were long and flowy. Athena liked the shorter dresses best. She looked good in all of them, and they weren't *too* short.

"What's your favorite dress you ever wore, Bea?" she asked through the dressing-room door as she changed out of a salmon-colored dress into the last option.

"Me?" I checked over my shoulder, making sure Bax was still in compliance. His eyes met mine, then narrowed beneath his hat, but he shook his head and looked away. "Oh, I don't remember. I've never been to a dance. I think the last dress I wore was in elementary school."

"Really?"

Actually, now that I thought about it, the last dress I'd ever worn was to my mama's funeral, but Athena didn't need to know that. The last thing I wanted to do was remind her that her own mom couldn't be here to help her, and instead she got stuck with me.

"Yeah. I like long skirts 'cause they're comfy, as long as they have pockets, but I've never been super girly."

"It doesn't matter what you wear," Athena said. "Can you zip me up?" The door creaked open, and she stood with her back toward me. "You could wear a garbage bag and you'd still be pretty."

Stepping into the little closet-sized cubicle, I swept Athena's braid over her shoulder, zipped her up, and met her eyes in the mirror. She smiled softly and fiddled nervously with the neck of the dress.

Normally, I would've ignored her compliment or dismissed it with a self-deprecating comment, but it seemed important to show her that accepting a compliment like the one she'd just given me was a good thing to do. When I pictured someone telling her she was pretty and her blowing it off because she didn't believe it was true, like I normally did, it made me sad.

"Thank you, Athena."

When she came out of her dressing room and spun slowly in front of a mirror, fluffing the skirt as she turned, I couldn't help my smile, and said, "You're a knockout."

Athena beamed. "Thank you."

The lavender dress she'd finally chosen fell to just above her knees, cinched at the waist with a ruffled band, and it had a matching high, lace neckline and lace-capped sleeves. The lace highlighted the freckles on her arms and added a simple, feminine edge to the dress, and I couldn't put my finger on what it was, but something about the design said "western."

Bax tipped up his gray hat with a finger. He'd been silently peeking and watching us the whole time, his body rigid. I'd bet my truck he wished he could snatch his daughter up and run out of the store, but at least he'd kept his mouth shut.

Now, as he looked at the stunning young woman she had become, he was just speechless.

He tossed me a quiet smile, a "thank you" that tried to stop my heart, and he told Athena, "She's right, baby. You look just like your mama."

Athena's eyes lit up. Tears filled the corners, and she smiled so big. "Thank you, Daddy. Do you really mean it?"

"I do. You're beautiful, and the color is perfect. I'm sorry I was grumpy before, but I still remember when you were little and I was the only guy you wanted to hang out with. It's hard sometimes, seein' you so grown up." I saw something glisten at the edge of his eye, too, but before Athena noticed, he nodded down to the tennis shoes she'd worn to go dress shopping and cleared his throat. "You gonna wear your trainers to the dance?"

She giggled and looked at her shoes. "No."

"Well then," Bax said, pulling his wallet from his back pocket. He held it out to her and she grabbed it, and then he pushed himself up on his crutches. "Guess we better head over to the boot shop and get you some fancy purple cowgirl boots to match, and then we can grab some dinner."

And just like that, the little pinch and burn was back, the one I'd felt in my chest when I'd first arrived in Wisper and realized that the rude, argumentative man I'd met back in Sheridan was nowhere to be found. The pinch had carved a tiny hole inside me that first night, and it had been silently and steadily growing. Now, it was a gaping chasm edged with girly flowers and hearts.

The void had been there a long time, I realized. I'd just never found anything to fill it that fit the shape.

This man and his daughter had filled the space inside me easily. I would never have thought it possible a month ago, but they'd packed me full of laughter and light and family, and they had me questioning my own resolve to leave when my job was done.

Thinking about driving away now made the pinch feel angry and raw, and I thought I'd do anything to stop it burning.

CHAPTER TWENTY-FOUR

BAX

SUNDAYS, according to Merv, were for prayer and rest.

She'd shown up like she did most Sundays, hoping to get Athena and me to accompany her to church, but as usual, trying to convince her there was no rest on a cattle farm and with new businesses to navigate proved to be an exercise in futility. But there really was no rest for the wicked, the weak, the strong, or the mired. Not for anybody around here, so Merv headed to Sunday services alone and disappointed, and I felt a pang of sadness for my mama. She'd spent her whole life trying to find God's love, but didn't she know she'd just driven away from it?

It was right here, in Athena and in me. In the land she'd raised us on, in the sky, and the wind. A lot of bad things happened, sure, but so many good things had happened to us here too.

Finally, I could see it, could see past all the pain.

I wished Merv could see it too. I hoped someday she would. Maybe when her house was finished and she lived on the property again instead of in the run-down trailer she'd insisted on buying after my dad passed. I still had no clue why she'd punished herself like that. And when Candy and the baby died, she became almost a recluse. I had the feeling she was in the same fight with God I had been in the last three years, and if that was the case, she'd need to figure out how to let the Almighty off the hook when she found him.

I'd come around to it, and if I could forgive, then so could she.

The ranch was the only place I wanted to be. This land was slowly bringing me back to life. Rye and his crazy ideas had lit a fire under my ass again. Last year, after I'd made the decision to let go of the sheep farm that had been a burden my whole life, I got lost again, just like I'd been when Candy and Duo died. And then I broke my leg and the world had become a shitstorm once more.

But now, the wavy, nauseating heat lifted from the road in front of me, and I could see the many paths just waiting for me to stand up and choose one. Rye, my brother and sister, and Athena hadn't let me get truly lost. They pulled me off the pavement and gave me reasons to look for the sunrises and sunsets again every day.

And Bea, she'd shown me that those sunsets could light my world on fire again.

Plus, there really was a fuck-ton to do.

Sitting on a folding chair in the shade at the mouth of the barn, I used two small, stacked hay bales as a desk, logging expenses into a spreadsheet on Rye's laptop. But really, what I'd been doing the last hour was watch my little girl learn to command Tulsa, wishing I could be out there in the ring with her.

Rye and Presley had the physical tasks covered while I recovered, but I was itching to feel dirt under my fingernails again. I missed my nightly showers when I could feel the strength in my mind and my body after a hard day's work.

There was a certain euphoria after a shower like that, when I'd sit on the porch, watching the sky darken and feeling accomplished. Even if I'd failed at the larger task of life, I still felt proud of the work I'd done with my hands. It was when I drew the best. I had clarity then, could see what I wanted to bring to life in my sketchbook easily.

I set down the computer and picked up my sketchpad to start on a drawing of my brave daughter as she listened to the guys while they instructed her and taught her how to be a rider. She had no fear, and she looked so confident that I thought the pride inside me might break open my chest to get out of my body. Seeing her like that reassured me that she could handle some teenage boy. If he put the moves on her on their date, I hoped she'd use the same confidence to punch—

"Whatcha drawin'?"

Bea's quiet voice behind me nearly caused a heart attack.

"Jesus! Warn a guy before you sneak up on him like that." I couldn't put my finger on why, but all day, it felt like I'd been being watched. How ridiculous was that though? No one cared about my mundane, disabled activities.

Bea laughed softly. "Then what would be the point of sneakin'?"

"S'pose you're right," I said. "but if I'd been standin', you would've brought me to my knees just then." I looked up at her, and she stroked two fingers over the brim of my hat. "I thought you had work to finish."

"I do, but I was gettin' kinda lonely over by the cabins all by myself. Plus, it's not safe for me to do any hard labor without at least a buddy. Wanna be my buddy?" She smiled as she collected her long hair in one hand, then twisted it into a bun and secured it on her head with a band she wore around her wrist. "I have to tell you, this hat is *really* doin' it for me."

Was I blushing? I totally was, and her smile grew naughtier.

"There's no one at the cabins today. Mine, for example, is empty." She wiggled her eyebrows.

Reaching out, I tugged her closer by the belt loop on her jeans. "I've got a better idea. Pull up a chair. There's a show for you right here. Look." I waved my arm out toward Athena as she led her mare into a controlled canter around the edge of the ring. Rye and Presley watched from the middle, turning in circles, looking for any sign that the horse might buck or spook. "The guys have been workin' with both of them separately for several weeks, but this is their first ride together."

"Really?" Bea squinted beneath the shade of her hand. "She looks so good."

"She really does," I said as Bea snagged an old feed bucket from the side of the barn. She flipped it upside down next to my chair and sat on it.

Crossing one leg over the other, she propped her elbow on her knee and leaned forward to watch. "Athena's so beautiful up there. She looks like a proper cowgirl."

"Yeah," I agreed, but I was watching Bea as she watched my little girl. She was proud of Athena too. I saw it all over her face. "What about you?"

She didn't take her eyes away from Athena and Tulsa. "What about me?"

"Ever ride?"

"Oh God, no. I'd fall off."

I shook my head. "No you wouldn't."

Athena slowed Tulsa to a walk to cool down, and I turned toward Bea. Presley stayed in the ring with the new dynamic duo, but I saw Rye out of the corner of my eye, walking over to the fence to grab his water bottle.

"Oh, young squire?" I called to him.

He stopped in his tracks with the water bottle almost to his lips. "Uh, yes, *my liege*?"

"Saddle my horse."

He snorted and rolled his eyes. "My liege, if I may be so bold, are you out of your fuckin' mind? You ain't gettin' on your horse with a broken femur."

I waved my hand toward Bea. "Not for me, but for the princess."

"No way in hell am I gettin' on a horse!" She stood and backed away, shaking her head. "Nuh-uh. No dice."

"Scared?" I taunted.

Her beautiful smile wilted into a grimace. "Terrified."

"IT SMELLS like cow shit in here."

"It's a cattle farm," Presley said, holding Bea's hips to keep her steady when she climbed onto her feed bucket next to Purdy, my eleven-year-old sorrel gelding.

There was no other word for it; my horse was lazy, which was how I knew he'd be the perfect first ride for Bea. Purdy wouldn't buck her because it would take entirely too much energy on his part. He'd gotten far too comfortable standing around munching hay since I'd closed down Lee Family Fleece and then broken my leg.

"I know that," Bea argued, "but is the smell s'posed to be this strong? I feel like it's burnin' the inside of my nostrils."

Presley rolled his eyes, and Athena and Rye snickered like two old ladies as they watched from the other side of the barn aisle.

"Get down," Presley grunted, his gruff demeanor made clear in the rough sound of his voice.

Bea wasn't deterred. "What? Why? I was just jokin'," she

said. "I promise to stop complainin' about the putrid smell of bovine feces."

"C'mon, Pres," Rye said. "Where's your sense of humor?"

"Don't have one, but that's not why she needs to get down. This ain't the right horse for her. Their energies don't match. Get Blue. He's the one for miss Bea."

Athena winced, Rye's eyebrows rose in tandem, and I crutched closer.

"Uh, Pres," I hedged, "you sure?"

"I'm sure." He nodded toward Blue's stall, his eyes on Rye's. "Get him."

"Wait a minute," Bea said, stepping down from the bucket and backing toward me. Anxiety radiated out around her like a force field. "Why do you all look like this man just signed my death warrant?"

"It'll be fine, right, Rye?" I said. I needed his reassurance that his horse would not, in fact, kill Bea or put her in the hospital. If we both had broken legs, we'd be doomed.

Rye pursed his lips for a few seconds. He studied Blue and then Bea, and back to Blue again, but then he nodded. "I trust Pres's judgment. If he says Blue's the horse for Bea, it must be true." He turned and opened his horse's stall.

Presley led Purdy back to his stall across the way, and Bea turned to look at me. "Are *you* sure?"

"Yeah, 'course," were the words that came out of my mouth, but my head moved side to side as I said it.

"Thanks," she griped. "Thanks for that vote of confidence." But when she heard Blue's hooves on the barn floor as Rye led him into the aisle, she turned and gasped in awe. "He's beautiful."

"That he is," Rye said proudly. "Don't you break him.

Now c'mon. Come closer. Talk to him. Introduce yourself. Let him smell you and feel your heartbeat."

Athena moved next to me, and we held our breath as Bea approached Blue with her hand out, like he was a snarling dog instead of a rowdy horse. Sitting next to my broken leg on the dusty barn floor, even Fig was nervous. He yelped softly and ran out the open door.

It wasn't that Blue was mean or dangerous, but he was a horse meant for an experienced rider. Rye had bred and raised Blue for himself, and they had an unexplainable bond and connection, like two pieces of a whole. I'd never seen Blue take to anyone other than Rye. The horse hated me. Every time I walked by him he tossed something at me: water, hay, spit—whatever he had at his disposal.

But Bea was brave, too, and when Blue slipped his nose beneath her hand and tossed her arm up in the air, she didn't cower away; she stayed her course slowly and laid her other hand on Blue's chest.

"Hello, you regal creature. You're so handsome."

I swore he could understand her. He chuffed and nosed at her hair.

It was unlike anything I'd ever witnessed as Bea laid her cheek against Blue's neck, and he lowered his big head until it rested on her back.

"Look, Daddy," Athena whispered. "He's huggin' her."

Rye stared at me, his eyes nearly bugging out of his head, but then he shook the surprise off his face. "Okay, okay, that's enough of that. If you steal my horse, I'm gonna have to ban you from the barn."

Bea laughed, and she stepped back, but she didn't stop touching Blue. She stroked his wide cheek and asked, "May I ride you?"

Rye passed Blue's lead to Bea, and when she led him down the aisle, Presley mumbled, "Told ya so."

"I've never ridden before," Bea told Blue. "I've never even had a pet. Please be patient with me."

Blue nodded and whinnied quietly, and they left the shade of the barn. In the sun, his speckled roan coat was striking, but his dark tail and mane matched the color of Bea's hair. They looked like they belonged together.

Rye noticed it, too, and he croaked out his jealousy to his horse. "You're breakin' my goddamn heart here, buddy."

"Oh shush," Bea said. "I'm just borrowin' him. You'll get him back."

Athena and I stood off to the side while the guys prepared Blue, saddling him and adjusting Athena's saddle's stirrups to fit Bea's shorter legs.

Something kept tickling at the back of my neck, an awareness that had me turning and searching the trees. For what, I had no idea, but it felt again like someone had been watching us. There was no one, though, so I slipped my arm over Athena's shoulder and tugged her closer, leaning on her a bit.

When Bea was seated and visibly scared out of her mind, Rye gave her a quick tutorial. The unsure scowl on her face didn't have him convinced she'd listened, so he started over.

"Don't pull on the reins. Hold 'em in your hands gently. If you want to turn—"

"I heard you. I got it," she snapped. And then she clicked her tongue twice and carefully squeezed her legs around Blue's big body. He loped forward toward the gate, and Bea let out a nervous laugh.

After they'd walked two slow circles around the ring, she nudged Blue into a trot with a squeeze of her calves and called out to me. "Do you see this, Bax? I'm ridin'!"

"I see you." She was all I'd been able to see since the day

she showed up in her beat-up Chevy with a little chip on her shoulder and a light in her green eyes.

"Look at her go," Athena said. "She's fearless."

"Kinda like somebody else I know," I replied, and I flicked the top of my daughter's white cowgirl hat.

I'd been so mesmerized watching Bea that I hadn't even heard Aubrey's car coming up my drive. "What's goin' on?" she asked when she came to stand between Rye and me.

"Hey, baby." Rye leaned down to kiss her cheek, and he slipped his arm around her waist. "Didn't expect you till later. Slow day at the bookstore?"

"Yeah. I closed early, and then on my way here, I almost got into an accident. Some jerkoff was speedin' down Old Fish Creek Road, and he nearly ran me into the ditch."

Rye kissed her again, but this time she lifted her face to him and caught his lips with hers.

"You okay?"

"Yeah," she said, waving away his concern. "I'm fine."

"Well, good then, you're just in time to see that woman steal my horse. I think he's in love with her."

"Is that Bea?" Aubrey asked, squinting against the sun to see better.

"Yeah," Rye said, "except now we're callin' her Stealer of Horses, kinda like that white-haired chick on *Game of Thrones*—the Mother of Dragons."

At the end of our line of observers, Athena snorted.

In the middle of the ring, Presley called out to Bea, encouraging her, but also reminding her what to do.

"Shh!" she said. "You're ruinin' my moment."

Presley grumbled something but stopped talking.

"Y'all are lucky I don't have big boobs!"

Athena and Aubrey chuckled on either side of me, nodding in solidarity.

The bouncy up-and-down of the trot had worked the messy bun off the top of Bea's head. Her hair slipped out, the elastic fabric she'd wrapped it with fell to the dirt, and her dark brown locks flowed down her back, licking at the wind as she squeezed Blue again and he increased his speed and eased into a canter.

Bea was a natural; she and Blue had found some kind of communion. She pushed up in the stirrups and leaned forward a bit, like she was ready to fire out the gate at the Kentucky Derby, and then Blue really took off. Everybody on the sidelines whooped it up, and the smile on Bea's face was one for the books.

She'd never been more beautiful, and that was saying something since every single time I looked at her my heart tried to lurch right out of my chest.

"Athena! We're goin' ridin' together," Bea hollered back to Athena as she passed us. "This is so fun!"

Athena laughed. "It's a date!"

"Beatrice Baker," I called back, shaking my head in wonder as Bea passed us again at the gate. "If Athena's a road trip, you're a goddamn runaway train!"

She heard me, and she threw her head back, laughing. "Oh yeah? Well this train's leavin' the station. Choo-fuckin'-choo!"

CHAPTER TWENTY-FIVE

BEA

THE NEXT FIFTEEN days passed like a whirlwind.

I spent the nights with Bax in his bed, like it had always been that way, and I spent the days working, watching the cabin crew toil away and the house crews finish their builds. I felt pride seeing them find completion. I hadn't designed the structures. I'd barely lifted my own hammer to craft them, but I'd guided them to the end, and that felt just as good.

Abey and Devo had already come to check out their new digs, and they'd screeched and hollered, and I found myself jumping up and down right along with them in the middle of their new living room, helping them plan their move in. I was ecstatic for them, and my cheeks had cramped and hurt for all the grinning. A little part of me was envious though. I wanted what they had. I wanted the life they had, one filled with work they loved but with family and friends they loved even more.

I had the work part down, and it felt like the rest could be mine. All I had to do was reach out and take hold of it.

Athena and I were in a serious, long-standing discussion about how she should wear her hair to the dance, which was less than a week away now. After the fifth time we'd brought it up at dinner around Bax's table, he suggested shaving it all off. Athena rolled her eyes so hard, I thought her eye sockets might be sore in the morning. She thought she should wear her hair up, but I insisted down and free and flowing. She really had no idea just how beautiful she was. Her awkward, early teenage phase seemed to be passing right before my eyes, and I had no doubt that by the same time next year, she'd have a whole line of boys asking her to dances.

She and I had gone on trail rides with Presley leading the pack. Once, we even saw a bear far off in the distance, rooting around at the base of a tree. Thankfully, he wasn't on Lee property when we spotted him, but that didn't do much to assure me he wouldn't wander over there. Presley said he probably wouldn't, but I still had my doubts. I wouldn't even have noticed him if Athena and Presley hadn't pointed him out, and I'd had to use Presley's binoculars to get a good look, but sure enough, it was a flipping grizzly bear!

We'd also seen my bison. Of course, there was no sure way for me to know it was really Wooly Wally, but I felt it was him. And when he lifted his big ol' head and stared me down, I knew it. He stood at the center of a small herd grazing in a field a football field away from our little trail-riding group, and there'd been two calves jumping and playing around him and the smaller females. Wally had a family.

Trail riding was like getting a brain massage, with warm sunshine sifting through the boughs of the trees above us while we listened to birds sing and fallen branches and leaves snap and crunch beneath the horses' hooves as they carried us over mountain paths.

And then when we returned to the barn, the cool-down tasks of rinsing the horses with cold hose water, feeding, and brushing them relaxed me even more. I'd started wondering how much horses cost. Maybe I could buy one for myself, keep it at the ranch with Bax and Athena, and come back to visit and ride.

But if I did that, what would that mean for Bax? If I left and went back to Sheridan like I had planned, he'd move on. It wouldn't be fair of me to ask him not to, but the thought of him with another woman brought that pinch right back to my chest and made it rage.

Bax and I were good together, but it hadn't even been a month. It wasn't like we were in lo—

Or were we?

Was I?

It was crazy that I'd spent years in a marriage that had about as much intimacy as a rock garden, but I'd only been around Bax for three short weeks, and he already knew me down to my soul. And it was bonkers to me that Bax's ranch felt like home even though it was two-thousand miles away from the graves of the only people I'd ever really loved.

But it was the truth, and it didn't feel too fast or scary or weird.

It felt right.

Bax was everything I'd ever wanted: steady, supportive, loving, trustworthy. The way he cared for Athena showed me not all fathers failed their kids. I'd known it in the pit of my stomach, but until I spent time with Bax and Athena and saw it for myself, I couldn't admit my dad had failed me. I wasn't mad at him anymore. I knew now that his grief had robbed us both of his love, and there was a freedom in admitting it to myself.

Bax had lit some kind of fire inside me, and when he smiled at me and crooked his finger? Hoo boy, I had to take note of which side of the sky was up when he kissed me 'cause the man could knock good sense right out of me.

How did he do that? No one ever had before.

But there was something missing. It felt like Bax had tried many times to say something to me, to tell me something important, confide in me. But it never came.

We'd talked about everything under the sun: his wife, his loss, our dreams, and even the future. He knew that I was a marathon belcher and that I had an excessive new-tool problem—if DeWalt made one, I had to have it. I'd told him about the day my dad overdosed, and he told me about his youngest brother, Dixon, and how he'd been bullied by their dad, and how that had helped lead Dixon to alcohol and drugs too.

Maybe it was me. Maybe thinking Bax was hiding something from me was just my tendency to see the cup half-empty. Or maybe it was my own self-preservation trying to give me a reason to leave when my job was done, so I wouldn't get hurt. So I couldn't hurt Athena or Bax.

The job *would* be done soon. Maybe I needed to figure out how I felt about Bax sooner rather than later.

Clay waved and flashed me a bushy lipped smile when I parked in front of the cabin Monday morning and climbed out of my truck. I was dragging ass because Bax and I had stayed up way too late playing strip checkers, and I was a sore loser, so I'd made him play again and again until I'd won. But I knew he was the real champion, so I'd rewarded him with the longest and sexiest blow job in the history of ever, and it had gotten so heated that my jaw was still sore, and he was nursing some deep fingernail divots in his ass cheeks this morning.

"Mornin', Clay. How you doin'? You know, you've never said and I've never asked, but are you married?"

"Naw. I was married once upon a time, but you know how that goes. Didn't last." He shrugged.

Oh yeah, I'm quite aware of "how that goes."

"Oh, before I forget," he said, "I have to take off Friday."

"Sure, everything alright?"

"Yeah, damn doctor wants me to have an angiogram or an EKG or some bullshit. He says my old ticker's not doin' its job the way it should. I can come Friday mornin' but I'll have to leave around ten."

"No, don't worry about work. Take the day. Sleep in and rest up before your tests."

He tipped his hard hat like it was a cowboy hat. "Thanks. And I've got some good news for you. Final checks will be done for houses two and three today."

"That's great. Thank you. That makes me feel so much better about our deadline."

My eyes rose to the flurry-free sky, hoping hard that winter would keep her distance for one more week. Two if I was lucky, but I wouldn't hold my breath because the tip-tops of the mountains got snowier every day.

"Looks like things are movin' along nicely here too," Clay said.

"Yeah." I looked around at the cabins, noticing things I hadn't really thought about in the last two weeks. All the cabins' siding and roofs were done. I was surprised I'd missed that really important detail, but I'd been so preoccupied with Bax that I'd been slacking.

That wouldn't do. Brand hadn't sent me here to screw up my job just so I could sleep with his brother. *Shit.* Just what the hell did I think I was doing? Had I put my job in jeopardy because I'd fallen in love with—

"Ohh no."

Yep. You are totally and completely in love with your boss's brother.

"What?" Clay asked, his eyebrows lowering in concern. Thank God I hadn't said that last thing out loud.

"I-I, uh…" I looked around the build site, trying to figure out what to do. Suddenly, I had no answers. All my la-di-da musings about relaxing trail rides, soul-deep love connections, and naked games of checkers seemed silly when I compared them to the pride and love I had for the job Brand had given me. "I forgot somethin' inside," I told Clay. "I'll be right back."

Jogging to my cabin, fear finally kicked in and my heart felt like it might beat right out of my body. My job was important. It was all I had, and I'd clung to it the last two years like it was the last little pocket of air in a car sinking under a lake. I excelled at my job. It was what made me feel special and necessary, but five minutes ago, I'd been all lovey-dovey about Bax and ready to give it up, and now I couldn't get inside the cabin fast enough so I could scream into a pillow or something. I felt like I had whiplash.

And now that I'd admitted to myself that I was, indeed, very much in love with Bax, Athena's wellbeing smacked me upside my head. I had no clue how to be her mom. Or mom adjacent. Athena had been playing matchmaker, but if Bax and I did get together officially, she probably wouldn't really even want that. No one could ever replace her mama. How foolish was I that I'd even considered trying to fit into Athena's life like that? She and Candy had years of history together, years of laughter and skinned knees with smiley-face Band-Aids and kisses and melting popsicles on the front porch.

All I had was one trip to a dress shop.

Shaking my head at the audacity, I slipped my key into

the cabin's lock but then realized it was already unlocked. I could barely remember the last time I'd been inside. Had I forgotten to engage the deadbolt before I left? But the knob lock was open too. The crews were arriving, truck after truck, so if danger lurked, I wasn't worried. Clay was a holler away, and it couldn't be the bear, could it? Not with all the people and noise going on around the build site.

Opening the door, I did a quick scan of the living room and kitchen and shivered. Had I turned off the heat? I thought I'd left it at sixty-eight. That was the temperature I kept my apartment at, but as I rubbed my hands up and down my arms to eke out a little warmth from the friction, it felt more like thirty-eight.

Nothing seemed out of place though. No hungry grizzlies waiting to pounce on me, so I stepped inside and shut the door behind me, listening for movement, but I heard none and walked to the bedroom. The bathroom and closet were both empty, doors open, lights off.

When I got back out to the living room, I noticed a basket on the floor under the south window, tucked just behind the arm of the loveseat.

Odd. I hadn't noticed it when I came in, but to be fair, I was looking for bears, not baskets.

Outside the cabin, someone dropped something, and I heard their exclamation a little too clearly. When I followed the noise, I found that the kitchen slider had been left open a crack, but not by me. I'd never even used the back door.

I went back to the basket. Was there a bomb in there? A small plastic tarp with frayed and loose edges looked like it had been cut and ripped off a bigger tarp, and it covered the basket's handle and its contents, but the light-wood-colored bottom and weaved-wicker part of the basket was easy to see.

I took one more look around, but other than the open back

door, found nothing out of place, and then, out of the corner of my eye, I saw and heard the tarp move. Something underneath squeaked and cooed.

What the fuck?

Dropping to my knees, I pulled the cover away, and staring out at me from a cocoon of baby blankets with red cartoon tractors on them, two big, round, clear blue eyes blinked.

The baby cooed again and reached out with his chunky little arm. His cheeks looked flushed, and when I touched his face with the backs of two fingers, his skin was still warm, but the cabin was freezing. Whoever had left him hadn't been gone long.

"Oh my God. Who are you? Where'd you come from?"

My head swiveled back and forth, searching again for the baby's parents, but I already knew they were gone. They'd escaped out the back, but I had no clue when. Too bad we hadn't installed security cameras. *Dammit! We should have.*

"Are you okay? You poor thing."

I lifted the baby and cradled him in my arms, and he began to cry. He couldn't have weighed much more than my cordless drill. I held him to my chest, trying not to crush him, but I was freaking out. What in the actual fuck? Who would leave a defenseless baby in the middle of a construction project alone?

It didn't take long for Clay to come barging in. "Miss Bea? You okay in here? I thought I heard a—"

"A baby," I said, finishing Clay's sentence as his boots squeaked and he stopped in the doorway.

A baby with blue eyes that looked extremely familiar. I'd just looked into another pair not twenty minutes ago, right before I left Bax's house and he kissed me goodbye. I'd seen another pair the other night when Abey told a terrible joke and we'd belly laughed together around Bax's kitchen table. And I looked in yet another pair every day at work back in Sheridan. Brand, Abey, and Bax all had the same crystal-blue eyes.

That was why the guy with long hair looked so familiar. He had to be Dixon Lee, the only living member of the Lee family I hadn't yet met. And this bundle was the thing he'd been carrying the day he showed up.

Clay nodded to the tractor blankets. "Where'd he come from?"

"I have no idea. He was here when I came in."

"Someone just left you a baby?"

"Not me. Why would they leave him for me? I-I don't understand. You didn't see anybody in here when you pulled in?"

"No," Clay said. "Not a soul. Maybe they were waitin' for you?"

"Um. Okay. Can you take over here? I need to—"

What? What exactly was I supposed to do with a baby?

"Sure thing," Clay said. "Not to worry. You better call the sheriff."

Oh. Good idea. I released the breath I'd been holding when he said it and finally realized that Abey would know what to do.

I set the baby back in his basket and covered his arms and legs with one of his blankets. He'd stopped crying, but he whimpered and puckered his lips. Was he cold? Scared? I had no idea. I tucked Athena's green throw around him too, to keep the morning chill off his skin, and Clay held the door open for me as I lugged the bundle to my truck.

The crew had all stopped what they were doing to stare at me, and just as I set the basket on my passenger seat, a car started up down the lane. I recognized the sound of the faulty muffler and turned my head to see the sedan from a couple weeks ago peeling away.

"Get the license number!" I yelled to Clay, turning and pointing to the dust cloud the car made behind it as it raced away, and the baby wailed. Bax had told me that no one had seen Dixon in a long time. They had no clue where he'd been living. What if they couldn't find him now?

"Too late," Clay called loudly over the crying, "but I'll ask around. Maybe one of the crew noticed somethin'."

"Shit." I shut the passenger door and rushed to mine. "Oh man. I gotta go."

Clay stepped away, and I started my truck as fast as I could and threw it into Reverse, but then I remembered there was a baby in a goddamned basket, sitting unsecured on my seat. I didn't have a car seat or a carrier or whatever the hell they were called.

I put my truck into Drive and steered with one hand while I held the basket handle with the other, trying to avoid potholes and checking every other second to make sure the baby hadn't decided to jump out. He didn't seem like he'd be able to command his little body that effectively quite yet, but I had no idea how old he was or what babies did. The only baby I'd ever been around was Mrs. Ortiz's granddaughter when I was nine years old, and then I'd held a couple of my dad's employee's kids years ago at the company Christmas party.

I was so not equipped for this; my little freak out about being a mother figure to Athena was so spot on, it made me sick to my stomach.

Bax's kitchen door banged against the wall when I pushed it open with my hip.

He stood in front of the sink, leaning on one crutch and slowly swiping the scratchy side of a sponge around the pan in the sink he'd used to make eggs. He was humming. Seriously out of tune humming.

"Bax."

On my way in the door, I noticed the extra cabin key wasn't hanging from the hook like it had been every other time I went in or out of the house. It was possible someone had knocked it behind the garbage can below, but with the basket in my hand and the memory of the car kicking dirt behind it as it drove away, I had my doubts.

"Did you forget you wanted to kiss me again?" Bax asked with a goofy smile on his lips, still facing the window over the sink looking out at a view of the barn.

"Where's Athena? Has she left for school yet?"

He turned when he heard the breathless sound of my voice. My heart was still pounding.

"Yeah, Abey picked her—" Bax stopped mid-sentence, confused at my question, but then he zeroed in on the delivery in my hand. The dish sponge splattered on the floor, and the whites of Bax's eyes showed as he looked at the baby, like the kid really was a bomb.

I set the basket on his kitchen table, and he swung his wet hand toward it, pointing at the baby with a shaking finger. "What is *that*?"

CHAPTER TWENTY-SIX

BAX

"IT'S A BABY," Bea stated simply, like that explained away the fact that there was a baby in my house.

She looked like a completely different woman than the one I'd made love to early this morning. I saw real fear etched into her usually confident features.

"He was in my cabin alone. The car. The car from the other week and the man with long hair, he just left him! Clay and I watched him drive away. I bet that's who took the key, but he couldn't leave through the front door because of the crew."

"*Him*? What key?"

Just then, the baby let out a cry, and he opened his eyes. They were the same blue I'd seen in my youngest brother's eyes my whole life. The same blue I saw when I looked in a mirror. The kid was the spitting image of Dixon.

"I think it was your brother, Dixon. Is that possible?" Bea lifted the kid and tucked him into the crook of her arm. He whimpered and cried harder as she swayed from side to side, shushing him. "Bax, look in the basket. There's an envelope.

I didn't notice it till now." When I didn't move, Bea stepped closer to the basket. "It's addressed to you."

"Me?"

"Yeah." Like she knew instinctively not to get too close to me with the baby in her arms, she held the note out to me and waited for me to take it from her hand.

The letter had been sealed in a thin, nearly see-through, white envelope, and my name had been scribbled on the front in Dixon's chicken-scratch handwriting.

Panic swirled in my chest, and the sight of Bea comforting a baby wasn't helping.

Somebody else needed to come and deal with this. I couldn't. I couldn't stop shaking. I whispered, "Can you call my sister?"

Afraid she hadn't heard me, I looked up, and finally Bea said, "Of course."

I hadn't hid the panic as well as I'd hoped. Bea had no clue what was wrong with me, but she knew it was something if the worried look on her face was anything to go by. She fumbled her phone, trying to unlock it and search for Abey's contact while she bounced the baby.

Trying not to crush it in my hand, I pulled my own phone from my pocket and leaned on my crutch. I swiveled on my foot, turning away from Bea, and opened my contacts. I hit Dixon's name with my thumb so forcefully, I was surprised the screen didn't crack.

For more than a year, my family's and my calls had gone unanswered, but today, surprisingly, my brother answered, and my temper got the better of me. "What the fuck, Dixon!"

It took him a minute, but he said, "You can take care of him, Bax. You're a good dad. I'm not. I can't do it."

I lowered my voice so Bea wouldn't hear. "You knew what this would do to me. Goddamn you."

"I'm sorry. I know, but I love you, brother. You've always looked out for me, but now I need you to forget about me and look out for him."

"It doesn't work that way, asshole."

"I'm not worth your worry, Bax. Take care of him. He needs love, and you got lots of that to give. I owe this to you."

"You can't owe a *child*, Dixon," I seethed through clenched teeth, my voice getting louder and louder as my heart thundered inside my chest. And fuck Dixon. I knew exactly how he'd ended up in this situation. "How fuckin' high are you?"

"I'm not," he said. "I know you don't believe me, but the minute he was born, I got sober. But I dunno if I can keep it up. Better to stay away. Everybody's better off without me."

"Dixon," I pleaded, falling forward under the weight of the panic now, but I caught myself on the edge of the kitchen counter and leaned on it. "I-I can't."

"Everything you need's in the basket under the blankets. He's healthy. They detoxed him in the NICU and he's had all the shots they said he needed. I left you his birth certificate, and Kel and I signed a paper that says we give our rights to you. It's notarized."

"Kel?"

"Kellie, she's the mama. She's in bad shape, Bax. I tried to keep her sober as much as I could durin' the pregnancy, but once he was born... I've tried gettin' her to go to rehab, but she won't go. She wants nothin' to do with Stu, but her parents are dead, and she doesn't have brothers or sisters."

I couldn't remember ever being so goddamn mad, but all that came out of my mouth was, "You named your kid Stu?"

"It's short for Stuart. It means he'll always have a guardian lookin' out for him. It's just a nickname. You and

Athena can name him whatever you want. She's good at that. And I met that new chick you been hangin' with. She seems nice. Maybe she can help out, but don't give him to Merv. I put that in the paper. I love her, but she'll ruin him.

"It's also written in the paper that if you don't take him in, he goes to foster care."

Motherfucker!

I wanted to scream at my brother, but the inevitable heartbreak made me whisper. "How can you do this to me?"

A scuffle sounded at the end of Dixon's line. "I gotta go, Bax. Don't try to find me. I won't be in Wyoming." He got quiet for a minute. "I wish Candy could see him."

"This ain't the same k—"

"I *know* that," Dixon said. "But he can be. He can heal that part of you I broke."

Hearing the guilt in his voice exhausted me. My wife's and child's deaths had nothing to do with him. Dixon had just happened to be in the truck with Candy when she had the aneurysm. I'd said it till I'd gone blue in the face, but he wouldn't listen. He'd blame himself till the end of time. "Dixon, it wasn't your—"

"I gotta go," he said, and he cut the line.

"*Fuck.*" I shoved my phone back in my pocket. What the hell was I supposed to do now?

"Bax?" Bea tried to get my attention as the baby screamed. She was freaking out, the strained sound of her voice like a blaring siren. "Abey's on her way, but why's he cryin' like this? Is somethin' wrong with him?"

"He's probably hungry."

"You have milk."

"He can't have cow's milk yet," I said woodenly. "He can't be more than a few months old. He needs formula or breast milk, neither of which we have."

Fuck. I couldn't think with the kid wailing like that. It filled up my whole house, and it nauseated me.

"Bax? Look at me."

I couldn't. I made my way to the table and fell into a chair.

Still rocking from side to side, Bea slipped her pinky into the kid's mouth, and he latched on. I knew that wouldn't work for long, though, once he realized no milk was coming out.

Devo. Devo had said they kept baby formula at the community center for mothers who couldn't afford it.

The baby opened his mouth and let out another wail, and Bea groaned miserably as I pulled my phone from my pocket again. I pounded my finger over the sensor till it unlocked, found Devo's contact, and called her.

"Bax? What's up?"

"I need formula."

"What's that noise? Is that… a baby?"

"Yeah," I yelled over the incessant crying. "Abey's on her way, but he's hungry and I got nothin' to feed him. You said you have formula at Ace's House?"

"I'm on my way," Devo said, and she hung up.

"OH GOD, Dixon, what have you done now?" my sister said as she looked over my shoulder at the baby sitting on my kitchen table in a fucking picnic basket that looked like it was ready to unravel and fall apart.

Bea held him as long as she could, but the wailing hadn't stopped once, and she was more than freaked out.

Abey raised her voice over the crying. "He didn't even come to the house?"

I shook my head and looked at Bea, who happened to resemble a little girl, scared and worried, like Athena when her favorite lamb sprained his knee.

"No," I said, "but he's been around. Like a goddamn skulkin' cat for weeks! I knew it. I felt it. Bea thinks he snuck in here and stole the extra key to her cabin."

"The baby was alone in there this mornin'," Bea said. "I wasn't plannin' to go inside, but I… forgot somethin', so I ran in real quick, and thank God I did. I think your brother was lurkin' around in the trees, makin' sure somebody figured out that the baby was in there, but as soon as I carried him out the door, Dixon took off in his car."

"Clay tried to get the license plate number, but it was too late." Bea shook her phone in the air. "One of the guys from the cabin crew just texted me and said it was an older, silver Honda Accord, but he has no idea what year and he didn't see the plate. He said he saw it parked off the edge of the road where not a lot of people would notice it. Hell, I didn't even notice and I drove right by it."

"*Goddamn* you, Dixon." He had the thing I'd spent the last three years mourning, and he just left it? Gave up his kid just like that? "What the fuck is wrong with him?" But I knew the answer. His and my fates had been intertwined the day Candy and Duo died, even more than they had already been.

My good knee jumped so fast beneath the table, I thought it might launch me to the moon right alongside Red Pepper the bull. "He did a good job of hidin'," I said. "And the long hair probably kept any of the guys from recognizin' him. He went to school with half of 'em."

"He doesn't look exactly… *healthy*, either," Bea added.

"Bax?"

I didn't answer Abey. I couldn't. There wasn't anything I

could say that would help the situation. No matter how hard I'd tried, I'd never been able to fix my brother. He'd been a fuck-up his whole life. Our dad did a good amount of the fuck-up himself. Dixon was confused about who he should be. He always had been, and Merv hadn't made that better by coddling him and excusing every stupid thing he ever did.

He'd been drinking heavily since he was sixteen years old, but the drugs hadn't started until after Candy and Duo died.

"Bax, look at me, please?"

When I finally did, my sister saw the anger and the devastation on my face.

"Breathe," she said.

Clenching my fists around my crutch handles, I stood and screamed, "I can't! I-I don't understand. I need to get out of here."

"Go, brother, but come back soon so we can deal with this. I'm callin' Mama."

"Fuck! Well then I really need to leave."

"C'mon," Bea said. "I'll drive."

I didn't say a word. I slapped the kitchen door open and almost fell down the stairs to get to Bea's truck because the anger and pain were bigger than my body could contain.

BEA DROVE for miles without a word. I knew she had to be confused, but she must've understood that I couldn't say the thing she wanted to hear.

An hour passed at least, and all the while I seethed and I tried so fucking hard not to cry.

The day Candy and Duo died came back to me in violent waves—the feeling of fear I'd felt when I realized I would have to raise my daughter alone, the look on Athena's face when I had to tell her that her mama wouldn't ever come home, and the loss I'd felt when I knew I'd never hold Duo, that there would be no baby boy. He was just gone, and it felt so fucking wrong.

The memories rocked me so hard I almost asked Bea to pull over so I could puke out the window.

All the sadness, the lost hope and excitement, the feeling that I'd failed my wife, my son, and my daughter all tried to strangle me. It was choking the life out of me.

Finally, Bea pulled off Highway 26, east of Moran. She parked somewhere—I had no idea where we were—and I tried not to break her passenger door when I threw it open, but the fucking crutches stopped me from running away like I wanted to.

I made my way past the tree line along the highway, banged my head against the trunk of a lone quakie, and let the crutches fall.

"Fuck!"

Bea sat next to the base of my tree on the ground and crisscrossed her legs. She must've grabbed my Bob's Feed sweatshirt off the back of my kitchen chair, because now she draped the thick, green fabric over her knees.

"I'm so fuckin' sorry," I said, "but I'm about to lose my shit."

"It's okay. I'm just here to make sure you're safe. You scream, cry, kill a tree. I don't care. Do what you need to."

When I looked down at the patience and acceptance on her face, I lost it.

Pivoting on my foot, I slid down the tree. Rough bark tore at my back but I couldn't feel the pain. All the heartache clawing at my insides made it hard to for anything else to get my attention.

"You didn't just lose Candy, did you?" Bea said softly

while I curled into her lap and cried. "That's what you've been strugglin' to tell me. You lost a child too."

She didn't need to hear me say it. The information had been written in every cell inside my body, and the pain had been etched on my face and rang in the sound of my voice all this time. I was surprised Bea hadn't guessed it sooner.

Sobs ripped from my soul and it all came out, and I clutched at her like I was chasing the wind. I couldn't hold on tight enough. Bea moved with the violence of the anguish coming out of me, like a tiny boat in the ocean, trying hard as hell not to sink in a squall. I still felt like I might be sick, and the ringing in my ears threatened to deafen me.

We stayed like that for so long that I thought time had stopped.

The rush of pain finally receded enough so I could speak. I wiped my face with the sweatshirt and tried to clear my throat. "When Candy died, sh-she was seven months pregnant with our son. That's why the third bedroom's locked. I couldn't bring myself to get rid of his stuff."

"Oh, Bax." Tears streamed down Bea's cheeks, and she cradled my face in her hands, rubbing the beard growth I hadn't yet shaved today with her thumbs. "I'm so sorry." She covered me with my sweatshirt, patting it closer to my body to hold in my body heat, trying to protect me from the wind blowing through the trees, rustling the leaves and whispering things I didn't want to hear.

"Dixon was with her in her truck that day."

"Was he... Was your brother high at the time? Was he drivin'?"

"No. Candy drove, but I suspect Dixon had been drinkin'. The drugs didn't start till after she died. He thinks it's his fault. The doctors said there was nothin' more he could've done. They just pulled up to a stop sign in the middle of town, Candy braked, and she never moved again. Dixon had to shove his leg over the console to get to the pedal to stop the truck from rollin' onto the sidewalk.

"They died almost instantly. Nobody could explain it. Duo should've been able to survive. Dixon did CPR until the paramedics got there and took over. They delivered Duo in the OR, but he was gone. Nobody knows why.

"I couldn't bring myself to hold him. They offered to let me hold him in the hospital. They said sometimes that h-helps, but he wasn't breathin', and he was too small. It didn't make sense. And now Dixon thinks he can just drop his kid on my doorstep and everything will be okay? How fucked up is that?"

"Very," Bea whispered. "Duo?"

"Baxton Brennen Lee II. Duo for short."

The thunderstorm in my head had passed. I could breathe again, but every time I drew in a new breath, all I could think about was that my son couldn't, and the air scraped and rubbed me raw inside.

"I'll never know him. I'll never know the sound of his laugh or what his eyes would look like when he's happy. I can't get past that.

"And I feel so fuckin' guilty because I never grieved Candy like this. I missed her, you know? But her death didn't eat at me the way his did. I don't know why. I can't make sense of it."

"I don't think grief is s'posed to make sense, Bax. It just is."

"Yeah, but how can I explain this to Athena? Oh shit." I sat up. "Athena. We have to go. I have to figure this out before she gets home."

"Okay." Bea stood slowly, brushing fallen leaves and dirt

off her jeans, and she jingled her keys in front of me. "You drivin' or am I?"

With a soft smile, she held out her other hand. I pulled the sweatshirt over my head and took the hand she offered, and for the first time in three years, there was no weight behind my smile. Telling her about Duo had lifted it. I knew it wasn't gone. The reprieve was temporary, and the pain still lingered behind my bones, but for right now, it let me breathe and feel and laugh.

"You better."

"I'm probably a better bet," she said, nodding. "You're right. Plus, I've run down a bison before on this road, so I know what to do if we encounter my old friend Wooly Wally."

"Wooly who?"

She pointed to the northeast, past the trees, and there in the distance in a big open field guarded by the Tetons stood a grazing herd of bison. "He's my best friend."

I looked at her, at the glittering green sparkle in her eyes when she looked back at me and her face softened in sympathy. "Have you lost your marbles?"

"I don't think so," she said, and she laughed, and the sound filled up the emptiness I felt since all the pain I'd been carrying had released, like the sound of her voice had been made just for me. Just to ease the ache that had carved out holes inside my body these last three years.

CHAPTER TWENTY-SEVEN

BEA

"DADDY?" Athena rushed to Bax when we walked in his kitchen door. "Are you okay?"

She wrapped her arms around him and tucked her head against his chest, and a memory so vivid punched me in the gut. I saw myself at Athena's age, running into my own daddy's arms after Mama died. He didn't hug me back like Bax was hugging Athena. My dad pushed me away because, unlike Bax, he'd forgotten how to love me and that I'd lost the most important person in my life too.

"Yeah, baby. I'm okay." Bax stroked his fingers through Athena's hair and closed his eyes. It looked like the contact reinforced him so that he could face this thing, and I fell in love with him even more than I already had. "I'm sorry I wasn't here when you got home. Did you have a good day at school? Wait, why are you home early?"

"Granny came to school to pick me up. But I got an A on my English paper right before the principal called me to the office," she said and smiled, and his responding smile hurt my heart. He was trying like hell to hold it together.

Bax's mom called his name from the living room. "Son?

Come in here, please." He narrowed his eyes at the sound. He wasn't happy Merv had interfered.

"I don't understand," Athena whispered. "Why'd Uncle Dixon leave his baby here? Where is he? I didn't even know he had a baby. Did you?"

"No. I found out today, just like you. I don't know where he is. Aunt Abey will look for him."

"I will," Abey said softly when she walked up behind Athena still looking up at Bax with wide, questioning eyes. Athena turned at the sound of her aunt's voice, and gently, Abey swept Athena's hair off her shoulder and let it fall down her back. "But I don't know that I'll find him."

"C'mon," Bax said, and he looked at Athena and then me. He flexed his fingers away from his crutch handle, like he wanted to hold my hand.

I nodded and followed him, and we all walked into the living room to see Merv holding the sleeping baby in Bax's recliner. She'd already fallen in love with the kid. That was clear as she gazed down at him with wonder.

She smiled at Stu sleeping in her arms. "He has my eyes."

Bax looked at his sister. "What do we do?"

"I'm not sure there's a lot we can do, Bax. I've put a call into child services just to have somebody in the loop, but Dixon must've done some research because everything seems to be in order." Abey walked to the coffee table and lifted an unfolded piece of paper, and I saw the raised notary seal from where I stood clear across the room.

"We'll do a DNA test just to be sure," Abey said, "but he's ours. I know he is. Doctor Whitley will come to check Stu over, make sure he's healthy, and he'll take a swab so we can do the test. Given his history, we'll need to take him to a pediatrician, to check for any lastin' effects from the"—Abey glanced quickly at Athena and then her mom—"the drugs."

"I think I need to lie down," Bax said when he swayed on his feet, but he pushed into his crutches to steady himself.

"Go," his mom said. "Get some rest. I'll be here with Stuey."

Abey nodded. She'd stay too.

Bax sighed heavily, but he asked, "Athena, are you okay?"

"Yeah," she said. "I'm fine, Daddy. I still don't understand, but I'm okay."

Holding his crutch under his arm, he reached his hand out to her. She took it and squeezed, and then she sat at the end of the couch closest to Merv, draped herself over the arm, and became transfixed with the baby still sleeping peacefully in her grandma's arms.

Bax looked at me. "Will you come with me?"

"Of course."

Merv didn't bat an eye this time. She couldn't see or hear anything besides her grandson.

"HOW THE HELL am I gonna explain to Athena that the reason her uncle dumped his kid on us is that he feels like it's his fault her mama and brother died?"

I didn't have a good answer for that, so I said nothing.

We'd made our way upstairs, and I helped Bax out of his sweatshirt and T-shirt because they had been covered in dirt and leaf debris still. I grabbed a clean white tee from his drawer, and now we lay on his bed, side by side on top of the covers, staring at the ceiling.

I was so fucking far out of my depth. I had no clue what to say or do.

I had zero experience with a big family. And even less with babies.

And Bax and I weren't a couple. Not a solid one. We hadn't talked about kids, other than Athena.

Now that I knew about Duo, I realized Bax had been avoiding the subject completely. Everything made sense now; he'd opened up to me, but I'd still known something was missing. And now I knew what it was.

What exactly did he want me to do in this situation? But I wasn't sure he had the answer to that question either.

I wanted to be with Bax like I couldn't remember ever wanting anyone, but I wouldn't give up my job for a man. I couldn't. Not again. And now there was a baby?

Oh God. How had I ended up here?

Oh yeah, that's right. You're in this mess because of your damn hormones, you idiot. You should've stayed at the cabin and braved the goddamn bears by yourself.

"I think Athena's old enough to understand drug addiction," Bax said. "They talk to the kids about it at school, and she and I have talked about her uncle. And she can understand abandonment, but the rest will break her heart. I can't tell her that."

Bax grew quiet. When I turned on my side and looked at him, I saw the war going on inside his head. I could only imagine the thoughts fighting for dominance up there.

My own thoughts weren't much calmer.

Abandonment wasn't something felt only by people who'd been left on purpose. I felt it every day after Mama passed. I'd screamed and cried and begged God to tell me why she'd left me. Why he'd taken her. And after my dad, it got worse, which was probably the reason I'd ended up married to someone I'd never really loved. Not like I loved Bax.

"What're you thinkin'?" he whispered.

"Just thinkin' about my parents."

"I'm sorry you're in the middle of this," he said, and he rolled onto his side and faced me.

"Oh, it's… It's fine."

His laugh lacked humor. "You wanna run, don't you? Go back to Sheridan as fast as you can?"

My mouth popped open to respond to his question, but nothing came out.

The situation was fucked up, that was for sure, but I didn't want to run away. When I tried to picture getting in my truck and leaving, a sickening feeling filled my body. I couldn't leave Bax and Athena. Not like this.

It hurt to even think about.

Still wrapped up in thought, Bax rolled onto his back again. "Shit. Brand. Somebody needs to call him."

"I will," I said. It seemed I needed to talk to my boss too.

"Thank you. I'll call him soon, but I… I dunno what to tell him right now."

"It's okay. I'll call him now."

Bax nodded, but he didn't say anything more, and I got up and left the room quietly. Downstairs, Merv and Athena were still enamored with Stu. They both stared at him, but he hadn't moved since Bax and I had gone upstairs.

As I walked into the kitchen and headed toward the door, Abey stood and followed. "You okay?" she asked.

I turned to face her. "Me? Oh yeah, I'm…"

"This is a lot for anybody, but you and Bax are new. Nobody would blame you if you wanted to wipe your hands of us."

"I don't. I don't know what I want, but I can't leave them."

"You love them"—she tipped her head to the side, trying to read me—"don't you? Both of them."

I nodded, and tears filled my eyes, but I couldn't say the words out loud.

I'd cry like Stu if I did.

<hr>

CLAY HAD TEXTED that he'd sent everyone home early but promised a full day's pay. I knew Brand would be fine with it as soon as I told him what was going on.

I passed Merv's finished blue house as I drove back to my cabin. The back door was still open when I got there, but it didn't look like anyone else had been inside, and still no bears.

I closed and locked the door, jacked up the thermostat, dropped my keys on the kitchen table, then fell onto the loveseat in the living room. And then I called Brand.

"A baby?" he said. "Whose baby?"

"Your brother's."

"Bax doesn't have a baby."

"It seems Dixon does."

"Fuck."

"Yeah. That's pretty much what Bax and Abey said too."

"*Fuck*," he said again, and a garbled static noise filled my ear. I could picture him falling into his desk chair and swiping his hand over his face. "I can't believe Dixon did this. I'm comin' home."

"You can't leave, Brand."

"Fuck this goddamn court case."

"Just stay in Sheridan for now. There's nothin' you can do here. Bax is hurtin', but he's handlin' it. How's the case goin'?"

He sighed. "It's almost done. A couple more days I think, and I can come home. I should already be there. If I'd gotten off my ass and made the move, I probably would be. I wanna talk to you about that soon."

"Okay," I said, but panic began to build in my stomach. It worked its way up my throat until I thought it would choke me.

"You haven't checked in about the builds lately," Brand said. "Everything goin' alright?"

"Y-yeah. We're gettin' down to the wire, but everything's on track. The last two houses are done."

"Good. Thanks again for doin' this for my family."

I didn't respond because now I was imagining what would happen when my job was finished. I didn't like the images I'd conjured up, flying around in my head like a swarm of angry bees.

Every single one had me leaving soon. Winter would hit. Snow would fall, and I'd leave for home. But where was that exactly? Because when I pictured rolling back into Sheridan alone in my truck, pain cracked through my chest like someone had punched it into me.

But if Brand was really planning to move headquarters… What would that mean for me?

"Sweetie?"

"Mm?"

"What aren't you sayin'? I've known you two years and you've never failed to tell me exactly how you felt about a situation, but you're awfully quiet now."

"I—"

What could I say? Not one thing that had happened in the last few weeks made any sense to me.

"Spit it out, Sweetie. Just say whatever it is."

"I-I think I'm in love with your brother."

Brand cracked a laugh in my ear. "Oh, is that all?"

"'Is that all?'" I nearly screeched. "That's what you have to say to me right now?"

"*There's* the Sweetie I know. And yes, that's all I have to say. I saw it comin' a mile away. Bax has had his eye on you since the moment he met you. Why do you think he got so drunk that night we all played poker?"

I stammered, "Uh, well I, I mean… Huh?"

"When I put my big, drunk brother to bed, all he could talk about was how beautiful he thought you were, and how guilty he felt for feelin' that way. So maybe he's finally figured out he has nothin' to feel guilty about?"

"Maybe," I said. "I'm not sure. We haven't actually talked about it. Not really."

"Well, my friend, it's probably best now you do."

CHAPTER TWENTY-EIGHT

BAX

"DADDY, CAN WE KEEP HIM?"

Athena jumped up from the couch when I came down the stairs. I was so exhausted, I actually thought for two seconds about sliding down on my ass. Bea hadn't come back yet, and I could only imagine what Brand had to say when she told him everything that had happened.

"Athena," I warned. She couldn't know what this was doing to me. Things always looked so simple in her eyes.

Merv looked up at me when she heard the tone of my voice.

Athena ignored it and insisted, "Stu needs a home, Daddy. If Uncle Dixon isn't comin' back, it's up to us."

"Apparently, *my* house ain't an option," Merv muttered bitterly.

"Mama, don't you start. This has nothin' to do with you. And the next time you decide to pull my daughter out of school, you had better call me first."

"She needed to be here. This involves the whole family, and it has everything to do with me," she yelled in a whisper, trying not to wake the baby, but he startled in her arms. "He's *my* grandson!"

The poor thing probably hadn't had a full belly in a long time, maybe never, and now that he did, he slept like the d—

"Mama, I don't have any say in the matter. It's not up to me. We'll have to hire a lawyer to figure it all out, but for now, we're gonna follow Dixon's instructions to the letter so it doesn't come back to bite us in the ass later. You hear me?"

"Fine."

"So we're keepin' him?" Athena asked. God, there was so much hope in her voice.

"For now," I answered. "But Athena, I can't be his dad. You know that, right?"

"Why can't you?"

"I… I just can't."

"So you want him to go to people we don't even know?" Athena argued. She planted her hands on her hips. "Your answer's not good enough. Make me understand, Daddy." She plopped back down onto the couch, her irritation with me giving her attitude. "'Cause right now, I don't."

"Me neither," Merv said. She stared me down but pushed with her shoes on the floor, rocking gently in my chair, and the baby settled. "You've been lost for three years, but here's a map right here." She looked at the baby and lifted him up, like an offer at some altar.

"No," I said. "Don't you dare offer that to me. I didn't deserve it the first time and look what happened. Besides, he's not mine. I can't."

"Son—"

"*Goddammit*, Mama, I said no. I can't fuckin' do it! He's not my kid. He can't replace what we've lost. I've already let Athena down. Don't make me let him down too."

"Daddy," Athena said softly, "you didn't let me down. You've been grievin'. You were sad."

"So were you, and I left you alone with this." I sat next to her on the couch and set my crutches to the side. "I never talk about your mama. I never let you talk about her. I don't deserve you either."

"Yes you do! And you're talkin' about Mama now. Just the other day, you told me I looked like her. But it's not Mama's memory I'm worried about. I know it makes you sad that we lost the baby, but Daddy, he never got to be born. If *we* don't talk about him, who will remember him?"

"What is there to remember, Athena? We didn't know him. I never got to hold him. I don't even know what his voice sounded like."

Sobs worked themselves up behind my heart. I'd never said these words to Athena, and it hurt more than I expected. I curled my shoulders to keep the anguish trapped inside me, still trying to protect my little girl from all the shit in my head.

I was trying to hold onto my sadness so it couldn't leave the same way the people I loved had.

"You're right," Athena said, and she slid off the couch and knelt in front of me. She reached out and held my face between her hands, making me look up. "But I remember how he made you smile and laugh when he'd kick Mama's tummy. I remember the look on your face the day you guys told me I was gonna be a big sister. You were so proud. You had so much love inside you, Daddy. Where'd it go?"

I held her face between my hands too. "Baby, it's not gone. It didn't go anywhere, it's just that it hurts. I've only got room in here for you." Pulling her hand from my face, I placed it over my heart. "I can't love that baby. If somethin' happened to any of you, I don't think I could handle that. And what if someone comes to take him away? We don't even know if he's really our family."

"Daddy," Athena said quietly, "he is. Just look at him. He looks just like Uncle Dixon. He looks just like *you*. He's ours."

"She's right," Mama said.

"There's love all around you," Athena said softly, pleading with me now. "Bea loves you too. All you have to do is open your eyes and take it, and we can be a family again."

When I pictured it, when I saw all that love she talked about, I thought I might die on the spot. My heart beat so fast. Bile rose up the back of my throat, and all those happy imaginings faded quickly because all I could see was the broken man left in the aftermath when it all got ripped away.

I dropped my hands. "No!"

CHAPTER TWENTY-NINE

BEA

"WILL YOU DRIVE ME SOMEWHERE?" Athena asked when I pulled up in front of Bax's house and found her sitting on the porch stairs in the sunshine, with red, swollen eyes.

"Sure."

"Now?"

"Should we let your dad know—"

She sighed. "He doesn't care right now."

Merv poked her head out the kitchen door, her shrewd eyes locking on mine. "Can you come in here, please?"

Standing in front of her in Bax's kitchen, I felt like an imposter, like I didn't belong anywhere near this house. Bax was nowhere to be found, but Merv was front and center, holding the Lee family together by a flimsy thread.

Did she have any clue how deeply I'd fallen for her son and granddaughter?

I couldn't have cared less what she thought about my job or my ability to do it well, but the thought of disappointing her if I walked away from Bax and Athena now bit at my confidence like hungry piranhas in some jungle river.

"It's okay," she said, still holding the baby and rocking

him gently in her arms while she bottle fed him. "Please get Athena out of here for a while. She needs a break."

The tables had turned, though, because now Merv was asking something of me, begging really. She was just as confused and worried as Bax, but now she wanted my help.

"Bax is asleep upstairs. He needed some time, too, and they're just buttin' heads anyway. She'll probably want to visit her mama's grave. Do you know where the cemetery is?"

"No."

"Athena does. She can give you directions."

I nodded. "Okay."

"Thank you, Bea. Thanks for lookin' out for my family."

Smiling, I patted Stu's bare foot sticking out of his blanket. At least one good thing had come from all this pain and confusion. I wouldn't make the mistake of thinking Merv and I were friends now, but maybe we understood each other a little better.

Back on the porch, I waved my arm, dangling my keys in my other hand. "C'mon, Athena."

She climbed into my truck and snapped her seatbelt in place, and as I shut her door and walked around to my side, I felt her sadness and hopelessness like it was a heavy mist surrounding us.

"Where would you like to go?"

"The cemetery."

"Okay. Can you show me where it is?"

"Yeah," she said. "It's on the other side of town, out past the Duck & Bowl."

"What is a Duck & Bowl?"

"It's a bowlin' alley with ducks," she said, like that made it all make sense.

"Oh. Sure. 'Course it is."

As I drove, Athena was quiet. Unnervingly so, but I knew, like me, she'd talk when she was ready.

"I'm here," I said quietly, "if you wanna talk."

She nodded as she stared, unseeing, out her window, and we made our way through her hometown.

Wisper, Wyoming was a cute little place. Every time I'd driven through, it felt almost like I'd stepped back in time. There were maybe only five or six stoplights lining the main drag, and lots of quaint avenues and lanes lined with big trees, old cottages, and newer log cabin-style homes. The streets seemed familiar with names like Lincoln, Washington, and Main, and people walked and strolled down every one of them, despite the growing cold in the air.

We drove by a busy diner, where a line formed at the door and wound halfway down the block. We passed the library and a charming bookshop, Your Local Bookie, which I knew was owned and run by Rye's girlfriend, Aubrey. And we passed Devo's community center, Ace's House, a big, brick, three-story building set in the middle of town.

The afternoon was sunny but crisp, and everywhere I looked, I saw happiness and the world passing us by.

Athena led where she wanted to go, and when we passed through the cemetery's gates, the snow-capped mountains loomed around us like wardens sent to protect all the secrets buried beneath the ground.

"Park right here."

Pulling to the side of the gravel lane, I listened to the gravel pop and crackle beneath my tires as I slowed, and Athena pushed open her door with great effort when I parked.

Sadness slowed her movements and made them heavy, and I watched as it crossed over her face. I wouldn't cry for her. Not in front of her, but holding back tears was proving to be harder than I'd imagined it would, and the lump in the back of my throat was making it hard for me to swallow.

I never went to the cemetery back home, not since my dad's funeral. I had to pass it nearly every day on my way to work or the grocery store, but I'd always forced my eyes to stay on the road. I hadn't thought there could be anything good to come from looking back.

I followed Athena silently as she walked along the edge of the cemetery until she cut across the still-green grass and stood in front of a large headstone lying flat in the ground.

"Here they are." She sat next to it and looked back at me, reaching to touch the rectangular stone with the soft tips of her fingers. "C'mon. I wanna introduce you."

"Oh. Um. Okay."

"Granny brings me out here sometimes. And sometimes Aunt Abey takes me for milkshakes after school. We stop at the Dairy Dream on our way here. I guess she knows sometimes a girl needs her mama.

"I know it's dumb, but sometimes I feel jealous of my brother, 'cause he gets to be with Mama every day."

When I sat next to her, Athena brushed dried, fallen leaves off the stone. "This is my mama, Candy Adela Lee." Beneath Candy's name, I saw Duo's: Baxton Brennen Lee II. "And this is my little brother. Daddy was gonna call him—"

"Duo."

She looked at me. "He told you?"

"Earlier today," I said. "Yeah, he did."

"I think he loves you, Bea."

"Athena, I-I don't know if this is the right place to—"

"It's fine," she said. "My mama knows you're here. She watches over me, and I think she's been watchin' over Stuey too. I think she brought you into our lives, and I think she wants us to be a family."

Whoa.

"I know. You think it's too soon. You're not sure. You live far away. Blah, blah, blah."

Yeah, well, that about summed it up.

She stared straight into my eyes, looking for answers from me. "But you love him too, don't you? You love my daddy?"

I wasn't sure if I should tell her. I hadn't even told Bax I loved him yet. I wasn't sure if I ever would. Was he anywhere near ready to hear it? But I came to the decision that Athena needed the truth. As someone who was already fully aware I loved her dad, she deserved at least that from me.

"I do."

She nodded. "I knew it."

"But Athena, it's not so easy as one, two, three. You know that, right? Just 'cause two people have feelings for each other, it doesn't mean they can be together. Live together. Be... a family."

"I know." She sighed. "But why not?"

"I don't know the first thing about raisin' kids," I said, dipping my head and trying to hold her gaze. Trying to get her to hear the reality coming out of my mouth. "And your dad has his hands full now. The baby could change a lot for him. For you both."

"You're right," she said. "So why not change everything all at once? Why not grab hold of this gift, this happiness? Why not embrace it all?"

"It's not that easy."

"Why not?" She plucked at the grass next to the grave and looked away. "I don't understand."

"Well, for one thing—and it's a pretty important thing—I live seven hours away from here. My job is in Sheridan."

"Yeah, but Uncle Brand said he wants to bring Lee

Construction here. Or maybe he'll start up a second company. I dunno, but he could, and you could work there. Or you could work at the farm with us."

"I love my job. I'm really good at it. I don't wanna give it up."

"Okay, then I'll just have to convince Uncle Brand to move home. He'll listen to me."

"And what if your uncle Dixon comes back and wants to take Stu with him?"

"Well, then at least I'd still have you and Daddy."

"Oh, sweet girl, you don't really know me. Your dad barely knows me. How do you know you want me?"

She turned, and tears streaked down her face. "Because I just do! Because I love you, and my daddy loves you. Why won't you love us back?"

She stood and stormed away, and I rushed to follow.

"Why can't anybody love anybody around here? I'm sick of it!"

"Athena, wait!"

"No! I wanna go home."

She stomped her feet into the grass, and I nearly tripped on it and fell on my face, but I used the top of a standing headstone to catch myself and pushed to gain back momentum, apologizing to the unknown dearly departed in my head.

Finally, I caught up to her back at my truck and stopped her from yanking open her door with my hand over hers. "Athena, please just listen."

"I don't want to." She pulled her hand away from mine, refusing to look at me. "I want to go home."

This was going to take some heavy emoting, something I'd practically sworn never to do again.

Here goes nothing.

"I lost my mama when I was your age."

That stopped her, and she turned to face me.

"And I lost my daddy when I was nineteen."

"You did?" she asked, flicking away the tears beneath her blue eyes with two fingers. She looked so much like her dad that my heart squeezed in on itself inside my chest.

I nodded.

"So then, you get it. All I want is a family. Why's that so bad?"

"It's not bad at all," I told her, tucking pieces of her messy hair behind her ear, "but it's harder than you think."

"So? Hard doesn't mean impossible."

"You're right," I said. "It doesn't. Here, sit down."

Pulling open her door, I waited for her to get in. When she did and she turned toward me, I tried to explain.

"When my mama died, it broke my daddy in ways I didn't understand back then. I think I do now. I see the same things in your dad. My daddy loved my mama with all his heart, and I think yours did too."

"Yeah, he did."

"Okay, so when a person is lucky enough to have love like that and then they lose it, it's hard to imagine ever lovin' someone else. And I can't even imagine losin' a child."

"Did your dad ever fall in love again?"

"No," I said, shaking my head. "He wasn't ready. Some people might never be ready."

"But my daddy *already* loves you."

"You can't know that. *I* don't even know that."

"But I *do* know. Haven't you seen the way he looks at you? Haven't you noticed that he smiles when you're around? He laughs. He eats more. He sleeps better. Everything's better when you're around."

"You feel like it's up to you, don't you? That you have to keep watch over your dad, that you have to take care of him?"

She nodded. "It's my job. At the funeral after Mama died, I promised her I would."

God, that broke my heart. Athena and I had more in common than I wanted to admit.

"I know it feels that way, baby, but it's not. It's not up to you. You're just a kid. It's not meant to be your responsibility."

"I'm not a k—"

"You are," I interrupted, lifting and holding her hands in mine. "You're not little anymore, but you're a kid, and it's not your job to make sure the adults around you are happy."

"Then whose job is it?"

"It's theirs."

"And if they don't *do* their jobs?"

"Then it doesn't get done," I said, "but that doesn't mean it falls on you. Do you think your dad would like to know that you think his happiness is your responsibility? Do you think he wants that for you? It's a really big job."

"No," she whispered. "He probably wouldn't."

"You can't just add a little of this and a little of that to make a person happy. They have to find and accept happiness for themselves."

She narrowed her eyes and speared me with them. "So if you know this, then why haven't you accepted it for yourself?"

CHAPTER THIRTY

BAX

I SPENT most of the afternoon and evening in my room, working hard not to scream.

Images of Dixon's baby kept flashing like neon lights in my head, and they warred with the image of Duo I'd conjured up and held tucked beneath my ribcage, behind my heart for three years.

It wasn't the same goddamn kid! Had everybody forgotten that?

I fell in and out of sleep and dreams until I succumbed to exhaustion. And Bea never came back after she went to her cabin to call Brand. Where the hell was she? Maybe she decided to run after all. I couldn't blame her if she had.

But when she was by my side, the strength I felt allowed me to act like a semi-normal adult again, and when she was gone, I felt like the same sorry guy I'd been the last few years. The shit dad, terrible son, brother, and husband. I felt like a failure, but how did that make sense? My wife and child died, but it wasn't my doing. How had I managed to make it my fault?

Why had I done that to myself?

And just to fuck me up even further, Candy was there again in my dreams, screwing up the deepest sleep I'd had in forever.

"You like that show I told you about?" she asked.

It was clear this was a dream because the dead mother of my children was dressed in flowing robes. I felt no wind, but the yellow thing billowed out behind her in the bedroom we used to share, and it fluttered like she stood on the tallest mountain peak.

She almost glowed, she was so bright with love. Her light reminded me of that song from the '80s about wearing sunglasses at night. Candy loved '80s music. We used to argue about it 'cause I could never stand it, but she hated country.

"Yeah, I like Bea." I answered her question directly 'cause I was damn tired of talking in metaphors. "I love her."

Candy nodded. She closed her eyes and smiled, like it was the answer she'd been looking for all along.

"It's a good show."

"And the baby?" I asked. What was her answer for him?

Candy shrugged, and she lifted her arms as if she wanted to give me something, but her hands were empty. "Watched over him as long as I could."

Watched over him… like a guardian?

The delicate color of her skin began to fade, but somehow I knew this would be the last time she'd come to me in my dreams.

This was goodbye, and it was overdue.

"Thank you, Candy. I love you. I always will, but it's time for me to move on now."

Half solid, half see-through, she stopped in the middle of her disappearing act. "The hard road is behind you, Bax. Take care of them and yourself and follow a new one now."

And then she was gone.

BEA WOKE me gently with her warm hand on my shoulder.

"The doctor was here," she said as I opened my eyes.

The baby cooed behind me, and when I flipped on my lamp and rolled over, he lay between us, sleeping soundly in the middle of my bed as Bea sat on the opposite edge.

Shit. I slept through that? "What'd Dr. Whitley say?"

"Stu's okay. Everything's fine, but he wants Stu to see a special pediatrician in Jackson just to be safe."

The relief was overwhelming.

"I'm sorry," I whispered, looking hard into Bea's bright eyes. God, did she have any idea how beautiful she was or how hard I'd fallen for her in less time than it took for my heart to beat?

"Bax, stop apologizin'. You didn't do anything wrong."

"I know," I said, "but I'm about to."

"Huh?"

"I love you."

Her sharp intake of breath told me she'd heard me loud and clear, even though my voice wasn't any stronger than a breeze.

"I love you, and I know it's fast. I know this is all so fucked up, but you and Athena are the only good things for me in this world right now. I'm just gonna say what we've both been thinkin' about: don't go. Don't leave when the cabins are done.

"I'm part of a package deal. I know that. You didn't ask for that, and maybe right now, it doesn't look all that attractive to you, but there's a beautiful life here for you if you want it."

She stilled and watched as I smoothed my hand over Stu's foot and held it between my fingers, feeling its plump warmth beneath the thin blanket tucked around him. I hadn't made a conscious decision to touch him; it was some kind of automatic compulsion to connect with him, to make sure he was breathing and content.

But once I had, it wasn't enough. I sat up and scooped him into my arms, holding him to my chest below my heart so he could feel it beating, so he would feel that there was love in the world for him despite the fact that his parents had abandoned him.

Bea watched as tears rolled down my cheeks, splashing onto Stu's blanket.

"I love you too," she said. "I tried not to—"

Her words stuck in her throat as I lifted the baby and kissed his warm cheek, and I curled him even closer, trying not to break him or crush him between my arms. He smelled so good, clean and sweet and milky. His hair, a light brown color, was as soft as down, and I wondered what color it would be when he was ten. Dixon had brown hair like mine, but I had no clue what Stu's mama looked like.

Holding him eased something inside me. I knew it shouldn't, but it did.

Suddenly, Bea's arms were wrapped around me and the baby both. She cried with me.

"I love you too, Bax," she whispered. "I tried not to, but the way you love Athena, the way I can already tell you love this baby, that you'd do anything for them? I really never had a choice in the matter."

"Yeah?"

"Yes." She kissed my cheek. "I love you. I don't care if it's too soon. I don't know what it means." She held me tighter. "I have no idea what to do now, but Athena's right. It's pretty simple."

When she pulled away, I smiled. Feeling her love, hearing her say she loved me too allowed possibilities to bloom inside my head, possibilities of things I never thought I'd feel or have again.

"You'll stay? You'll figure this out with me?"

She straightened and nodded, wiping her tears away with soft brushes of her fingertips. "There's nowhere else on this earth I'd rather be. We'll figure it out."

"Come to me." I reached for her with one hand. She leaned in again and kissed me softly. "Things have definitely taken a turn. It wasn't even four weeks ago when you showed up in the dark, and I concocted plans to fuck the daylights out of you."

Embarrassment and shock showed on her face, and she swatted my arm. "Bax!"

I chuckled, drying the tears under my eyes with the neck of my T-shirt. "And now there's a baby, and my impossible mother downstairs, and a whole lot of complicated history. You sure you're up for this?"

"I-I think so?" She sighed. "I always wanted to be a mom, but at my age and with my own history, I never thought I'd get the chance. I mean, not that I'm saying I'm anybody's m—"

"That's what I'm askin'," I said, interrupting her and the doubt I heard in her voice. "I know we have a long way to go with all of this." I lifted the baby gently, and he startled, but his arms were tucked tightly to his chest inside the blanket, so he snuggled back in and settled. "But wherever the road leads us, I want you with me."

"And *you're* sure?" she asked. "You've lost so much. I can't replace that. I can't replace your w—"

Smoothing the hair away from her mouth, wet from her tears, I tucked it behind her ear. "I don't want you to replace Candy. I'm not tryin' to get back what I lost." Holding her chin in my hand, I brought her lips to mine and kissed her. "There's so much life left to live, and I'm finally excited to live it. With you. *You*, Beatrice Baker, my sweetheart. My friend. My love.

"I'll always love Candy. How could I not? She gave me Athena. But she gave me more than our beautiful daughter. She gave me the permission I thought I needed to move on."

Bea's eyebrows lifted, and her green eyes twinkled beneath. "More woo-woo?"

"Yeah," I said and laughed. "But it turns out, her permission wasn't what I needed."

"No? What did you need?"

"I just needed you."

A smile broke across her face, like the sun shining through heavy rain clouds, but then someone knocked on my bedroom door. It opened a few inches and Rye's head popped into my room. I had no idea when he'd arrived or how much he knew, but it made sense for him to be with my family. He'd been a better brother to me than Dixon had in a long time.

"Come in," I said, holding Bea tight to my side, both of us careful not to wake the baby.

"So," Rye hedged, pushing the door open wider and tucking his hands into his front pockets awkwardly, which wasn't like him at all. Where was my brash, can't-keep-his-mouth-shut loud-mouth best friend? "Uh, Merv wants me to ask you where the key to the extra bedroom is. She says we need to fix up a place for little Stuey to sleep." He winced 'cause he knew in the past the unoccupied third bedroom had been a tough subject for me. "I can pop the hinges if you don't know where it is."

As soon as I saw Stu, I'd known this was coming. And even before that, everything in my life had been building toward me and Bea finding and loving each other.

Taking a deep breath, I let the acceptance I now felt about my past settle inside my chest. It still hurt. I couldn't lie about that, but it had come time for me to live again.

Kissing Bea one more time quickly, I handed the baby to her, and she eased back against my headboard as I hobbled to my dresser with one crutch and slid open the top drawer. I pulled the single key from underneath a rolled-together pair of socks. "Here."

"Thanks, buddy," Rye said, opening the door wider and walking forward, and he took the key from my hand.

"Just, all I ask is that y'all let me take my time with it?"

"'Course." Rye nodded and gripped my shoulder "I got you, man," he said, and he left my room.

I looked back at Bea and smiled, testing the tentative feeling of happiness starting to finally take root inside me. Handing over the key hadn't been as hard as I'd thought.

"Do you mind if I go see?" she asked. "Show Stuey his room?"

"Oh God, not you too." I groaned. "We really need to figure out a different name for this kid. Stuey makes me think of that cartoon, *Family Guy*."

Bea grinned. "I know, right?"

I tried to think back. Was that where my brother had gotten the name? I couldn't remember if Dixon had ever watched the show, but it would've made sense. Brand had been named after a character from *The Goonies*. Although, I was pretty sure Dixon had spelled Stu's name wrong if that was the case.

But when I tried to think of a different name for the baby, it occurred to me that I'd be stealing from Stuart the only thing his father had given him.

But that wasn't true at all, was it? Dixon had given his son a chance. A better one than he would've had if he'd been raised by his parents.

I sighed, finally seeing Dixon's gift for what he was—Stuey was a chance. A chance for my whole family. I could already feel Stu stitching the sorry lot of us back together, patching us up and offering a little more hope for the future. And hope was the only thing making me desperate for Dixon to sort his shit out and get back here, clean and healthy so he could accept some love for himself.

"No, sweetheart," I said, refocusing on Bea. "I don't mind. Go ahead."

"You sure? If you're not ready—"

"I'm ready, Bea. Athena was right. If I don't remember Duo, who will? Maybe Stu can help us carry Duo's memory into the future. It's not right for me to forget him just 'cause the loss hurts. I don't *want* to forget him, and I want him to be proud of me."

Bea rose easily from the bed, walked to me, and tucked herself and the baby in the crook of my open arm. I pressed my lips to the tops of their heads, and Bea reached up on her tiptoes to place a soft kiss beneath my jaw. "I love you," she said, and then they left me alone in my room.

I heard Stu's new bedroom door squeak open in the hall when Rye unlocked it, and then Athena's voice in there with Rye and Bea. "Ooo! Look at that. I remember when my mama bought that. Hey! That used to be *my* stuffed tiger. I wondered where she went."

The creaky floorboard at the top of the stairs squeaked,

and Merv joined everybody. "I made that blanket," she said. "Crocheted it myself when Athena was born."

I found myself moving closer to my bedroom door. It wasn't lost on me that I'd locked Athena's childhood away when I locked the memory of Duo in the bedroom he never got the chance to fall asleep in. *Damn.* I was sorry about that. What had she missed because of my refusal to face the pain?

That realization cemented the decision for me, and when I finally made my way to the third bedroom and stood on the threshold, holding myself up with the crutches beneath my arms, everyone turned to look at me.

Soft light from a standing lamp in the corner flooded the ceiling, painting the nursery with warmth and illuminating my past and a path to my future.

I nodded to the Wyoming wildlife mobile hanging over the plain birch crib I still remembered building. The little stuffed bear, moose, bison, and wolf dangled motionlessly from a hook in the ceiling. "Your mama made that herself," I told Athena. "Stuffed the animals with the filling from an old couch pillow."

"She did?" Athena asked, wonder in her eyes.

"Yeah." I moved into the room slowly and stood next to the crib. "She worked on it at night, after you'd gone to bed while we watched—" I laughed as a realization hit me. *No shit? Really?*

"What did you watch with Mama, Daddy?"

Dumbfounded and believing in woo-woo more every second, I replied, "*Sons of Anarchy.*"

"Good fuckin' show," Rye said, nodding.

"Watch your mouth," Merv scolded. "There's babies here."

Athena rolled her eyes. "Granny, I am *not* a baby."

Bea tried to hide her laugh, and Rye mumbled, "Yes,

ma'am." But then he chuckled and wrapped his arm around Merv's shoulders.

I set a crutch against the side of the crib and reached for Athena, and she tucked herself beneath my arm. Bea moved closer, still holding the baby, so I leaned on Athena and held my other arm out for Bea. Stuey squeaked and opened his eyes while Bea hugged my side.

The women in my life held me up, and Merv smiled a true, genuine smile for the first time in a long time.

"Life goes on," she said. "How it should."

EPILOGUE

BEA

WITH MY FACE raised to the spring sun, I sat next to a grave, feeling the cemetery's cold grass beneath my butt, dampening the ass of my jeans.

My boss had officially decided to move Lee Construction down to Wisper, and I had been appointed to lead the bunkhouse project starting next week, which meant I was free to move in with Bax.

Brand hadn't cared at all that I loved Bax. In fact, Brand had seemed more than happy about his brother finding love again.

It had felt weird not working my normal job over the holidays and early spring, but I'd been swept up into family life, and I helped out on the ranch a lot. It kept me busy, but I was excited to get my hands on some raw lumber again and a new group of men I could boss around.

Brand wasn't planning to move home permanently until later in the fall, but I'd driven back to Sheridan as soon as the cabins were finished, with Athena, Stu, and Bax in tow, but only to retrieve all my stuff from my studio.

Athena had ridden in the front of Bax's truck with me so she could be my navigator, while Bax got stuck in the back seat, trying to entertain Stu for seven hours. It took more like ten 'cause that baby had no interest in being strapped into a car seat for extended periods of time. He wanted out to explore. Just like Athena, Stuart was a road trip too.

Relocating my entire life had been another whirlwind. A good whirlwind, but a whirlwind all the same, and some days, Bax's stubborn streak drove me up a wall. Athena took after her dad in that regard, so when one of them pushed me to a limit I'd never even known I had, which was kind of often, I'd drive over to the cemetery and hash it out with Candy and Duo.

Bax and Athena had both gotten their stubbornness from Merv, and since she'd moved into her new house, which was, like, a country block away, she could be a little… over the top. But she'd backed off as much as I could've expected her to. She saw that I loved her family just as hard as she did, and now that she had Stu to fawn over, her reality was a little sweeter than her usual salt.

Bax said he didn't feel Candy and Duo's presence anymore. He was confident Candy had moved on. She didn't linger in his dreams anymore, but I wasn't so sure.

I saw Candy every day in the curve of Athena's smile, her hair, and in the kindness she displayed toward every living being.

Candy lived on in the little ways Bax showed his love: the wildflowers he picked for me and left in a Mason jar next to my side of the bed, the spicy little drawings he'd leave in my underwear drawer of the two of us locked together, making love with the moon lighting us in its glow through our bedroom window.

But mostly I knew Candy was still around because Bax didn't make a decision without asking me first. He always wanted to know what I thought or how I might tackle a problem. He sought my opinion in all things, and I felt Candy's love then.

And it was hard not to see Duo in Stu. Or at least I imagined Duo would've been like Stu. I still couldn't believe everyone had agreed to keep the name. But Bax had said that Stu's daddy had given him his name, so if it was the only thing Stu would have of his dad, we were going to honor it. But I'd looked it up, and Dixon had been wrong about the meaning of Stu's name. The name Stuart didn't mean that *he* had a guardian looking out for him; it meant that he *was* the guardian, the steward of a family. And it was fitting, because Stu had reconnected the Lees easily.

Dixon was in the wind. No one had heard from him. Abey thought he might be in California for a while, and then the Portland, Oregon area. She'd been searching, but so far to no avail.

Dixon's absence in the Lee family's lives and the way it made them all ache was plain to see, but they never said a word of it around Stu. He was only ten months old, so he wouldn't have understood, but it was an unspoken rule.

Instead, we filled Stu's days with laughter and snuggles, kisses and hours spent playing in the dirt, taking him for rides in the skid steer, and chasing all the farm animals he could ever want to pet.

Anyone looking in from the outside thought Bax was Stu's bio dad. They looked so much alike, the color of their hair and eyes, and the way Stu laughed when Bax did something silly or when he'd toss Stu in the air, catch him, and blow wet raspberries on his pudgy, round belly, like Bax was the most important person in Stu's life. In that baby's eyes, Bax was everything.

He was in my eyes too.

And already, people mistook me for Stu's mama. We still had no idea who his birth mother was really, besides that her name was Kellie Gale. Kel. Abey had found her expired driver's license photo and a mugshot from when she was arrested two years ago for driving under the influence in Omaha, Nebraska. Somehow, Dixon had come up with the money for her bail. It was the only thread connecting Dixon and Kellie that Abey had been able to find, besides Stuey's birth certificate, but the addresses and information were old now. Useless.

God, did Kellie have any idea what she was missing by not being in Stu's life?

So much!

I wasn't so selfish to think Kellie wasn't an important part of Stu's story. She was his mother, but I was his *mama*.

In the quiet nights, I felt it in my bones when he'd cry and I'd rock him back to sleep, or when I'd give him a bath before bed, and we'd splash and giggle together. I felt it when he was feeling shy or scared and he'd tuck his little face into my neck and hold onto me tight.

Funny how those small things added up to something so overwhelmingly huge: motherhood.

Stuey began to babble and baby talk around nine months old, and last week, when he called out "mamamam" to get my attention because I had looked away while I fed him pureed bananas, I knew it was true.

Just like we'd promised each other, Bax and I had figured

things out. Every day brought a new challenge, but it also brought more smiles and kisses. More love, and it was all I'd ever wanted.

Bax referred to me as Stu's mama all the time, and even Athena claimed me as her mom occasionally. The first time she'd slipped and called me "Mama," she'd cried and I'd cried right along with her. Then she said she wanted to call me Step-Bea. Which was weird but kind of adorable. But still, when she was upset or angry about something happening at school, it would slip out.

When she broke up with her boyfriend, Logan, after three very serious months of "dating," which had amounted to the date at the fall dance, a trip to the movies with Shaylene, and a ski day up in the mountains with Logan's parents, Athena said, "Mama, I dunno what happened. We just have irreconcilable differences." And every time, when she caught herself calling me Mama, I'd smile and shrug. She knew I wasn't trying to replace Candy, and that fact bonded us even more than we already were.

Every day, Athena and Stu healed a little bit more of Bax's heart.

And every night, I worked on it too.

There really was no comparison between Candy and me. Athena told me all the time how different we were. Sometimes it frustrated her, but most of the time, it wasn't a thought in Athena's mind. She loved me no matter how different or alike her mama and I were, and she told me all the time how happy she was to have me in her life.

I tried to tell her how she'd changed my life, too, but words never seemed to be enough.

Now, as I looked at her mama's grave, I said, "Your dumb husband asked me to marry him." I huffed a breath into the cold April air. "Can you believe that? He wanted me to move to Wisper, so I did. He wanted me to move in with them, so I did. I moved my job. My whole life! Now, he wants me to marry him? And he thinks, what? That I'll just do what I always do and acquiesce to his wishes? Nuh-uh."

I swore I could hear Candy's laugh on the wind. She knew I was full of BS.

"You're right. Why am I even questionin' it? I *do* love him. With my whole heart. I've never loved anyone the way I love Bax. Athena and Stu too. So why shouldn't I marry him?"

Plucking at the grass beneath my hand, I took a deep breath, getting ready to ask the question I'd really come to the cemetery to ask.

"But are you sure *you're* okay with it? Are you sure it's what you want?"

A warm breeze rushed around me, a quiet whoosh that held me within its strength. It lifted the ends of my hair and tangled them gently as it rustled the new green leaves of the nearby trees, making them glitter in the afternoon sun.

I had my answer, even if it was a little too woo-woo for my liking. With everything inside me, I believed Candy could hear me and had given her blessing.

And then a squirrel with tufty ears scurried down the trunk of a budding red maple twenty feet away. He ran right up to me and stood five feet away on his hind legs. He stared into my soul for what felt like forever. It had probably really only been five seconds, but it seemed like time stood still. And then the little critter lowered himself onto all fours and slowly scampered away, looking back every few steps.

Duo had given me his blessing too.

Your fucking brain is cracked, Bea. First a bison, and now this? It's a squirrel for fuck's sake!

But whether I'd gone nuts or not, I felt Candy's and Duo's love in the air and in my gut.

I was sure of it, so I stood, watching the squirrel disappear at the edge of the cemetery, under the rusted iron fence. I dusted the cut grass off my jeans and looked at the grave once more, noticing the pretty curve in the script on their headstone that spelled out their titles beneath their names. Candy's read, "Beautiful Mother, Wife, Daughter, and Friend." And under Duo's name, a sleeping lamb had been carved into the stone, and the phrase "Gone mudding with the angels," made me smile.

"Thank you," I said to the wind. "For givin' me the thing I've been searchin' for since my mama and daddy died. I love you for what you made and for what you gave up. They'll never forget you, not so long as I'm around.

"Rest well, Candy Adela Lee. Rest well, Duo. I'll spend the rest of my life lookin' after your hearts. They're my heart now too. And say hi to my mama and daddy if you see them."

As I walked back to my truck, I knew this was my last visit. At least for me. I'd bring Athena back when she wanted a little time with her mama and brother, and Bax had finally come to pay his respects and spend some time with his loss. I hoped he'd come more often. He'd breathed a little easier after the first visit.

But I didn't need Candy's reassurance anymore. Knowing that Bax loved me with his whole heart, too, told me everything I needed to know. He couldn't have given himself to me if Candy's memory was still holding onto him.

And love me he did. Now that his leg had fully healed, he'd proven it down on one knee in the dirt by the barn when he proposed with a bouquet of road reflectors and a golden ring. But it didn't have one diamond. It had four. One for every member of our patched-together family.

One for every chamber of my heart and the love held within.

Under an autumn sky...
BAX

"NO TURNIN' back now," I whispered to Athena, who was my "best person," as she'd called it.

My little girl smiled, standing next to me while we waited for our future to meet us at the end of an aisle, and it hit me right in the face that she wasn't a little girl anymore. Athena had grown into a beautiful young woman, who looked like her mama and worked hard like me. The roundness of childhood had gone from her cheeks, and in its place were the smooth, contoured cheekbones of a teenager. She was already taller than Bea.

Rye was still a little butt hurt that I hadn't chosen him to be my best man, but he'd already had that honor when I married Candy years ago. We were boys then, or it seemed so now that I had grown up and weathered so much life.

But that life was unfinished, and I was more than ready to get on with it.

This time around, Athena was the only person I could picture standing up for Bea and me both, and she was so proud to do it.

Happy tears filled my daughter's eyes as we watched Stu toddle down the short aisle in his first pair of Wranglers, cutting through the middle of three rows of metal folding chairs at the edge of Lee Lake. He held a little ring pillow in one hand and Fig's leash in his other. The dog practically dragged Stu down the aisle, both of them trying to get to Athena. There was no ring attached to the pillow though. No way would I let the kid anywhere near it. He'd probably eat it.

Fig lay at Athena's feet when they reached us, and she lifted her cousin who'd quickly become her little brother into her arms, and he wrapped his legs around her waist, giggling and waving to our guests.

As soon as Bea and me were hitched, we were adopting Stuey officially. Dixon was long gone. Maybe he'd come back someday. I hoped he would, but Stu was our kid now too.

Athena handed Stu to Merv as Presley began to play a soft song on his fiddle off to the side of the festivities and our family and friends stood from their chairs. Among the attendees were many of the guys working for my brother and Bea on the construction of another barn and the new bunkhouse. And we had plans for more to come.

Clay Marveaux, now a permanent fixture on Brand's team and Bea's right hand, sat in the row behind my mama, and the man couldn't seem to take his eyes off the back of her head. He had this weird, dizzy look on his face, and I thought, *Uh-oh*, wondering if Merv would have any clue what was happening if Clay decided to flirt with her. The thought made me smile though. Everyone deserved to be loved the way Bea and I loved each other, with everything we had inside us. It certainly would be a new experience for Merv since my old man hadn't loved much of anything at the end of his life.

Warm afternoon sun reflected off the lake beside our small gathering, and the preacher behind me cleared his throat. I'd booked him when he married Abey and Devo in the spring, in the shade of their house next to their newly planted community garden. I'd booked him before I'd even asked Bea to marry me.

But even before then, I'd known she'd say yes. She and I were meant for each other. Written in the stars, as Athena liked to say. Three weeks had stretched ahead of us into forever.

Finally, Bea appeared from behind a tall white spruce at the end of the aisle with white and yellow daisies clutched between her hands, and she took my breath away.

She'd convinced me we didn't need all the pretense of a white dress and tuxedo or suit, so I was dressed in new pair of Wranglers, too, and a "dusty lavender" button-down that matched her skirt. Her silk tank top was white and her feet were bare.

Rye had relented from his firm position that he should stand up with Athena and agreed to walk Bea down the aisle, but as soon as her eyes locked on mine, she pulled her arm away from Rye's. She hiked up her skirt with one hand, ran to me, and jumped into my waiting arms beneath the altar we'd built together over the summer, wrapped in more daisies and sprays of lavender climbing roses.

"I love you," she breathed against my lips as I twirled us in a circle. She kissed me and said, "Marry me already."

As I chuckled and set her on her feet, she tossed her bouquet behind her. Everybody sitting in the first row of chairs ducked, and the bouquet hit my sister's deputy, Roxi, in the head, but she didn't seem too mad about it. Roxi grabbed it and held it close to her chest, blushing. A few available men smiled in her direction, but Brand sat still as stone next to Abey, refusing to look behind him at Deputy Fitts, even though every other person in attendance watched her.

Hm. Is there somethin' goin' on there? I can't wait to tell Bea!

A lock of hair slipped from the braid Athena had twisted Bea's hair into. It fluttered in the light breeze coming off the lake, and I tucked it behind her ear.

"I think you have the order of this whole thing backwards," I said, unable to hide my smile, and I stared into Bea's green eyes, trying to memorize the emeralds twinkling back at me and the happiness etched onto her face like they could disappear at any moment, 'cause I knew they could. "You're s'posed to wait to toss the bouquet till *after* we're married."

Bea shrugged, grinning. "You knew I was weird before you asked me to marry you. Deal with it."

"Gladly," I promised, and I took hold of my future wife's hands and squeezed them tight. "I'll take your weird and raise you one. You're bizarre and beautiful, and you're mine."

If you liked *Roads Behind Us*, please consider leaving a review—even just a few words would help—wherever you buy your books, Goodreads, or Bookbub. Self-published indie authors rely heavily upon reviews to get our stories out to the masses. And thank you. I know it takes time to do this.

I appreciate the time out of your day and the effort.

DEAR READER,

Thank you for reading *Roads Behind Us*!

I probably shouldn't admit this, but when I meet a new character in my head, I don't really know much about them. This was true of Bax Lee. I knew Abey had brothers, and I knew their dad had screwed them up pretty good, but that's as far as I got before I started writing Abey's book. But then I met Rye Graves, and his and Bax's friendship bloomed in my imagination.

The rest came as a kind of cathartic purging. My parents lost several pregnancies and a daughter before I was even born. Her name was Tawny. She's buried next to my dad and my grandparents back home, and I've always felt her presence in my life. Writing this book broke my heart, but it also let me feel and know a little bit more about the sister I lost before I even knew she existed. The loss shaped my parents into the people they would become, and it carved out holes inside them that I couldn't understand as a kid, but now are so easy for me to recognize.

I wrote Bax's character with my dad in mind, as weird as that might sound. But my dad's stubbornness and his unwillingness to let go guided me. They're things I loved about him, but also things that sometimes made life harder for him.

And Tawny was the inspiration for Duo and all the woo-woo, and I imagine her smiling up in Heaven cuz she got to be a part of my fictional world and because she's proud of me.

But because I have never myself lost a child or a spouse, I tried very hard to write this story with grace. I hope I succeeded. I got some feedback from someone very close to me who has gone through that devastation. She knows who she is, and I love her and will always be grateful she was willing to read something that made her remember how hard that loss hurts.

If you want to know what happens with Bax and Bea and the kids a year after their story ends, join my newsletter for the password to my super secret extra content page on my website (or go to www.gretarosewest.com/VIPS). Bax and Bea are there waiting for you. You'll also get a free short story just cuz I'm so grateful you're reading my books.

Brand and Roxi's story is up next in *Forever Finds Us*. It's right up there at internal-combustion heat levels. I won't apologize. And you won't be sorry when you read it!

xoxo

Greta

Preorder **Forever Finds Us.**

Coming September 25th, 2025!

From internationally bestselling small-town western romance author, Greta Rose West, the seventh book in the Wisper Dreams Series, Forever Finds Us, is a forbidden search for love…

Brand Lee is the prodigal son. The corporate cowboy. The Lee family success story and the guy in control.
The second he turned eighteen, he got the hell out of dodge to escape his father's temper, but he's returned home decades later to Wisper, Wyoming, hoping to find whatever it is he's been missing in his life. He knows it. He feels it when he

wakes at night, clutching his chest and gasping for air. He has a thriving company and millions of dollars at his disposal, but when he thinks of his brother and sister and the lives they've built without him, he feels the missing piece strongest.

He's ready to roll up his crisp, white sleeves and find that elusive happiness.

But Brand is holding onto secrets his family may never forgive. The guilt eats him alive. When his inevitable punishment comes due, he's terrified it will cost him what he craves most.

Sheriff's Deputy Roxanne Fitts carries handcuffs and zip ties.

She follows all rules, upholds them every minute of every day, but when she rescues a sexy billionaire from a broken-down Ford on the side of the highway, she recognizes his name on his license and registration: Brand Lee, her boss's older brother.

Roxi's been searching for some happiness of her own. All five of her sisters have found it, and they popped out a bunch of kids, too, which makes her parents happy, but leaves Roxi feeling all of her forty-one years and... different. Her above-average height hasn't helped, and the fact that she'd rather spend a day at the shooting range or hiking a mountain than she would shopping for baby clothes or getting a pedicure. She's dated every available man in the tri-state area, looking for love, and she has the hilarious, but sometimes creepy, stories to prove it.

She's a dollar-store girl, an Oklahoma tomboy, so what the hell can some perfectly handsome rich guy see in her?

She has no clue, but when she unknowingly responds to his question with, "Yes, sir," and his eyes flash with heat, she's ready to find out.

The seventh book in the Wisper Dreams series, *Forever Finds Us*, is a steamy, forbidden power struggle of a romance. It might make you clutch your pearls, but you'll do it willingly and beg for more... *won't you, good girl?*

COMING SEPTEMBER 25th, 2025

EXTRA CONTENT

Join my newsletter for a FREE short story, *Wild Heart: Welcome to Wisper*. This is where you can get all the Wisper news and sexcapades—naughty little interludes for my subscribers ONLY! There's a little somethin' somethin' there about Bax and Bea!

Sign up on my website: gretarosewest.com/VIPS

LETS CONNECT!

You can also join me in my Facebook group, Wisperites Unite. We get up to a lot of fun there. Mostly we drool over sexy cowboys, but we do other things there too, I promise, like giveaways and fun games, and my Wisperites always get new book news first, teasers, and we chat about life. We'd love to have you!

Go to: https://www.facebook.com/groups/wisperitesunite

I would love to hear from you. Email me at greta@gretarosewest.com. I'll reply. Or find me on Facebook and Instagram.

@gretarosewest

ABOUT THE AUTHOR

Greta Rose West was a floundering artsy flake until cowboy Jack Cade showed up, knocking on the door of her brain, pounding on it, and then he just plain kicked it down. She's a boy mom to a grown freakin' man, who has recently gifted her with the title of GRANNY! She comes from the "Region" of NW Indiana, but Greta, her husband, and her two precocious kitties, Geoff Trouble and Sally Mae Midnight, now reside in the Denver, Colorado area, where she often makes her husband drive her out into the mountains so she can look and dream. When she's not writing, she's reading and devouring music. She enjoys indie films no one else likes, and her favorite food is Aver's Veggie Revival pizza.

You can find her on Instagram @gretarosewest, in her Facebook group, Wisperites Unite, or on her website.

gretarosewest.com

facebook.com/gretarosewest

instagram.com/gretarosewest

bookbub.com/authors/greta-rose-west

goodreads.com/gretarosewest